North of Channing Street

This book is a work of fiction. Names, and incidents are used by the author fictitiously, and any resemblance to actual persons, living or dead, is strictly coincidental. Names of Certain places and business establishments are taken from the author's memory or imagination with no intent to advertise or criticize.

Library of Congress registration number:TXu1-292-725

This is a self published novel by Gloria Spivey Flecker using Booksurge, an Amazon.com company.

Cover art by Travis Teate

Poem/Flawless: by Ryan Z. Ricciardi
Used with author's permission

ISBN: 1-4196-4156-5
Library of Congress Control Number: 2006905427

To order additional copies, please contact us.
BookSurge, LLC
www.booksurge.com
1-866-308-6235
orders@booksurge.com

North of Channing Street

Gloria Spivey Flecker

2006

North of Channing Street

TABLE OF CONTENTS

ACKNOWLEDGMENTS

My thanks to all of you. My oldest son, Rick, for his faith in my ability to write this. My oldest daughter, Fran, who always had faith and trust in me, and believed I could do anything I set my mind to. To Michael, dear strong and gentle Michael. Although we lived far apart, were always close in heart. Brenda, my fourth, we've shared so much, good times and hard times during your childhood, and as two adult women, raising your son and believing in one another. Tamera? Thank you sweetheart, for your sweetness and undying love and faith in me. Last, not least by far, my youngest child, Ronald. Always the believer in himself and our family. No matter what!

My love and thanks to my grandchildren. You're all very special to me.

A special thanks to my grandson, Travis, for the art work. And my grandson, Ryan, for allowing me to use your poem.

I could write a book about each and everyone of you, but those books shall stay in my heart for eternity.

Thomas, my husband, who was such a huge help with my computer glitches and understanding my moods. I love you to the sky and back.

My step-daughter, Lori, for your input in the dream about the strawberry fields. Thank you so much for that. It got me started on a day when I could think of nothing to write.

To my instructor at CCU, Dave Zinman. You are the best!!

To my classmates and writer friends, Georgiana, Nancy, Gail, Peg, Judy, Sue, Kjersti, Barbara and Anna Louise. Also, my dear friend, Jeanette.

A very big thank you to the staff at Booksurge,for the editing, formatting and all of your help. My thanks to anyone that I may have failed to mention. I apologize.

Thanks again!! May god bless all of you.

This book is dedicated to my six children
And their children.

THE PLAY

Here in the autumn of her days
She looks at pictures of children,
Grown.
And a mother, long passed away.

With eyes closed, she sees a stage
The audience applauds as she acts in
the play
She didn't know she could have it all
The children and the curtain call.

For the love of a man
In heat of passion.
A dream was lost, a soul unfulfilled.
A fantasy became her fashion.

So search your souls, young girls
Today.
Know your desires, don't throw them
Away.
Marry your men and have their children
If you're sure you need them, more than
the play.

By: Gloria Spivey Flecker

RETURN TO CHANNING STREET

The sobbing was almost unbearable. We had to drag the woman away from the coffin at the cemetery. Who the hell was she, anyway? I didn't remember Dad telling me about anyone with bleached blonde hair. I knew he had managed to court many women after Mom died in 1961, at too young an age. He hadn't, however, told me about the person I saw that day at his graveside. She was fairly attractive, very well dressed, and I guessed in her mid-sixties. I walked over to her and said, "Excuse me, ma'am, I'm Richard's daughter, Molly. I don't believe we've met." She looked at me with such sad blue eyes and did not speak, but took me by the hand and began walking away from the grave, leading me with her. I said, "Listen, I don't know who you are, but we have to leave so they can close this grave." She said she understood, and asked if I could just let her ride with me back to the house. I said I supposed it would be all right, since there was plenty of room in the car. As we were being driven to my home on Channing Street, she told me that she was Sally, Dad's fiancée, and showed me her engagement ring. I was shocked! My father was gone; I was the only person left of my family of four. Now I would be forced to befriend this person. How would I ever deal with this? I took a deep breath and said a silent prayer that I would come through this awful ordeal with my sanity intact.

Back at the house on Channing Street, I managed to remain calm as I talked with the mob of people who kept coming to pay their respects to my father's memory and to celebrate his very active life. My dad had been a very popular man in our neighborhood in Portsmouth, Virginia, but no one seemed to know much about Sally. According to Grace Callahan, my friend Rosalie's mother, an engagement party had been planned for the following week, but now there would be no need. I kept thinking the woman looked familiar, but couldn't place her. Eventually everyone had gone, including Sally, and I could relax and reminisce.

The telephone rang just as I finished putting the food away. I almost didn't answer, but decided that would be rude since it was most likely Rosalie, my best friend, calling to check on me. I picked up the receiver and said hello. The man's voice on the other end was strange, yet oddly familiar.

He said, "Hello. Is this Molly Peale, my old girlfriend?"

I said, "This is Molly. Who is this?"

"Molly, it's Nick Graziano. I was in town this week visiting my uncle, and I read about your father's death in the *Pilot*. Let me offer my condolences. I hope you don't mind my calling. I would like to stop by the house, if it's okay."

My heart fell to the floor. He was actually talking to me, after forty years! I couldn't believe my ears. I invited him for lunch the next day, stating that I was much too tired for any more company that night.

Knowing that my life could have been different, that I could have taken a different path, I stood in my room and looked out the window at a beautiful sunset. I remembered how it was in the summer of 1955. I had often looked out this same window and wondered where and how he was. I knew on this June night, as a full moon rose over this southern place, I would once again look out onto Channing Street and wonder. Only this time, I could look forward to tomorrow, when I would know.

I went downstairs and flopped on the couch to relax and watch television. I couldn't get interested in anything, so I made my way back upstairs to read. I stopped by my father's room and looked in.

His bed was unmade and exactly the same as when they had carried him out. I could picture the terror in Martha's eyes when she found him lying there, dead. Martha was Dad's housekeeper, and had worked for our family since I could remember. She had moved with us from the creek house in North Carolina when I was nine. Looking back, I could hardly believe so much time had passed, and now I was fifty-five years old and all alone. I felt like an orphan, and I guessed that was exactly what I had become.

I decided to telephone my friend Jeff in New York, to let him know how things were going. He wasn't in, so I left a message saying that I would call again in a few days, and got in my bed to read. I closed my eyes for a moment and, as usual, began my specialty of thinking and daydreaming. Pictures of the past came rushing into my mind. I remembered the summer that I met Nick, at the beach in Ocean View. Rosalie and I were walking off the beach when we saw him. His wet black hair glistened in the sunlight. He stood up to show off a tall muscular frame. He was the best-looking boy I had ever seen. I was fifteen years old and had just completed my freshman year of high school.

He smiled at me and said, "Hey, Blondie, where are you going so fast?"

My heart raced and my hands felt cold and damp, but I smiled and said, "Why, I don't believe we've met, sir; therefore, it's none of your business where I'm going." I remembered from charm school — which my parents had subjected me to the previous year — that if a young lady is approached by a gentleman, she should at least give him the opportunity to introduce himself. He said his name was Nick, and he would like very much to buy my friend and me a Coke and a burger. I told him I didn't think so, right then, but he could come to Craddock at two o'clock the next day, and buy us a Coke at the luncheonette on the corner by the high school. I told him how to get there. He said he would be there, and we walked away.

On the way to meet my parents at the car, Rosalie stopped dead in her tracks. "Are you out of your ever-loving stupid mind, my idiot friend? You just invited that strange boy to our neighborhood, and you know damn well that shit is totally against everything we've been taught."

"Oh, pipe down, Rosy", I said."Saying 'damn' and 'shit' is also very much against the rules. You know as well as I do that he may not even come, and if he does, that luncheonette is a public place and he has as much right to be there as we do."

She continued to complain all the way to the car. I promised her that if she squealed on me to either of our parents, it would be good-bye friendship. There was silence all the way home.

The next day at one thirty I got a call from Rosalie. "Listen, stupid, I can't let you take a chance like this. As long as we don't show up, there is no harm done." I told her to back out if she wanted to, but I would be there on schedule. She yelled into the phone like a screaming cat. "Okay, okay, you idiot! I'll meet you at one forty five."

I knew from Nick's accent when he had spoken to me that he was from someplace up north. I planned to show off my southern demeanor straight out of cotillion. He walked in the door at exactly two o'clock and the show began. I found out that he was from New Jersey and had been in the navy for the past six months. He was seventeen and homesick. We made a date for the following day. He would pick me up at five thirty. I would tell my parents that I was having supper and going to a movie with Rosalie, and she would swear to it — or else. This was my first dating experience and the first time I had ever deceived my parents. I felt excited and scared.

We went to a drive-in theater and filled up on chilidogs and French fries. He kissed me and my hormones went wild. I was confused and afraid, but he became an addiction and I knew I was in love.

The whole summer we continued to see each other, always sneaking out and lying to my parents. Rosalie finally threatened to tell if I didn't. I said I would, but the next day Nick told me he was being transferred and asked me to go with him. He was going to Rhode Island; a big city called Providence. The thought was so scary that I almost peed my pants. I told Rosalie and she freaked out.

"This is crazy," she said. "If you don't come to your senses now, I will go straight to your mother. This boy is everything they warned us about. He is a sailor, and he is also Italian. You are a fool, Molly Peale. Have you forgotten what you're made of? What about your dreams? If you go away with this boy, you'll be giving up your dream of ever being an actress. Went all the way with him, didn't you? Tell me the truth."

"No, not yet," I said. "Although I almost did, once." All of the things Rosalie was saying suddenly started making sense. The thought of never going on the stage again, the way that I was deceiving my parents — I knew I had to say good-bye to Nick. That night, I told him how I had always dreamed of being a famous actress someday, and even though I loved him, I would have to say good-bye. He left the next day. It was August, 1955. I was fifteen and my heart was broken over a boy for the first time, but my dream was still alive. My parents never knew about Nick, and I was forever indebted to Rosalie for helping me wise up. Even though Nick's uncle lived in Virginia Beach, only a few miles away, I never had the nerve to call and ask about him. I never stopped loving him and now here we were, forty years later, about to meet again. Only this time, there were no parents to tell.

I continued to lie on the bed with the lamp on, attempting to read a short story in the *Reader's Digest.* My mind wandered again. I found myself remembering my high school days. It was September, 1955. I sat in a classroom, looking at pictures on the wall and feeling so much older than my fifteen years. After what had happened that summer with Nick, I wondered if I would ever be the same again. The bell rang and I moved on to my biology class. Mr. Nahaas, the biology teacher, barely said good morning and never cracked a smile. Most of my classmates had him pegged as a fag, but I wondered if he was that, or just an eccentric person. Mom always told me not to judge other people, so I tried to refrain from it. I was wishing that I didn't have to take biology. I couldn't imagine how that sort of thing could possibly help an actress. Nine o'clock in the morning and there I was, dissecting worms. I put my face in my hands and cried.

The morning dragged on and lunch break came. After lunch, I went outside with Rosalie and we hid behind the equipment shed to smoke a cigarette. The bell rang and we crushed the cigs and went back inside. Rosalie and I bonded as best friends the first day we met, and vowed that nothing would separate us. I admired her then for her strength and will power. She knew exactly where she wanted to go in her life and how she intended to get there. She wanted to be an accountant because she liked working with figures. I was the opposite; I liked English and drama, so we were able to draw on each other's talents. Rosalie wasn't really beautiful, but she was attractive and had an athletic look. Her hair was jet black and she had large brown eyes. She was five feet three inches tall, and was well liked by most for her outgoing personality. She had a round face with thin lips and small teeth, and she always walked with her chin up.

I wasn't really beautiful either, but I guess I was cute. I had gotten my first short haircut just before the start of school. My blonde hair looked nice with the lighter blonde streak in the front. It was a fad back then to put peroxide on the front of our hair, sit in the sun, and allow it to lighten. My aqua eyes often got attention from the boys, as did my large breasts, of which I was ashamed. I tried everything to flatten them under my sweaters. I weighed in at one hundred thirteen pounds, which was pretty thin for my five foot four inch frame. My teeth protruded a little, but were very straight and even. I've never worried about my smile.

Rosalie and I split up in the hall to go to separate classes. We agreed to meet after school at Jeanne's luncheonette, our favorite hang-out. I rushed down the hall to drama class, the highlight of my day. My heart began to pound as I remembered it was the day to audition for the school play. When I arrived at the classroom, we were told to go to the auditorium if we were interested in taking part in the play. I rushed to the auditorium to audition for a part in *Arsenic and Old Lace*. I was hoping for Abbey Brewster, the leading old lady murderer, but I would take anything.

My wish came true: I got the part. I was excited and must have shown it because other students were congratulating me and commenting on how I blushed with excitement. Marsha Wilson and Mildred Turner walked up to me with their bouncy step and confident air. Marsha was a pretty blonde with the largest, most beautiful blue eyes of any girl in the school. Mildred, a brunette, was almost as pretty. Both were slim and athletic. They were the two most popular girls in school. Both were cheerleaders. I was never much of a cheerleader, but I knew I was the best at acting. I was on top of the world as they congratulated me for getting the part I had wanted. I thanked them, and remembered how often I had wished I was a cheerleader and would have liked to have been in Marsha's shoes. Right then, I was happy to be me.

Rehearsals started that same day, after school. I became Abbey Brewster. I dreamed her and lived her. I spoke her words, drank her drinks, and ate her food. I was Molly Peale as little as possible. To be me meant that I had to remember the summer and him. I prayed to God to let me forget him. I wanted to forget how I could have run away with him and given up my dreams. Mostly I wanted to forget how handsome he was, and how very warm he had made me feel when he held me in his arms, kissed me, and told me he loved me.

The next three years went by quickly. I starred in three high school plays and did some work with local theatrical groups. Graduation came and went, summer turned into fall, and we went off to college.

BIG SISTER WOES

The campus of William and Mary was buzzing with activity as students moved into the dorms and crowded the bookstore, talking and laughing. There was also some crying from those people with the unending umbilical cords as their parents left them behind. Rosalie was busy tripping on the sidewalk and walking into bushes as she watched all the men go past. Some smiled and said hello, but most seemed wrapped up in their own stuff and didn't look back.

"Will you watch where the hell you are going?" I said. "Can't you see these men are trying to focus on getting checked in?" I looked up at the beautiful sky for one second, and wouldn't you know I tripped? I fell flat on my notebooks and had to start school with a bruise on my nose. "Just great," I said, dragging myself up off the cement.

"Look at your face, you stupid ass. I'm the one getting pleasure out of looking at these studs, and Miss Graceful of the Year falls flat on her face. What a pity! Now, let's go get you some ice. You've already grown another nose," Rosalie teased.

Our first year at William and Mary was fun and exciting. We worked hard to get good grades, but were still able to enjoy the festivities around Williamsburg. We loved the area and spent a lot of our time sightseeing. The term went by quickly, and before we knew it, we were back in Craddock for the summer.

I hadn't dated since the previous summer, and was looking forward to hooking up with old friends from high school and letting my hair down. Although I had dated some cute boys throughout school, I found myself comparing each one with Nick — and so far, no one had measured up. My memory soared back to the summer of '55, and I wondered where he was and what he was like now, and if I would ever see him again. Somewhere deep in my soul, I felt that we would meet again someday; our lives would once again be filled with love, and everything would be perfect.

My brother, Jesse, had graduated from high school that year and was dating a pretty girl from Winston High. My parents teased her because her name was Sarah Winston. My Dad said they had probably named the town after her because she was so pretty. Teasingly, he would say to her, "How is Queen Sarah Winston from Winston?"

"Oh, Mr. Peale," she would answer, "You're making me blush again." There were many Winstons in Winston and not one was considered royal. Sarah didn't come from a wealthy family, but her parents were fine, hard-working people and Sarah was a credit to them. I could tell by the way Jesse looked at Sarah that he was in love with her. I told him someday she would be Mrs. Jesse Peale. He laughed and said he didn't see a future. He said he didn't have any idea of what he wanted to study in college the coming year, and somehow did not think it was all that important at the time. I was bothered by his indifference about school, and wished he could be a lot more positive about his future.

"That is because you're a boy," I said, laughing at my remark, but somehow I didn't think it was funny. The subject never came up again, and I wouldn't remember the conversation until months later.

The summer of 1959 was filled with fun and part-time jobs for those of us who wished to take advantage. I worked at a five-and-ten store downtown, making just enough to pay for beauty parlor visits and good times, and barely saving a cent. Jesse worked at a gas station in Winston and made pretty good money. He spent most of it on Sarah. My parents didn't seem to mind. My dad was an officer in the navy, and Mom was a seamstress and owned a dress boutique. We never heard them discuss money or the lack of it, so we never worried about how much we were spending or saving. Things were good for us back then.

September came and we went back to school. I went back to Williamsburg and Jesse went to a school up north. He had decided on Trenton State in New Jersey. He said something about becoming a teacher, but didn't really elaborate. I mentioned to Rosalie that I was concerned about him, but said nothing about it to my parents. They were very much against Jesse or me leaving the South. I vowed to Mother that as long as she was around, I would never leave Virginia.

CHANGING TIDES

The historical scenery of Williamsburg removed me momentarily from the present, and I dreamt about the past once again, so impossible to touch. Thoughts of my brother came rushing into my mind. I thought about last June, and how he seemed to have no interest in where he was going with his future. I pictured his blond hair bleached by the sun over the summer. I had always admired his good looks, with his blue eyes and bright smile that showed white, even teeth. He was five feet eleven inches tall and had light skin like me that tanned well in the sun. When we were kids, we would have a contest to see who could have the best tan by the end of summer. Jesse won every year. I didn't mind because I loved my brother, and his happiness meant a lot to me. I was proud of him. I had high hopes for his future and worried now about his disinterest.

It was Wednesday night, one week before Thanksgiving, when I received a phone call from Jesse. He told me that he was planning to spend Thanksgiving in Fort Lauderdale with a buddy, and would not be home until Christmas. He asked me to tell Mom and Dad because he was afraid the letter he had written would not reach them in time, and a call from him might generate an argument. I thought, *How cowardly*, but I had always been a go-between for Jesse when he wanted to avoid a confrontation with my parents. We both knew this was going to upset them, so I agreed to spare Jesse the experience. To this day, I am sorry I didn't let him make that call himself.

I went home the following Wednesday and broke the news to our parents. They were hurt and disappointed. "Mom, Dad, Jesse will be here in less than a month, and we should look forward to good times with him then," I said. "Besides, we'll have a wonderful time despite his absence." So we did. Mom and I shopped until we dropped on Friday. I bought a beautiful sweater for Jesse for Christmas, with light colors that would go well with his skin and eyes.

That night, I stared across the table at my father. He looked exactly like an older version of my brother. I thought it ironic that Jesse had Daddy's features and I was the spitting image of Mom. Her blonde hair had turned gray in places, but she sported those blue eyes and a mouth that protruded slightly that she had passed down to me.

Saturday was spent mostly with friends, just taking walks down Channing Street and later enjoying cups of tea by the fire. That night, after a light dinner with my parents, I went up to my room and read until I fell asleep.

I awoke to a beautiful, sunny Sunday morning and felt exceptionally good as I rolled out of bed. I looked out the window and there was not a cloud in the sky. After Mom and I finished the breakfast dishes, I went upstairs and started packing my things to return to school the next day. I didn't hear the phone ring, but I heard my mother scream.

"Molly, come down here!"

I ran down the steps with my heart in my throat. Something wasn't right.

"Mom, what is it?" Her face was as white as a sheet.

"Grab some clothes. There's been an accident. We have to go to Florida. It's Jesse."

"Oh, my God!" I said. "How bad is it?"

"I don't know, honey," she said.

I looked at my father. He was sitting at the table with his head in his hands.

"Daddy, are you okay?" I asked.

"I'm afraid, sugar," he said. "My boy, my buddy," he cried.

I picked up the phone and called the airlines. There was not one available seat from Norfolk to Fort Lauderdale. That meant we had to drive. Dad said a nurse had called from Lauderdale General Hospital and said that Jesse had head injuries sustained in a surfing accident, and the prognosis wasn't good.

Somehow we managed to throw our bags in the car, and we rushed out of town and onto the highway. We knew it would take us eighteen hours to get there, and I was terrified that because of my dad's grief. he would lose control of the car. I sat in the back seat of my parents' Nash Ambassador with my arm over the front seat and holding my mother's hand. She was squeezing my hand so hard, and we prayed together for God to please spare our beloved Jesse's life.

We arrived at the hospital on Monday at four o'clock in the morning. We rushed into the emergency room and they hurried us into the intensive care unit. We stood frozen as the nurse went down the hall to get the attending physician. The doctor came out and introduced himself.

"I'm Dr. Daniel Brown, the neurosurgeon who performed the surgery on your son. I won't beat around the bush," he said. "It doesn't look as though your son is going to pull through. Right now he is on an oxygen machine. My opinion is that if we take him off the machine, he will die. Would you like to see him before you make a decision?"

The three of us held onto each other and cried for what seemed like ten minutes. The doctor put his hand on my father's shoulder and said he was sorry. He said that Jesse had been hit in the back of the head with the surfboard, and his brain was so severely damaged that there was nothing he could do. We went into Jesse's hospital room and went through the worst time of our lives. We cried over him and told him we loved him. After about an hour, my dad said the nurse or doctor could remove the oxygen. Jesse left us at 5:37 a.m. on the Monday after Thanksgiving, 1959.

Somehow, we managed to arrange for the body of our beloved Jesse to be sent home to Virginia the next day. The funeral took place on Thursday, one week after Thanksgiving. Rosalie stayed out of school that week to help me through. After the funeral was over and all of the guests had left our house, she and her parents stayed with my parents and me. The six of us sat in silence, just sort of staring into space. I couldn't cry anymore. Finally, Rosalie and her mom got up and started cleaning up and putting food away. There was so much food that we couldn't fit all of it in our refrigerator. We gave some to the Callahans and asked them to share it with the neighbors, if they couldn't use all of it. After they left, I went upstairs and sat on Jesse's bed. I prayed and cried. Sometime during the night, I went into my own room and got changed and into my bed. I cried myself to sleep.

The bright sun shone in my window and I could hear things moving, so I knew it was morning. I got up and looked out of the window, and saw people outside talking. Cars were going along Channing Street and everything looked normal, but it seemed out of whack. The world, I mean. It seemed wrong that life should go on like nothing had happened when one I loved so deeply was gone forever. Someone at the church said time heals all and we must trust in the Lord and know that Jesse was in a better place. Heaven seemed so far away. I wondered if it really existed. Was Jesse really up there? Was he looking down on us?

I went downstairs and sat at the table with my parents. They said there was coffee made and danish on the table. I looked at my mom and thought how dreadfully sad she looked. *She will never be the same,* I thought. She never was.

I decided not to go back to school that semester. I stayed home with my parents through December and half of January. There was no Christmas celebration in our home, even though our friends told us that Jesse would want us to put up a tree. We didn't have the heart. I remained at home, watching my parents give up hope of ever feeling happy again. I wondered why I was there. My twentieth birthday came on January 15 and I felt guilty that I was alive. I knew I had to do something! I called a support group for people who had lost a son or daughter. I told my parents about it and begged them to go to a meeting, for my sake. They hugged me and said they loved me and I was all they had left. "We will do anything if it will help you feel better, sugar," my father said.

The next day they went to a meeting. After that, they started talking about Jesse for the first time since his death. For the first time since his death, I felt relieved.

By January 25, I felt okay about leaving Mom and Dad in the comfort of their new friends who had also lost children. I took what money I had in my checking account, went to Williamsburg, and rented a studio apartment. I found a job in a local restaurant and signed up for acting parts with the Williamsburg Theatre Guild. By the end of February, I was starring in a musical called *Hi-Fi Girl.* My character was a young girl who had lost both of her parents and sang in a nightclub to support herself and her brother. She eventually met the love of her life and married, to live happily ever after.

The following September, I went back to school a different person. I was there for my parents only, and wondered how long I could keep up the pretense. I wanted to be a full-time actress. I wanted to go to New York.

I went back home for Christmas. It was 1960, and I was less than a month away from my twenty-first birthday. My parents were doing a lot better by then, and thanked me for finding the "parents with lost children group" for them. I told them I was so happy that I could help. I also told them how very much I wanted to act on Broadway, and mentioned that I would like to leave school and go to New York. Dad didn't say much, but my mother wanted me to complete my education first. I agreed not to make a decision just then, and promised to wait until she felt better about it.

One chilly April morning in 1961, I was summoned to the dean's office. There was a call from my father. My mother had passed away during the night. They said she had a stroke. I signed out of school, and moved to New York one week after her funeral.

HELLO BIG APPLE

I arrived in New York on Wednesday, April 15, with the pain of Mother's death still heavy on my heart. I had read in a performing arts circular at the airport that there was an audition for a lead role in a Broadway play at four that afternoon at the Broadhurst Theatre on 44th St. I figured I would at least get some experience in try-outs in the big city, so I called from my room at the Doral. There is a saying that behind every cloud there is a ray of sunlight. The darkness that loomed over me as I grieved for Mother seemed permanent. Just when I thought I would never see light again, I received a phone call from Jeff Wilde, the director of that particular Broadway show, advising me that I might go to the theater at four that afternoon if I was serious about the audition. He was willing to give an unknown a chance to show her talent, if she had any.

I was onstage at five fifteen, auditioning for the part of Cass in *The Devil and His Angels.* I was given a script and a brief summary of the character's role. Cass was a young woman who tried desperately to hold on to a handsome young man who, even though he was in love with the lovely Cass, had an insatiable appetite for sex with as many other beautiful women as he could possibly charm into the act. The audition scene called for a painful experience, as Cass walked into a room to find her lover, Will, in the arms of the beautiful Maria. As I faced the director, and cried, "Oh my god! I have lost you," the thought of Mother brought tears to my eyes and they streamed down my face. Jeff called on Thursday morning to inform me that I had the part of Cass and would start rehearsals at seven on Saturday morning. The picture in my mind of Mother's casket as they lowered it into the ground would be my ticket to tears throughout my career.

The next day, I found a nice little apartment in lower Manhattan and moved out of my hotel room. I was filled with excitement and felt more adult than I ever had.

My relationship with Jeff Wilde developed into a friendship over the next few weeks as we worked long and hard on the play. We were into the third week when he asked me to join him and a few friends for dinner at a local restaurant. It was a clear, cold spring night that Sunday in May. We had hoped for warmer weather, but it seemed as though the winter had left us with still some chilly nights. The restaurant was quaint and reminded me of a place I had visited with my family in Richmond a few years before. I loved Italian food, and Vinnie D's had an excellent reputation for serving some of the best in New York.

The table was near a fireplace and I felt cozy and warm. Jeff introduced me to four people that night. Jason was an actor and had starred in Jeff's last play, *Spotless*. It was adapted from a book written by Cecilia Goodland, who also joined us for dinner. Calvin Albritton was another successful writer, with seven books to his credit. All seven had hit the shelves in every bookstore in the country as best-sellers. Martine Hamilton, a beautiful tall, thin model, stood by Jason's chair and smiled as though she were involved in a photo shoot. Her long red hair was braided and hung over her left shoulder like a rope. I thought how sophisticated she looked, and wondered if she would ever stop smiling. She finally moved to her seat in a sort of slinky fashion and the smile changed to a half grin. She said hello and told me that her friends often called her Marty,and asked me where I was from, "originally." I answered that I was from Virginia, and had been in New York only a few weeks.

"Well, you certainly are doing marvelous in a short time. I was in New York for two years before I got my first modeling job."

"Not everyone is as talented as Molly," Jason said.

I could see the hurt in Martine's face, and I smiled at her, winked and said, "I just happened to meet the right director. I think maybe not everyone recognizes good talent when they see it." I could tell by the relief on her face that I had a new friend.

After dinner, we took a cab back to Jeff's place in Manhattan. His apartment showed a rather bizarre taste in home decor, but I had to admit it was interesting and I enjoyed my visit. A bronze lion's head over the fireplace in the den was most unique. We enjoyed nightcaps of Sambucca with little coffee beans in pewter cups, and I remember thinking how medieval it all seemed. However, I felt a certain sense of security just being in Jeff's world. I knew that I could depend on him for virtually anything. His display of affection for his associates was obviously his way of letting us know he was there for us. He was wealthy and wise, and knew exactly how to get what he wanted. I was in awe of all he had managed to accomplish as a young man of thirty one. Jeff had been instrumental in the successes of each person he had worked with. He had become important in my life, and each time I looked at him he grew more handsome in my eyes. Although I had no romantic interest in him, I felt love for him. I was impressed with his six foot two stature and slender build, and his light hair and green eyes reminded me of my dear father. The party broke up around 1:00 a.m., and Jeff, Jason and Martine walked me home. Martine and I laughed and joked all the way, and promised to get together for lunch the following week.

A week later, I met Martine for lunch at the Carnegie Deli. I ordered a corned beef sandwich and I swear, it was the biggest sandwich I had ever seen. Martine ordered a turkey on white, and I was almost certain they had put an entire turkey breast on that one sandwich. I noticed a funny thing about Martine and her food. She took three bites and asked the server to wrap up the rest, and bagged it in the enormous purse she was carrying.

"Aren't you hungry?" I asked.

"Well, I had a very big breakfast. I think I'll save this for dinner," she said.

I admired her will-power, and decided that must be how she stayed so thin. I finished my sandwich, and we walked to Rosy O'Grady's and enjoyed a glass of white wine. After that, we took a cab to Martine's apartment on Twelfth Street. She invited me up for coffee and I gratefully accepted, hoping I could shake the effects of the wine.

"So, how did you meet Jeff?" Martine asked. "Was it really through an audition?"

"Yes, of course. Why would you think any different?"

"It's just that most of the models and actresses I've met have gotten their jobs because they knew someone in the business."

"Well," I assured her, "you are looking at someone who knew absolutely no one in this business."

"I'm sorry, Molly, I didn't mean to imply anything. Ah, well . . . I wasn't, I didn't mean . . .

"It's okay, I know you didn't mean anything by it," I said. She was quiet for a few seconds after that, then began talking about her situation. She confided that her relationship with Jason was strained, but she felt insecure about her career without him to promote her and get her bookings. I gathered from the conversation that he was possessive, and maybe verbally abusing her.

"Marty, I'm sure you could do well on your own. If you need someone to talk to, I'm here to listen. And if you need help with anything, I'm only too willing to help you."

"Thank you so much, Molly. I do appreciate your willingness, but I'll be fine."

We had another cup of coffee and I started home. I decided to walk a few blocks since it was such a nice day. I was five minutes away when I realized I had left my keys on Martine's table. I ran back, went up, and knocked on her door. The door opened and I went in, calling her name. I could hear choking noises coming from the bathroom, and I called out to her.

"Martine, are you okay?"

She came out of the bathroom, wiping her mouth. Her face was flushed and her eyes were red.

"It's nothing. I just felt a little queasy. Must have been the food."

"But you hardly touched your food."

"It's nothing," she said, smiling.

"Okay, kiddo," I said. I walked over to the counter and picked up my keys. On the counter where she had placed the food when we came in, the sandwich wrapper was empty. I guessed that she had eaten the food and forced herself to regurgitate.

Hey Marty, what's going on?" I said.

She stared straight at me and said, "Listen, Molly, I really want us to be friends. Heaven knows, I need a good friend. But if we're going to remain friends, you'll have to mind your own business. I gain weight at the drop of a hat and I refuse to be in *Fat Model of the Month* Magazine. Got it?"

"Okay. I just hope you wise up. You can learn to eat healthy. What you are doing is risky business, and no modeling job is worth it."

"Think about this, Molly, my friend. If the shoe were on the other foot, what would you do? Is your acting career worth a risk or two?"

"I think I would look for a part to fit my size," I said.

When I returned to my apartment, I took a long bath and got ready for evening rehearsal. At the theatre, as I was changing into my costume, I felt bothered about Martine's behavior, but tried to push it out of my mind. Once I was on stage, it was easy. I was no longer Molly. I was Cass, and Cass had no friend named Martine.

MARTINE HAMILTON

"I'm not interested in your excuses," the woman said.

"I don't know what you want me to say," the man said. "That woman means nothing to me," he continued. "I don't know why it happened. After this, I promise to make it up to you. If you will just be a little patient with me, we can work this out. You know I would do anything to protect Marty. We have to work this out for her sake. We must never let her know about this."

The woman began to sob. "I'll do whatever it takes to protect our daughter. As soon as she is grown and off to college, I want you out of this house and out of my life, once and for all," she said.

"Listen to me, Gail," he said. "I'm not even thinking that far ahead at this point. Your precious little affair with your physician wasn't exactly easy for me to accept."

"You bastard," she yelled, holding her left hand in a fist and looking up at the ceiling. "That was four years ago, and I have kept my promise to you — even though it has not been a picnic keeping up this pretense."

The fourteen-year-old girl stood frozen behind her bedroom door. She was unable to move a muscle as she listened to her parents fighting another war. She knew it was up to her to do everything just right to keep her family together. Martine Hamilton took a deep breath and called out to her mother.

"Mom," she yelled. "Have you seen my science book anywhere? I'll be late for school if I don't find it soon. Oh, never mind, here it is on my bedroom chair." Once again she had stopped the war by crying out to her parents, knowing that the sound of her voice was the only thing that ever worked. She felt so burdened sometimes with this responsibility that packing some luggage and walking out the door seemed like a wonderful idea.

"Get yourself down here, Martine," Gail called up to her. "Breakfast is getting cold. We don't like cold oatmeal."

Martine rushed down the steps carrying the missing science book. She took one look at the oat cereal and felt sick at the thought of eating it.

"Oh, Mom, why aren't we having our usual egg and pancake? I don't think I can eat this."

"That's very nourishing for you, Mart," her mother said. "Besides, pancakes are fattening and I have noticed you are getting a little pudgy around the middle. Tomorrow we'll have eggs with one piece of toast, but for now eat your cereal."

Martine reluctantly ate the oatmeal. Once she was finished, she felt so sick that she ran to the bathroom and upchucked her entire breakfast. Feeling better, she kissed her mother, put her coat on, picked up her books, and headed off to school.

Outside, the air was cold and crisp. Another Minnesota morning in December. The snow glistened in the sunlight, and Marty caught up with some friends and walked with them to school. She shared her breakfast story with her friend Sandy, who was probably the skinniest girl Martine knew. Martine noticed how she ate at lunch and wondered how she stayed so thin. Sandy told Martine to meet her at lunch and she would tell her the secret to staying thin.

That day, at age fourteen, Martine learned how she could control her weight without dieting. Sandy explained to her that any time she over-ate, she could get rid of the extra food by sticking her finger down her throat to make herself vomit. At first Marty thought that sounded like a drastic way to control her weight. Then she figured she had so much else to control with her parents and their problems, and trying to keep their marriage together, that she welcomed a way to be thin without having to worry about what she ate.

After six months, Martine was eating more and staying thin. She felt great, and Sandy was always there to support her. Together, they would have binge and purge parties.

That summer, Sandy went to the hospital with a hemorrhage in her esophagus as a result of the purging. Martine was frightened by this and discontinued the practice. She stuck to a healthy diet and remained slim the rest of her high school years and into her first year of college.

One dark July morning after her freshman year at Penn State, her father was killed in a car wreck in New York while he and his wife were on their way to see a play. Her mother was injured, but survived.

Martine didn't return to college after that. She took her portion of her dad's insurance money and moved to New York City to find a job as a model. By the end of the second year, she had depleted most of her savings by paying high rent and buying expensive clothes and a new car, which she said she needed to look successful on her visits to her home town.

On June 18 ,1960, Martine answered an ad for fashion modeling at Bloomingdale's. She was hired and given an invitation to a cocktail party that night, to give her a chance to meet others in the business. That's where she met Jason Carter. He was standing by the bar when she walked up to order a glass of wine.

"Hello," he said, putting his hand out. "I'm Jason."

Martine shook his hand and smiled. "Martine," she said. They exchanged information about each other, and he asked her to have dinner with him the following evening. She accepted. She left the party that night feeling beautiful and confident. The infamous Jason Carter had shown an interest in her.

Over the next few months, Jason took a personal interest in Martine. He became her agent and began getting bookings for her with different fashion magazines. She left her job at the department store and worked strictly with Jason.

One Saturday night in September, at a dinner party at the Sheraton in Times Square, Jason mentioned to Martine that she needed to be more careful about her diet. "I think you are putting on weight," he said, as she was finishing a steak. "Try eating fish from now on, and cut out the cocktails." Martine had to admit that her clothes had felt tight lately, and she had gone up a size at her last photo shoot. She vowed that she would be more careful, and was, for a while.

Eventually, trying to keep up with all her appointments and trying so hard to please Jason, the pressure got to her. Once again, she turned to food for comfort. She remembered her high school days and the purging, and began that method of control again. She lost weight rapidly and Jason could not have been more pleased. As time went on, she allowed him to control her every move. If she did not, he became very angry. He screamed and yelled at her, and sometimes grabbed her arm and shook her violently. She became more and more obedient, and soon felt as though she was losing herself. She was twenty-one years old and her life was a horrific, exciting mess.

CECILIA GOODLAND

Linda Jean Barkley was thirty-seven years old when her husband of twelve years died suddenly of a heart attack. Her daughter, Cecilia, was fifteen at the time, and had lived with Linda's mother in Ocean City, New Jersey since she was three. Linda's husband, Robert Barkley, refused to allow the child to live in his home in Los Angeles with him and her mother. He was a cold and rather sarcastic man whom any child would have been better off away from. Linda had married him only because of his wealth, and the fact that he could promote her modeling career. She had stayed in contact with her daughter over the years, and vowed to bring Cecilia to live with her in California as soon as possible. Linda was a very attractive woman and one of L.A.'s top fashion models. She was barely scarred by her husband's death, since life with him had been an unpleasant experience from the beginning of their marriage.

The fifteen-year-old Cecilia walked slowly up the steps to her grandmother's home on Third Street in Ocean City. She let the screen door slam slightly as she entered, to allow Nan and Pop to know she had made her entrance. Pop was Nan's live-in lover and companion, and Cecilia did not want to embarrass them or herself by walking in at an inopportune time. Her sixty-six-year-old grandmother was very healthy, and Pop was two years her junior. They spent a lot of time in Nan's room — just "spending time," as Nan referred to it. This day, though, Cecilia was surprised to see the two of them sitting in the living room and smiling at her as she walked in.

Cecilia stood in the middle of the floor with her eyes wide and her mouth open. "What?" she asked. "What is it with you two? You look like the cat that just ate the mouse. Tell me, hurry!"

Pop spoke first. "Your mother wants you to come to California," he said. "You'll be leaving the day after the school term ends. Your mother will arrive here next week. She phoned today to tell us that Robert died, and she wants you to go with her."

Cecilia looked at her grandmother, who was sitting there and smiling, as if in a daze.

"It is true; your mother is coming for you," Nan said.

"But aren't you the least bit upset that Mom has lost her husband of twelve years? I'm sure she will miss him."

Nan said, "Yes, we are sorry for her loss, but we're trying to focus on the good that will come from it. It will be good for you, Cel, to finally be with your mother."

"I'm going to my room." With her books in hand, she marched up the stairs. She felt a sudden surge of excitement as her mind began to take in what had happened. *I can't believe the old bastard finally croaked,* she thought. *I can't believe I can finally be with Mom. I'll no longer have to explain why I live with my grandmother to every new person that I meet. I hope the old coot left us a bundle of money.*

She took her rosary from her dresser, dropped to her knees, and began to pray. "Thank you, God, for answering my prayers. Please forgive me for hating Robert and please have mercy on his sinning soul. Please watch over my mother and keep her safe and well. Amen."

Linda arrived on Friday, May 15, 1953. It was a beautiful day. The weather man had called for rain, but it did not come. Cecilia thanked God once more for this blessing. Her mother stepped off the train in Atlantic City wearing a yellow skirt and a white spring sweater, with her blonde hair tied back in a ponytail. She smiled as she ran to Cecilia, who thought Linda was the most beautiful woman in the entire world. They engulfed each other in hugs and kisses. The dark circles around Linda's eyes indicated that she had had a rough time the previous week. Nan and Pop stood in the background, giving mother and daughter a chance to enjoy their reunion. Soon everyone had hugged and cried, and they were in the car and headed for Ocean City.

TWO YEARS LATER

The past two years, living with her mother, had been the best that Cecilia could remember. She was at the end of her senior year of high school and was happier than she could have ever imagined. She was dating a nice young man who was a freshman at UCLA, and was thinking about him as she walked home from school. Her eighteenth birthday was coming up in July, and she hoped to become engaged before she went off to college. There were so many things she wanted to discuss with her mother, and she planned to do that this very day.

Linda was not due to go in to work that day, since it was her regular day off. Cecilia called out to her as she walked into the house. When Linda didn't answer, she called out again as she walked into the kitchen. She panicked when she saw her mother's feet sticking out from behind the cabinet. She screamed, "Mom!" and ran for the phone.

She quickly called for an ambulance, and Linda was transported to the nearest hospital. She had been unconscious for a while, according to the doctor. There were no signs of foul play, so attempted murder or robbery were ruled out. After running several tests, it was determined that Linda had a brain tumor and needed surgery immediately. Cecilia prayed harder than ever as her mother underwent major surgery to remove the tumor.

After the surgery, Cecilia was told that her mother would live, but she had suffered severe brain damage and would not speak or walk. The young girl fell to her knees and cried.

A week later Linda was transported to New Jersey, where she was placed in a well-run nursing home. Cecilia vowed to spend her life taking care of her, if necessary. During the next year, she spent her waking evening hours sitting by her mother's bed, talking to her and writing a story. Linda died on June 10, 1956, only one year and one month after her surgery.

The following September, Cecilia went to college at UCLA. She hoped she would find Joseph Jackson and renew their relationship. This was hopeless, since Joseph had married and worked for his father-in-law. She threw herself into her studies, and graduated with her bachelors in English in the summer of '58.

She was still living on her inheritance from Linda when she moved to New York and rented an apartment in Manhattan. She found work writing for a local paper, and decided to revise the book she had written during her mom's illness. She called the story "Spotless," and within nine months it was published and she was on her first tour.

Cecilia met Rizzy that summer, at a little coffee shop in Manhattan as she was signing copies of her book for some fans. He purchased five copies for signature, and invited her to a party at his apartment at nine the next evening. He promised that she would meet other authors there, and she quickly accepted.

When she arrived at his apartment in Queens the next night, she found Rizzy alone. "Where are the other guests?" she asked.

"They will arrive around ten. I wanted to take this time to get acquainted with the new up-and-coming writer," he said. He poured each of them a glass of wine, and after they toasted to a nice evening and set the wineglasses on the table, he embraced her and began kissing her hard on the mouth. "I knew you lusted for me when you looked in my eyes yesterday," he said.

She pushed against him violently in an attempt to break his grasp, but he continued to hold her and forced her down onto the sofa. She screamed and begged him to release her, but was helpless against his superior male strength.

"Please let me go," Cecilia cried, but he held her tighter, forcing his hand under her dress and grabbing at her panties. He ripped them off and raped her, then went to the bathroom and left her whimpering on the couch. She pulled herself together, ran next door, and asked someone to call a cab for her. She went home feeling violated and stupid. She thought about going to the police, but felt no one would believe her since she had willingly gone to his apartment.

A week after the rape, Cecilia went to see a psychiatrist to help her deal with what had happened. She chose a woman, knowing at that point that she would not trust a man. The sessions were very helpful, and all during her six months of treatment, she noticed she had a warm and strange feeling for Dr. Feldman. On her last day of treatment, as she was saying good-bye, her feelings took control and she reached up and kissed the doctor on the lips. "You're so sweet," said the doctor. She kissed Cecilia on the mouth, and within seconds the two women were on the couch, kissing and fondling one another in heated passion. Nancy's mouth found Cecilia's hard nipples, and Cecilia moaned with delight as Nancy's tongue found even more excitable parts of her body. Cecilia moaned with pleasure at the wonderful feeling she experienced.

Cecilia's relationship with Nancy deepened over the next six months, and by Christmas she had been introduced to several of Nancy's close friends. She was invited to a New Year's Eve party by one of them who lived in Queens. She was a little nervous about going to that area of the city, since that was where she had been raped the year before. She told herself she was being silly; she would be with Nancy and other friends. It turned out to be a wonderful party, and it was there that she met Calvin Albritten. He expressed delight at meeting her and raved about her book. She was overwhelmed with excitement when he told her that he had been talking with a friend of his about possibly adapting it as a play. He said, "Cecilia, the fellow that I am talking about is Jeffrey Wilde." She recognized the name and became even more excited. She had heard that he was one of the best.

Before January of 1960 ended, Cecilia's book was a Broadway play in the making. It was to be produced and directed by Jeffrey Wilde. They chose Jason Carter to act as a preacher named John Kingsley, the perverted rapist in the story that actually got away with murder because of his spotless reputation.

Jason introduced his friend Martine Hamilton to Cecilia and they became close friends with her and Calvin. Calvin had a lover named Harold Rice whom he saw regularly. Harold was kept pretty much off the Broadway scene because Calvin never really came out of the closet about his homosexuality .He was concerned that gays were not well respected and worried about his reputation. It was believed that he was involved with this new writer, Cecilia Goodland, that he was promoting. Harold owned a flower shop in the city that kept him busy, and Calvin spent as much time with him as possible.

The play took months in the making. They all worked very hard to make the play a success. It was a smash on opening night and Cecilia was on her way to becoming a well-known author.

NEW YORK CITY SECRET

Richard Peale sat at his desk in his study at home on Channing Street. His thoughts lingered on the past, when his beloved family was alive and young. He pictured his beautiful wife, Jessica, with her hair pulled back and wearing her white robe as she greeted him in the morning. He thought about a little boy with blond hair, and a beautiful little girl getting ready for school. His thoughts brought him to tears once again, as so often in the past, and he prayed to God to help him understand and accept his loss. As usual, his prayer was answered and he was jolted into the present. *Call your daughter,* he thought. He knew the thought came from God.

He was always reminded that he still had this little girl, now a woman, who was off in New York starring in a play on Broadway. He picked up the telephone and dialed her number. Her voice on the other end of the line, to Richard, sounded angelic.

"Hello?" she said.

"Hello, Molly, how's my baby girl?"

"Oh, Dad, how are you, dear?"

"Well, honey, I'm just fine now that I have you on the phone. When will you be coming home for a visit?"

"I don't know. It will be months before I can get time off from this play. I would love to have you come to New York to visit me, though. I have a lot of nice friends who are just dying to see you again. Call the airline and make arrangements, and I will call you tonight for details. Gotta run. We'll chat later." She hung up.

Richard longed to see his daughter. He closed his eyes and saw her face as he listened to the dial tone from the receiver. He hung up briefly, and then picked up the receiver again and called the airline.

The plane landed at 11:45 a.m. on a Sunday in late May of 1973. Molly was waiting at the gate for Richard to make his grand departure from the plane. She spotted him as he entered through the passenger gate, and her heart leaped with love for her father. He was still as handsome as ever; or better, with his full head of white hair. He was wearing a light blue leisure suit and tan shoes. She called to him and they ran to each other, with arms outstretched and smiling from ear to ear.

"You look absolutely marvelous, dad," she said.

"You do likewise, my dear daughter." They picked up his baggage and walked to the limo that was waiting out front. The driver opened doors and greeted them as the porter put the bags in the trunk.

"Molly Girl," he said, "we've both been so busy. This much time should not pass without our seeing each other. Now that I'm retired, you will be seeing a lot more of me."

"That's wonderful, Dad. I hope you'll stay longer this time. I haven't seen you for three years and that is way too long. Stay for at least two weeks. I'll be busy a lot of the time, but I can have Martine show you around while I am working. She has slowed down a lot lately and is actually taking a month off. She and Jason are on the outs now, and he is seeing a girl from New Jersey. Martine is relieved to be out from under his possessive attachment, as she refers to it, but you know, Dad, old habits are hard to break. She lived in his clutches for over twelve years. It will take some time for her to get used to being on her own."

"Well, Moll, maybe we can keep her busy and help her forget. I can sure use the company while you're working."

The traffic in the city was as heavy, as usual, and it took them a good hour longer than expected to get to Molly's apartment in Manhattan. They arrived at 1:15 p.m. The driver carried the bags in and set them down on the living room floor in Molly's plush apartment. She had upgraded to a larger place, decorated with cream carpeting and furniture, and beautiful peach and mint green accessories. The windows were large and overlooked a small park.

"My God, girl! This is a beautiful place. Your career has taken you to a new dimension. This must have cost you a fortune."

"Oh well, I suppose it is worth it to be comfy for a while longer. I know I have not told you yet, Dad, but I have decided this will be my last play. I have always wanted to write a book or two, and acting is just so demanding. The rehearsals take up so much of my time. I feel that I need to be free of the stage in order to write my first book. With any luck, I could hit the best-seller list and make some real money. Jeff has a friend who is an agent and will handle the publishing for me, which will be a big help. So what do you think, Dad?"

"Sweetheart, I think it's a wonderful idea. If it makes you happy, then by all means, go for it. Will you have something about your old dad in your book?"

"I'll tell you all about it over dinner tonight. I have to run now, Dad. Martine will be over around five. I'll be back at six or so. We'll have dinner around eight, so for now, you just make yourself at home and get some rest. If you are hungry, there is food in the kitchen."

Richard took his things into the guest room and began to unpack. He looked around the room and thought how the decor had more of a masculine look. He wondered if Molly had had his visits in mind when she had it decorated. There were pictures of fox hunters on the tan walls, and a painting of their home on Channing Street hung over the bed. There was a caption at the bottom of the picture which read "To here I shall return someday." Tears clouded Richard's eyes as he read it. He would never sell the home, now that he had read this. His beloved daughter would need the house to invite friends and relatives to after his funeral someday.

He put his things away and lay down on the bed. The Hollywood-style bed was adorned with a black and cream comforter that matched the tweed shag carpeting. Eight large pillows with matching black and cream shams lined the top of the bed. Richard dozed off almost instantly and must have slept quite soundly. At four forty-five, he was awakened by the sound of the doorbell. He got up slowly and straightened his thick white hair. He opened the door to find the beautiful Martine Hamilton smiling up at him.

"Martine, you are even more beautiful than I remembered. How are you, my dear?"

She said, "Oh, just fine, Mr. Peale, and you are more handsome than ever."

They gave each other a huge hug, went into the living room, and enjoyed a glass of sherry and good conversation while they waited for Molly to come home. She arrived at exactly six, as promised. After giving her dad a hug and greeting Martine, she asked Richard where he would like to eat. He suggested the Captains Wharf at the Marriott Hotel near the waterfront and the women agreed. Martine had brought a dress and shoes to Molly's the day before, so in order to save time, Molly invited her to shower and change there. It was agreed upon, and soon, everyone was ready and Richard had called a taxi. Dinner and good conversation was enjoyed by all three. After dinner they took a cab back to Molly's, enjoyed a nightcap, and called it a day.

Monday morning brought a little rain and a slight chill to the air. Molly was up early and off to work. At ten o'clock, the doorbell rang. Richard dragged himself out of bed and threw on his robe. "Who is it?" he called.

The familiar voice of Martine came back with a little smile as she let him know it was only her. Richard opened the door and invited her in. Martine thought how handsome he looked for his sixty-something years, and desire stirred within her. She asked Richard if he would like for her to make a pot of coffee, and he said that would be great.

Later, over coffee and muffins, they talked about their lives during the past few years. He was saddened by Martine's story of all the abuse she had taken from Jason. He stood up and excused himself to go to the bathroom, and Martine got up and began picking up the coffee cups. They brushed each other as they passed in the kitchen, and instantly began to embrace.

Richard spoke first, as he held her in his arms and stroked her hair. "Poor baby, I wish I could do something to take away your pain," he said.

"Oh, Richard, just hold me. It feels so good to be held. It's been so long since anyone has felt this good to me."

"Likewise, my dear," he said, and began to kiss her on the mouth. Suddenly, he released her, walked over to the window, and looked out at the city.

Martine stared at his back for a moment, then said, "I'll be in your room, Richard. Please join me. Don't be afraid. We are both adults and have the same needs and desires."

She went into the bedroom, removed her clothes, and got into bed. About ten minutes later, he joined her. They made love as though they were starved for each other. Afterward, they lay in each other's arms and held each other as Martine cried out all the pent-up anguish that had built up in her over the years as a result of the abuse from Jason. Richard let her cry it out as he stroked her neck and back. She felt loved like never before. They made love again that afternoon, and Martine left around three o'clock.

Molly made her entrance into her apartment at precisely four thirty. Her jolly voice rang out through the rooms. "Hello, Dad. Come out, come out, wherever you are. I brought Chinese home for dinner. I can't wait to tell you about my new plans."

Richard came out of the bedroom slowly and tried to show some enthusiasm for what his daughter had to say. He smiled as he gave her a big hug and said, "Okay, baby, what's cooking?"

She said, "Well, I have decided to go home to Channing Street to write my book. With any luck, the realtor will have this place rented in a month or two. What do you think?"

"That's wonderful, dear."

"That isn't all. I would like for Martine to come with me, since she depends on me so these days. She has been so distraught over her personal life and I just do not want to leave her here alone."

Richard breathed a little sigh, as he agreed that Martine should come home with Molly. "We'll treat her as my daughter and your sister," he said. All he could think about was what had happened that afternoon. He vowed to himself that it would not happen again.

When Molly arrived home from work the next day, Richard was packed and ready to leave. "Dad, what are you doing? You have been here only two days, and you're packed to leave already! Why?"

"Sweetheart, since you're planning to move back to Virginia, I think it's best if I return and get your rooms set up. There are things I need to do there. I want everything to be perfect for you and Martine. I'm so excited about your decision. Please understand." He pulled her into his arms, hugged her hard, and said, "My girl is coming home. Oh, baby, I'm so happy."

"I'm happy too, Dad", she said, laughing. "I'm going home to Channing Street."

The next morning at nine Richard boarded a plane for Norfolk. It was raining and there was a slight chill in the air. Fog was developing over the waterfront. In another part of town, Martine cried as she listened to Molly on the telephone, telling her that Richard had returned to Virginia ahead of schedule.

FINAL PERFORMANCE

The theater was packed on the night of my final performance. As I took my last bow that night in early October, I felt only triumph. I was anxious to get out of show business and start my new career as a writer. My apartment in New York was under contract with a realtor for leasing, and I was planning to go home to Virginia to begin the first chapter of my first book. I wasn't ready to sell my place in the Big Apple yet, just in case I was unable to readapt to a more relaxed southern lifestyle. I had lived in New York for ten years and had become accustomed to its faster pace. Martine had agreed to go to Virginia with me for a few weeks before she started her new career as a fashion model instructor. Our dear friend Cecilia would also be making the trip south, to get acquainted with my home town.

We took a plane out of Kennedy Airport the next day and arrived in Norfolk at 3:00 p.m. I was happy to see Dad waiting for us as we deplaned and walked through the gate. I had spoken to him the day before, and he had told me all about a new lady friend he had met at a singles party he had attended in September. I was anxious to meet her, but he said he didn't bring her along because he wanted time with Martine and me first. Dad had not had the pleasure of meeting Cel, so there were introductions, greetings, hugs and kisses all around. I noticed Dad gave Cel a strange look, and I wondered if he had picked up on her homosexuality.

Cecilia had a different sort of look since her affair of several years with Nancy Feldman. The affair had ended two years ago, when Nancy fell in love with another female therapist she had met at a seminar. Cecilia seemed to have gone from a slightly feminine look to a more masculine appearance since the breakup. Her previously long brown hair had turned partially gray and was cut very short in a tapered style. She wore no makeup and favored tuxedo-style slacks suits. The only thing on her person that appeared womanly was a pair of gold hoop earrings that Calvin Albritten had given her before he died of an unidentified virus the previous year.

Cecilia had written another best-seller after Calvin's death. It was called "Calvin Lived," and was Cal's life story. He was a wonderful friend and a successful writer. We all loved him very much. His homosexual lifestyle led him into one major infection after another, and finally an undetected sexually transmitted disease took his life. He was only forty-eight years old.

The drive from the airport to Craddock was filled with conversation and laughter as we told of recent experiences and Dad told us a joke or two. He was filling us in on his new relationship as we turned off Highway Seventeen and onto Channing Street. The old house looked the same, except for some new paint and a new storm door on the front. Dad took our things upstairs and I showed our guests around the house. They were impressed with the way Dad had kept the house all those years and how nice everything looked.

My room looked exactly the same, with my old furniture and some of my old dolls on the bed atop a new white spread Dad had bought. The guest room had been completely redone in a beautiful pale yellow, with white accessories and a light beige carpet. I loved the way the window on the south side of the room allowed the light to stream in. It was almost heavenly. I thought how nice it was of my father to have this room fixed up for Martine to enjoy during her stay. I was beginning to notice a certain quietness about Marty, but I guessed she was probably just a little tired from the trip. I asked her if she would like to rest for a while, but she insisted that she was fine, and would rather change her clothes and hang out downstairs having tea with Dad.

Cecilia and I decided to take a walk around the neighborhood to stretch our legs. While doing so, I filled her in on who was who and who was new on the block. In my home town, if you hadn't lived in Craddock for at least twenty years you were new. We walked and talked for an hour, then went back to make plans for dinner.

As we entered the house, I was surprised to see Marty and Dad embracing and Marty in tears. He immediately stepped away from her and said that she had been telling him of her sad experiences with Jason, and he was trying to comfort her. It seemed like a logical explanation and I didn't give it a thought.

Dad offered to take us out to eat, but we insisted on making hamburgers and French fries, and just having a good old-fashioned, American-style meal. We pulled the hamburger meat out of the fridge and I made patties while Cel peeled potatoes. Martine made a pitcher of iced tea and Dad popped open a beer. We talked about my final performance over dinner, and Dad told us more about his lady friend. Her name was Connie Roper. She was a widow, fifty-nine years young, with salt and pepper hair and hazel eyes. He said he had invited her over for dinner the next night and we would all meet her then. I felt happy for my Dad, and expressed this to my friends and to him. Cel and Marty both said they were excited for him, but Martine had a sadness about her. I thought it was because she had been thinking about Jason, and dismissed my concern.

As Martine, Cel and I hung out in my room in our pajamas and chatted, I ask Marty if something was bothering her.

"It's nothing," she said. "Maybe I am a little tired." Cel and I assured her that if she was feeling bad about anything, she could talk to us about it. "I'm very aware of that. Both of you are wonderful friends, and if there is anything I feel I should talk about, I surely will," she said, and added that we shouldn't worry so much.

We shared stories about things and feelings that had occurred in our childhood days until midnight, and then Cecilia went into the guest room and Marty and I shared my room. We slept like babies until we heard Dad call us for breakfast at eight thirty the next morning.

I called my childhood friend Rosalie after breakfast, and the four of us drove to Virginia Beach to do some sightseeing and souvenir shopping. Rosalie had married in January of '63 at age twenty-three, and was the mother of two children. John, her first, was born on November 25 of the same year. It was the day of President Kennedy's burial at Arlington Cemetery. I remembered how we had felt the pain for the death of a great man and then the joy of a new birth. John was now ten years old and her daughter, Tammy, was eight. We had a great time buying for the children and had lunch at Duck Inn on the beach. Dad had reminded us as we were leaving that we were to be home by six, to have dinner and get acquainted with Connie.

At exactly four thirty, we drove onto Route 44 and headed back to Craddock. We invited Rosalie to join us for dinner, but she had to pick up the children from daycare and make it home before Jack, her husband, arrived home from his office. Jack was an attorney on the rise in the Norfolk area, and from what I heard he was not much of a husband to Rosalie and was very demanding of her services. She thought about divorcing him, but since she worked only as a substitute teacher at one of the local schools and didn't make much on her own, she felt she should wait until the children were older. I felt she should make her move to avoid further abuse; however, I didn't intend to put pressure on her for something that was none of my business. I loved Rosalie very much, considering she had been my best friend for so many years. We had shared so much fun and heartache, and oh so many secrets. I prayed so many times for her safety while with this man, and for her recovery whenever she was willing to make her break. She knew that I would be there for her.

CONSTANCE

We made it home just in time to welcome Constance to dinner. She arrived at exactly 6:00 p.m. Dad began introductions, but Connie stopped him by holding up her right hand and saying, "Please, let me guess."

She looked at me and said, "Hello, Molly. It is so nice to meet you. I recognize you from your picture. Oh, and Martine, I have had such a perfect description of you from Richard. Cecilia, I loved your last book. What a tragic story. I'm so sorry about your friend. I trust you are doing well?"

Connie had not missed a single beat.

"It's a pleasure to meet you, Connie," I said.

"Oh," she said, "I'm not Connie. I'm Richard's other girlfriend, Mary. Didn't he tell you girls he has a whole string of us?"

For a moment I was flabbergasted. I looked at my father in shock. He and the woman began laughing hysterically. We all caught on and joined in the laughter. I knew immediately that I was going to like this person. She was like a breath of fresh air after so many somber personalities of late. I was glad for Dad that he had found someone with a sense of humor and wit.

"Well, Dad, what can we do to help get dinner on the table?"

"Not a thing, dear. I have everything covered. If you ladies will take a seat, I'll put the food on the table." Dad had cooked his specialty: meatloaf, mashed potatoes, carrots and string beans. He announced that the carrots and beans had come from his own garden, which he had planted in the summer.

"Oh, Richard, do you really expect us to eat old food from the summer?" Connie said. This woman never missed the opportunity to crack a joke.

"Connie, you are a funny lady; however, I have to admit that your vegetable line was a wee bit corny. No pun intended," I said. Everyone laughed, and we enjoyed a healthy, hearty dinner.

I noticed that Martine had been exceptionally quiet again. Even though she laughed at Connie's cute remarks, her laughter was rather strained. I asked her about it as we picked up the dishes. She said she was tired, and shortly after doing the dishes she ask to be excused and went up to bed.

Dad offered us all dessert of tea-cake and milk or tea, but Cel and I begged off, saying we were about to burst from such a delightful meal. We excused ourselves and went upstairs to read and relax. We talked and laughed about the events of our day, and not long after we fell asleep. I dreamed about a man trying to make love to me, but when I looked at him, he had no face. I woke up startled, and then fell back into a deep, dreamless sleep.

I awoke the next morning at seven o'clock, and grinned to myself as I saw a sunbeam streaming through my window. I remembered my childhood and so many mornings I awoke to those beautiful sunbeams. I felt happy, and for the first time in years totally secure and without a single worry. I thought about the evening before and how very much I liked Connie, and how I looked forward to developing a friendship with her. I got up and went to the bathroom. As I sat on the toilet, I remembered the dream I had had and wondered who the man without a face must represent. I figured it to be someone I had yet to meet, and then forgot about it as I showered.

As I passed Dad's door on my way downstairs, I could hear him and Connie laughing and thought how nice it was that they were so close. It would be great to have a step-mom to share thoughts and secrets with. The fact that they were sleeping together wasn't an issue as far as I was concerned. I just assumed that eventually they would marry and live happily most of the time.

I started a big pot of oatmeal and put dishes on the table, along with milk and honey. I called up the stairs to everyone to come down and have breakfast, and then went out front to pick up the newspaper.

Mrs. Whitby, our next-door neighbor, came out at the same time. "Good-morning, Molly," she said. "It is so nice to see you home. How are you, my dear?"

"I am doing quite well," I said. "I would really love to talk with you Mrs. Whitby, but my dad and our friends are waiting for me and breakfast. Nice seeing you." I remembered Mrs. Whitby as a busybody from my childhood and wanted to escape before she could ask about my family's business. I was sure she had some thoughts about Dad and Connie and I wasn't in the mood to go there. I went in and sat down to breakfast with Dad, Connie and Cecilia.

"Where is Marty?" I asked.

"Oh, she said she isn't feeling well and won't be down until later," Cecilia said.

"Let her rest," Dad said. I said that would be alright, and we proceeded to eat.

After breakfast, Cel and I went up to check on Marty and found her talking on the phone. She hung up and told us she had answered an ad to audition for a commercial, and had an appointment at two that afternoon. We expressed our enthusiasm and started looking through our things for something to wear on a walk around the neighborhood.

Connie knocked on the bedroom door and asked us if we would like to go on a shopping spree with her later. Cel and I said we would love it, but Marty begged off because of her audition. Connie said she would pick us up in an hour to go and look at dresses at The Famous Shop downtown. I knew Famous as a formal dress shop, and wondered if Connie might be looking for something for a wedding. I asked her if she thought she would get a ring soon. She laughed and said, "Yes, probably around my bathtub."

She picked us up one hour later for shopping. We were surprised to find that Famous was having a fashion show, with tea and hors d'oeuvres. We enjoyed the show and the food immensely. Afterwards, we took a walk down High Street and looked in some of the shops. The old town of Portsmouth was not quite what it used to be when I was a child. I remembered when Rosalie and I used to ride the bus on Saturday to go to a movie. The thought of Christmas approaching reminded me of the first time I had seen *White Christmas* with Bing Crosby and Rosemary Clooney. I was fifteen years old; it had been the year that I met Nick.

"Molly, dear, what on earth are you thinking about?" Connie's voice pulled me out of my daydream.

"Oh, to tell the truth, I was thinking about an old boyfriend," I said.

"Oh," she said, "I would like to hear about the current boyfriend."

Just then Cecilia piped up with, "I can tell you about him," she said. "He is non-existent. If you ask me, I think our dear Molly is still carrying a torch for the old flame from her girlhood."

"Oh, I see. Do you ever think about looking this fella up?" Connie asked, looking at me with raised eyebrows.

I very emphatically told both of them that I had no intention of looking anyone up, and had to laugh a little. Then I found myself wondering if there was any possibility of finding him. I suggested we get on back and find out how Martine made out with her audition. We drove home in silence, feeling tired from such an active afternoon.

Martine was soaking in the tub when we arrived. She said she had gotten the job, and thought a bath would help her relax from all the excitement. Dad was in the process of making tea and seemed a little quiet. I hoped he wasn't upset with us for staying gone so long. He assured us that he was not, and said he hoped we had had a nice time. We sat in the dining room snacking on celery and peanut butter and everything seemed perfectly fine. Even Martine was in better spirits than she had been earlier. I smiled at her, congratulating her on the new job, and felt happy to have such wonderful friends and a perfectly great dad. I couldn't have asked for a better life.

Cecilia returned to New York the next day, and I pulled out my old typewriter and started writing my story.

CHRISTMAS 1973

"Give me back my umbrella, you idiot!" came a female voice from the street outside. I looked up from my typewriter at the clock on my nightstand. *Good grief!* I thought. *It can't possibly be three o'clock.* The school kids outside were on their way home and I was still in my pajamas. I stood up and looked out of the window. It was still drizzling, as it had been earlier that cold December morning when I sat down to write. My novel was in the fifth chapter and I had a hard time taking breaks. I loved what I was doing and was pleased with the way it was going so far.

Martine was still with us, and was doing one commercial after the other for a local dress shop. She was as beautiful as ever and seemed happier than she had since she came to Craddock. She had not mentioned her new career lately, and I wondered if she was still interested. I planned to ask her about it that evening when she arrived home for dinner.

Dad spent a lot of time out of the house these days. He said he was taking long walks and doing volunteer work at the hospital. I was ecstatically pleased with both of them, and was beginning to think of Martine as the sister I had always wanted but never had.

I lay down on the floor and began to stretch my muscles. I did certain exercises after a long session at the typewriter because I had a tendency to tense up as I typed. I was ready for a nice long soak in the tub after that, and right then it sounded wonderful. I turned on the water in the tub just as the phone rang. It was Connie, asking if I would please meet her at the restaurant in Holiday Inn at the waterfront downtown. She sounded upset. I said I would be there in an hour. My long bath became a short shower, and I quickly dressed, grabbed my coat and purse, and headed out to meet her.

I was very worried. Connie and I had become very close friends and I had come to love her dearly. Frightening thoughts consumed me as I drove. I knew that certain friends of my dad's had contracted illnesses and passed away in the last few years, and I couldn't help thinking that Connie was about to tell me she had a terrible disease.

I met her in the lounge at four fifteen. She was sipping a glass of wine, and looked up at me with tears in her eyes.

"Connie, for God's sake, what is wrong?" I was terrified.

"I don't know how to tell you this, Molly," she said. "Things have not been the same between your dad and me for about two weeks now. I knew he was busy with his volunteer work and I tried to pass it off as that, but then I got suspicious and started checking on him. My findings are devastating, Molly. It looks as though your dad and Martine are having an affair. I saw both of them coming out of this hotel four times in one week. Richard hasn't been at the hospital for two weeks. When I asked him about his activities, he said he had been working there."

I was horrified! How could this old woman make up such a horrible story about my father and my friend? I had actually loved her like a mother. How could she destroy my world like this? I ran out of the hotel. I went to a phone booth and called the hospital where he worked. What Connie had said was Confirmed; he had not been there in two weeks. I called the dress shop that employed Marty, and was told that she was on vacation and would not return until their Christmas show on the twentieth. This was only the tenth. My heart sank. I went back to Connie, who was still crying at the table.

"Listen, Connie, there has to be a logical explanation. After all, it is nearly Christmas and they may be shopping for gifts for you and me."

"Do you think that could be it?" she asked. I thought I saw a glimmer of hope in her eyes.

"Of course that is it. The idea that my dad and Marty could be interested in each other romantically is preposterous. She is like his very own daughter. Get yourself together now. Let's go to Channing Street and make a pot of coffee."

"I feel like such a fool, Molly. I'm so sorry to have upset you this way. I just love Richard so much, and the thought of him with another woman makes me lose my senses. Forgive me."

"There is absolutely nothing to forgive. If you were my mother, I would expect you to come to me with your problems, as I would to you. You are like a mother to me, Connie," I said.

She smiled and said, "I'm so glad you feel that way, Moll, because I think of you as a daughter."

We were in the kitchen sipping our coffee when Dad arrived from wherever he had been. We said hello, and he expressed how pleasantly surprised he was to find Connie and me together and getting along so well.

"Let me guess. You girls have been out Christmas shopping for the old man. Am I right? The presents are hidden in the trunks of your cars. Now, don't spend too much."

Connie and I looked at each other and laughed.

Connie answered, "Well, darling, how did you ever guess?"

His statement convinced us both that that was exactly what he and Marty had been doing. I asked how his day at the hospital had been, and his answer surprised us.

"Well, ladies, I didn't go there today. I had a few things to do myself." I breathed a sigh of relief, and looked up at Connie just in time to see the tension leave her face.

Just then I heard the front door open, and Marty made her grand entrance. I was sure her day had been filled with the joy of shopping for her friends and her mom, who would be coming from Minnesota to spend Christmas with us. Marty's parents had been in a car wreck in 1961, and her dad died as a result. She had been through a lot, and I was glad that all was well again and that a wonderful Christmas was on the way.

Nine days had passed since Connie and I had what we thought was the scare of the century. It was the nineteenth of the month and Christmas was fast approaching. I decided to take a break from writing and finish shopping. Martine and I had shopped most of the afternoon for gifts for her mom, my dad and Connie, and now I was ready to go with Connie to finish up for Marty and my dad. Marty, Dad and I had enjoyed a home-cooked meal for the first time in weeks, and I was waiting with my coat on for Connie to pick me up. Marty was due to start her Christmas show at work the next day, so she was glad to stay at home that evening and rest. Dad said he would be spending a quiet evening at home also. He had some reading to catch up on and would be going upstairs shortly. Connie's horn sounded at six thirty and I ran outside to meet her.

We were almost to the shopping center when I realized I had forgotten my purse. Connie said not to fret; that it would not take that much time to run back and get it. Ten minutes later, we pulled up in front of the house. I ran in the front door and, to my horror, there were Dad and Marty standing in the living room. Marty was not wearing a top and my father was passionately sucking one of her breasts. I froze in my tracks. They were so engrossed that they did not hear me come in. Marty was moaning and begging him to take her upstairs, and Dad repeated over and over, "I love you, I love you."

"Just what the hell do you two think you are doing?!" I screamed at them. "Connie was right about you two."

They looked at me with horrified expressions. Martine ran upstairs and Dad came toward me, saying insane things like he was in love with her and could not help himself. I grabbed my purse, swung it at him, and hit him in the face. I called him a pig and her a tramp, then ran back out to Connie's car. I was crying hysterically, and told Connie that she had been right in her suspicions; I had just caught them in the act. We held each other and cried.

After a good cry, we decided to go to Connie's house and spend the night. She opened a bottle of red wine and we drank, talked and cried until two in the morning. Connie went up to her room and I went to her guest room. Drunk and exhausted, I fell into a fitful, dreamless sleep.

My head ached and my eyes burned. Sunbeams streamed through the window onto my face, and for a moment I forgot where I was. Had it all been a bad dream? I opened my eyes and looked around the room, and knew it was not a dream. I realized where I was and sat up. I had slept in my clothes all night. The pajamas Connie had loaned me were still on the chair. I heard Connie moving around in the kitchen. Hers was a lovely little one-story home with two bedrooms, on Wooten Lane in Deep-Creek Shores, about ten miles from Craddock. The decor was so pretty, with a lot of yellow and light blue, which reminded me of our guest room on Channing Street. I called to her that I could use a cup of coffee and a shower, and she was quick to accommodate. She brought coffee into the room, insisted that I take my time in the bathroom, and said when I was ready we would have a nice talk. It was eleven thirty. The whole morning was shot, but we didn't care. We were both concerned about each other and where we would go from there.

We talked for an hour or so, sharing feelings and ideas. I decided that I would return to New York to finish my book, and invited Connie to join me there. She had a son in the military, and said she would call him about staying with him and his family for a while, until she felt comfortable being back in this area again. We were both embarrassed at the thought of our stupidity and inability to see through Dad and Martine's little subterfuge. I remembered my experience with the fairies when I was eight. My mother had told me that when you believed something so much it seemed real to you, even if it wasn't. Connie and I had wanted to believe so much that nothing was wrong; we couldn't see the truth, even though it was in front of us. I felt guilty about making excuses for Dad and Marty rather than working with Connie to find out the truth. Now we were faced with it, and it had changed our lives.

I needed desperately to talk to Jeffrey Wilde. I felt that he was the only man in the world I could trust. I got permission from Connie to use her telephone and dialed for a long distance operator and placed a collect call. I was ready to hang up when I heard the welcome familiar voice of my dear friend after the fifth ring.

"Hello?"

I began crying hysterically. "Jeff?" I sobbed. I was so overcome with emotion that I couldn't speak.

"Molly, is this you? What's wrong? Has something happened to your dad? Molly, speak up girl!"

I managed to pull myself together. "Oh, Jeff. Something very upsetting has happened, and I will be returning to New York. I'm going to try and get a flight out of Norfolk tomorrow. No, nothing has happened to my father, although I feel as if he has died. I can't tell you on the phone. I will call you as soon as I get the flight information. I will need to stay with you for a while because my apartment is leased for a whole six months. Is that going to work out? Tell me if it is an imposition and I'll ask Cel, although I would rather not."

"Molly, you are more than welcome to stay here. I'll start cleaning out my spare room immediately. Call me as soon as you get flight details and I will make arrangements to pick you up at the airport."

"Thank you, from my heart," I said, and hung up the phone. I called and made travel arrangements, and called Jeff again to give him the information. I felt the need to see Rosalie, and telephoned to ask if I could come over. She said, "Please do."

I left Connie to decide if she would stay at home or go to her son's. She was starting to feel better and was able to think more rationally.

Rosalie was waiting for me at the door when I arrived. I told her the whole story, and we held each other and cried.

"How could he do such a thing? Rosalie, I never want to see my father's face again as long as I live — or Martine's, as far as that goes. How will I ever cope with this?"

"You will, darling," she said. Then she held my face in her hands, looked in my eyes, and reminded me that time heals all.

"Not this time. I have lost everyone in my family now. There are only my wonderful friends to turn to," I said.

"I am always here for you, Moll," she said. I told her I knew that, hugged her good-bye, and drove back to Connie's house. I asked

Connie about her plans, and she said she had decided to stay in Portsmouth and get on with her life. She drove me back to Channing Street and I went in to start packing.

Dad and Martine were both out and everything seemed normal in the house, but I knew it would never be the same again. My father, whom I had loved with all my heart, had disgraced me and I vowed I would never forgive him. I packed as many clothes as I thought I could take on the plane, took my typewriter, and went back to Connie's. She was talking on the phone when I arrived.

"I have to go now, Richard. Molly is here. Please don't ever call me again," she said. She told me that he had apologized and asked her to forgive him, but insisted that he could not control his feelings for Marty. "He said he doesn't want to give her up, Moll," Connie said.

"Oh, Connie, I am so sorry. I hope you find the right person to share your life with," I said.

"I wish the same for you, my dear," she said.

I smiled and said, "Maybe I already have." I closed my eyes and thought of Jeff.

JEFF'S STORY
ACCORDING TO JEFF

I had loved Molly since I first laid eyes on her years ago, but had never expressed my feelings because of her distant nature. Sometimes she would stare straight ahead, almost catatonic, with her beautiful blue eyes slightly moist as if she were half-crying. I knew there had been one love in her life when she was very young, only fifteen, and how can a fifteen-year-old stay in love into her thirties with someone she never saw again? She always said she was just so wrapped up in her career, but I didn't buy it. I knew this time it was going to be different. I had to tell her; not today, but soon. She needed me now more than ever.

I was angry with Richard. I hated what he had done to her feelings for him and how he had destroyed her friendship with Martine. She had once confided in me that she could always depend on her father when she needed moral support. In a way I was hurt, because I had always told her that I was her friend as well as her director. She was so aloof at times. Then there were times when she was warm and friendly; a barrel of laughs. She had been the most dedicated actress I had ever worked with. She had given so much of herself to Martine and Cecilia, and now she had been betrayed by the one to whom she had given the most. I had to let her know how I loved her because she was in so much pain and needed love so desperately.

I was thinking that she must not have flown first class because it was taking her so long to come off the plane. Then I saw her. She was carrying a bag for an elderly lady and talking with her as they walked. Her face looked drawn and she had dark circles under her eyes, but this didn't hide her beauty. I had always thought she was sort of ordinary, yet beautiful. I watched as she handed the old woman over to her family, and saw how they appreciated her help. She looked up and saw me, and then she put her arms out. We held each other tightly, swaying back and forth. The words that came from me were meant to remain unspoken for a while, but I couldn't hold back.

"Molly, I love you. I'm sorry if it upsets you, but I had to tell you."

She didn't pull away, but very softly said, "It's okay, Jeff. I think I love you, too. I missed you so while I was away. It feels good to be in your arms."

I was on cloud nine after that. My mind was filled with serendipitous thoughts and I was hoping to make them a reality.

We chatted all the way to my apartment. Molly filled me in on the whole story of her dad, Martine and Connie. "I hope God will forgive them, Jeff, because I never shall," she said.

"Time heals, Molly. Maybe you will, too," I said.

When we arrived at my apartment, she was astonished at the condition of my living room. Everything from the guest room was piled into it.

"My God, Jeff! What on earth have you done?" she asked.

"Oh, I just made some room for my favorite lady," I said. I took her into my arms and carried her into her new bedroom. She loved the zebra comforter, white sheers with zebra drapes, and white shag carpeting with black throw rugs. She hugged me and laughed while trying to talk, and I was so in love. I was so happy at that moment that I was almost glad her father and Martine had screwed up. I knew it was wrong to feel that way and tried to think less selfishly, but began to feel guilty and angry at my thoughts. I just knew that I was glad to have her in my life.

The day went smoothly as I helped Molly set up her writing equipment and put her things away. I was in the process of directing a play. As much as I hated to, I had to leave at five to go to work. Somehow I got through the evening, and returned home at eleven thirty. Molly was busy at the typewriter and didn't hear me come in. I sneaked up behind her, peeked over her shoulder and read, "Marie was pregnant with her fourth child when she found the letter from the woman in the glove box of his car." I knew she was writing a story about a young girl who was married to a cad. In reality, I thought that making her character's husband a cheating scoundrel helped her feel better about staying single all those years. I leaned over and said in her ear, "Boo!"

She jumped and yelled, "Oh my God, Jeff! You scared the living shit out of me. How long were you standing there? Why didn't you say something?"

"I did say something. I said boo. So, are you ready to take a break? Let's have a little nightcap."

"Okay", she said, getting up from her work.

We sat in front of the fireplace and sipped on sherry, and talked about some of the things that had happened over the years. We wondered how it all came down to this. I reached over and touched her hair.

She looked over into my eyes and softly said, "Jeff, I have never had intercourse with a man. I'm not sure I want to go there at this point in our relationship."

God, I was shocked! I had no idea this woman was still a virgin. This was the last month of 1973, and I had not known a virgin since junior high. It was three days away from Christmas. I looked at the huge tree in the corner of my living room. My eyes went to the angel on the top, and silently I named her Molly.

She must have seen the disbelief in my eyes, and broke the silence by saying, "Hey, you, don't look so surprised. There are still a few of us around."

I said, "Hey, girl, I will never try to rush you into anything you are not ready to experience. I'm just overwhelmed with love for you, and the idea that I will be the first to make it happen is so fantastic I can hardly speak. You will let me know when you are ready. All I want to do is make you happy."

She laughed and said, "Don't count your chickens before they hatch, Mr. Wilde. I may never be ready."

I smiled at her and thought to myself, *Perish the thought.* We finished our drinks, said goodnight, and went to our rooms. It was 2:30 a.m.

Sleep came easily, as did the nightmares. I was riding a horse in a heavy snowstorm, with snowflakes flying into my eyes. I was tired and my horse could hardly move. I almost fell off, and then there she was, riding a zebra. Blood was spilling out of her eyes. I looked down at the stream of blood on the snow.

I awoke with such a jolt that I sat up in bed and quickly looked at the clock. It was 4:00 a.m., and my heart was pounding. I got up, and slowly and quietly went to Molly's room. I could hear the typewriter as I approached the door. I called out to her, so not to startle her, and the typing stopped.

"Jeff? Can't you sleep?"

"Well," I said, "I was sleeping, until I had this awful dream about a girl riding on a zebra with blood coming out of her eyes."

"Goodness, how awful. I couldn't sleep, so I decided to do some work. I'm writing a letter to my dad. I'm asking for an explanation from him about his interest in Marty. Then I'll write to Marty and ask her the same thing. Don't you think they owe me some kind of explanation?"

"No, not at all," I said. "Your father and Martine are both adults. They have a right to see anyone they choose, even each other. You have to let this go. Put it out of your mind. Try to think about your own stuff. Write your book and love your man, and that is me." She smiled and said she would sleep on it. I held her and kissed her, and I went to my room to try and sleep.

I was awakened at six thirty by the honking of horns and other street noises that go along with life in New York City. *I love this town,* I thought. *I love it more than ever, now that my love is here.* I showered and dressed for a meeting. She was sleeping when I left, and as much as I wanted to see her, I didn't wake her. I locked the door behind me and went into the street. I would meet with my staff for a few hours and then Christmas shop for Molly. I would buy her everything I thought she would want. It was zero degrees outside, but the sun was shining and life was beautiful.

FROM MY VALENTINE

A month and a half had passed since I had written to Dad and Marty. Valentine's Day was fast approaching, and I was feeling pain from the loss of closeness that I had valued with my dad and my friend. Christmas had been wonderful, with a shower of love and gifts from Jeff. New Year's Day had come and gone, and I had not received so much as a card from my father. I buried myself in my book and often worked into the night. My relationship with Jeff was the only thing that helped me break away from my work and enjoy life now and then. We had made many trips to Vinnie's for dinner and had seen a few plays over the last few weeks. We had even taken a weekend trip to Florida, just to escape the cold. I was basically happy, and wondered how I had taken so long to allow love to find me.

It was 10:00 a.m., February 13, and I was busy at the typewriter when suddenly the doorbell rang. I opened the door and was surprised to see my father standing there.

"Dad. Won't you come in?"

He said, "Hello, Molly," and stepped inside. We stood there, staring at each other for about a minute, before I finally broke the silence. "Please come on into the living room and have a seat. I'll make us some coffee."

"That will be good," he said, and we stepped into the living room. I took his coat and hung it in the closet, and then went into the kitchen to make coffee. My heart was pounding, and I said a prayer of thanksgiving that he had shown up here to visit. While the coffee was perking, I went into the living room and sat on the couch across from Dad, who had taken a seat on Jeff's red stuffed armchair.

"This is a very comfortable chair," he said.

"Please, Dad," I said, "let's cut through the small talk and get to the reason why you showed up so suddenly after you never bothered to answer my letter or even send me a holiday card."

He reached into his vest pocket, pulled out three envelopes, and handed them to me. There was a beautiful Christmas card, a New Year's card, and also a very nice birthday card.

"How is Martine?" I asked.

"I don't know, Molly. She left for Minnesota three weeks ago. I wanted to call you on your birthday in January, but have been so ashamed of what I had done. The shock of having my beloved daughter catch me in such a situation made me realize that this thing for Marty was just an infatuation. I was flattered to have such a young, beautiful girl give me that kind of attention. Please try to understand. I tried to make up with Connie, but she would not see me because of Martine's presence in the house. I didn't want to throw Marty out, and let her stay until she decided what to do. After Marty left, I contacted Connie again, but she had started a relationship with another man."

"Well, Daddy, can you blame her?"

"No, I guess I can't. I heard from Rosalie that you and Jeff are in a sort of romantic relationship. Is that true?"

"Yes, it is true; however, I wish Rosalie would have kept it to herself until I had the chance to see you."

"I'm sure her intentions were good. She knew how worried I was, and I guess she knew that I would feel better knowing you had someone like Jeff in your life," he said.

"I can forgive her, Daddy. I forgive you, too. I have missed you so much." With that we stood up at the same time and embraced. It felt so good to be in my father's arms again. "I'm sure the coffee is ready by now."

I went into the kitchen, poured two cups of coffee, and served it in the living room. I didn't tell my father, but even though I forgave him, I did not feel the same respect for him that I had before. I thought that I would never be able to forgive Martine for destroying Dad and Connie's relationship.

We talked until twelve thirty, then I went into the kitchen and made some egg salad sandwiches for the two of us for lunch. After lunch, Dad went into my room to take a nap and I went back to my typing. I worked until Jeff arrived home from the theatre around three thirty that afternoon. He was elated when I told him my dad was there.

"That's wonderful, honey," he said. "Did you tell him about us?"

"I didn't have to," I said. "Rosalie beat me to it. Miss Big Mouth herself," I said. I had to laugh at my remark, since it reminded me of the old days when we were kids and used to call each other all kinds of silly names, like Molly Face and Rosy Face.

My dad was there, and I felt lighthearted for the first time in a long time. I went in to wake him while Jeff showered and changed. He awoke promptly, and asked me to call a cab to take him to his hotel so that he could dress for dinner.

We decided on Vinney's for dinner, and Dad insisted on buying so we let him. As we sat having a glass of red wine before dinner, Dad said he had something to tell us, but we shouldn't worry because everything would be fine. He said he had had a slight heart attack right after Christmas, but the doctor said it was very mild and there was very little damage, if any. He had been given medication and there was no cause for worry. I immediately began to panic. I am sure Dad and Jeff saw the horror in my face. I reached across the table, and Dad reached out and held my hand in his large and powerful one. I had felt the power of those hands all of my life, and now I was filled with fear that they would become weak and frail from his weakening heart. Jeff rubbed my back lightly, as if to comfort me.

"I'm so sorry, Dad. I wish there was something I could do. Do you want me to come home again?"

"No, dear. I'll be fine. There's a nice lady that I see on occasion and she is very helpful. Besides, I really am doing well now. Whatever happened is over, and as long as I take care of myself, the doc thinks I will be right as rain. It would be nice, however, to have the two of you visit soon."

The waiter came with our entrees and we ate in silence. The words "heart attack" kept running through my mind. To think that he could have died as quickly as Mom, and the fact that we had not been on friendly terms could have left me with a guilt complex forever. We invited Dad to stay at our place that night, but he insisted on going to his hotel. We dropped him off around ten o'clock and went back to the apartment.

I awoke the next morning to soft music and felt Jeff's presence next to my bed. When I opened my eyes, he was standing there holding three red balloons and a box of chocolates.

"Good morning, princess. Be my valentine?" All the pent-up emotion started to pour out of me in the form of laughter.

"No, I will not be your valentine until I am queen. Princess is not enough."

Laughing, he said, "So be it." He picked up a cardboard box from my trash can that I had recently brought home from a shopping trip. Tearing off a long strip, he laughed and said, "I crown thee Queen of My Heart." Then he made a circle with the strip of cardboard, pinned it together with a hair pin, and placed it on my head.

I smiled and closed my eyes to feel the moment. Then, in the darkness behind my eyes, I saw Nick's face. He was smiling and saying, "I love you, Molly." I opened my eyes wide and stared straight ahead, trying to get the picture out of my head.

"What is wrong, honey?" Jeff asked.

"Nothing. Everything is wonderful. I think I should call Dad now, to make sure he is doing alright. I just happened to think of him."

"Of course, dear. I'm sure he is fine, but let's give him a call. After your mind has settled about your dad, I have another surprise for you," he said.

I picked up the black telephone from my nightstand, placed it on the zebra comforter, and proceeded to make a call to my father. We said our good-byes on the phone, since his plane was leaving from LaGuardia that morning at eleven. It was already nine fifteen, so he would be taking a cab directly from the hotel to the airport. I made him promise to take good care of himself, and to call if he needed us.

I looked around the room and did not see Jeff. I got out of bed and began to tidy up. I put the phone back on the night table, straightened the comforter, fluffed the pillows and headed for the kitchen.

Jeff had made coffee and was beating eggs to make omelets. I got out the plates, silverware, napkins and cups, and poured orange juice into our glasses.

"Thank you, darling," Jeff said as he poured the egg mixture into the pan.

"Thank you for cooking," I said. I excused myself and went into the bathroom to pee. When I came out, there was a small, beautifully wrapped box on my plate. The wrapping paper was red and the ribbon was a lovely combo of red and white. A small package of Valentine's candies was attached to the ribbon — . You know the kind I mean. They were the little tiny hearts with little sayings on them, the really sugary kind.

"Well look at this," I said. "I really am the Queen of Hearts."

"Yes, you are. Only a true queen may have that present. Now go put on your crown before you open that box."

I immediately obeyed my king and fished the crown out of the trash can. I sat down at the table and proceeded to open the box. Jeff watched intently as I opened it. Inside the box was a note. It read, "Go look in my blue coat pocket." Laughing, I went to the coat closet. I found another box in the blue jacket, with another note that read, "Now go back and sit on your chair and eat your breakfast." I laughed hysterically and obeyed. I had a gut feeling that something special was about to happen.

When we had finished our breakfast, he asked if I would mind doing the dishes. I knew the maid wasn't coming in that day, so I obliged. When I got to the sink, there was a paper plate with large printing on it that read, "Look on the window sill." By this time I was at my wits end.

"Jeffrey Wilde, what in the hell is going on here?"

He laughed and said, "Come on, Moll, be a sport." I knew how he liked to play little games with me, so I looked on the window sill, and there it was. Sitting on a tiny crystal plate and covered with a tiny crystal cup was the most beautiful diamond ring I had ever seen. He took the ring out of my hand, knelt before me, and proposed, calling me the queen of his heart.

My heart was pounding as I said "Yes, yes, and yes!"

Typewriters were clicking away in our apartment when the doorbell rang at five thirty that evening. Jeff called out from his study that he would get the door, so I continued to write. I heard male voices from the living room and stopped typing.

"Molly, come and see what the florist sent to you. Hurry!"

I went into the living room, and there on the table was a long white box, with a card on top that read, "From your other Valentine."

"Oh, Jeff, what have you done now?"

"I didn't do it," he said.

"Well, if it wasn't you, then it must have been my father."

"Of course," he said.

"I'll call and thank him tomorrow," I said.

We returned to our typewriters and went back to work. Later that evening over chow mien, we talked about how wonderful our day had been. As I sipped my tea, I smiled to myself and thought how blessed I was to have two wonderful men in my life.

FROM MOFFITT TO FOREVER

The wind was howling outside my window on that cold March day. I looked out and saw a young lady frantically chasing papers that must have blown out of her hands down the street. I wondered why she had not had them in a bag or briefcase or some other thing to keep them secure.

My phone rang and I ran to answer it. Jumping into my bed, I grabbed the receiver. "Hello?"

"Hi there, Molly Face. It's me. How are you?"

"Rosy Face! I'm just fine. How are you?"

"Don't ask," Rosalie said. Her voice dropped a little and I knew something was bothering her. Having been friends since fifth grade at Moffitt Elementary School, I could read her expressions and she could read mine like a book, even if they were coming through a telephone wire.

"So, give me the lowdown on things. The tone of your voice indicates a not-so-happy note. Shoot!"

There was a brief pause and then she said, "Well, the state of my marriage isn't getting any better, for one thing. Jack is not 'Mr. Nice Guy,' as you well know, and if there had never been a Boston Strangler, my husband might be the meanest man on earth."

"I understand," I said. "You know, darling, I'm here to help you if you need me."

"I know that, dear. I hope it doesn't come to that, but if it does I'll call you. The next thing, Molly, is that I'm concerned about your father. He's getting a reputation as a man about town, in a not-so-nice sense of the word, if you know what I mean."

"Rosalie, be a little more definitive. Just exactly what is he doing that's so terrible?"

"Well, he doesn't go to church anymore, and I have heard that he brings home one cheap woman after another. Maybe we should talk to him."

"Okay," I said. "I'll make plans to fly down in a week or two. Meanwhile, keep me posted on all the news."

"Love you," she said.

I said, "Love you, Moffitt to forever."

She said, "Moffitt to forever," and we hung up.

I looked down at the clouds from the window of the airplane. *It is so beautiful up here,* I thought. The flight attendant leaned over to ask if I would care for something to drink and I said, "No, thank you." I started to put on lipstick, and suddenly there was turbulence and I smeared it onto my face. I turned toward the aisle to ask the attendant for a napkin just as the man in the seat next to mine turned toward me to try and get a look out of the window. He smiled and pointed to my face and we both began to laugh. He pulled his handkerchief out of his pocket and offered it to me.

"Here, use this. I swear to you it's clean."

I took it, thanked him, and began wiping the lipstick from my face. I pulled a mirror from my purse and looked to make sure I had gotten all of it, then I handed him back his handkerchief.

"Thanks again," I said. He smiled and took the handkerchief out of my hand. Our eyes met momentarily, and I couldn't help but notice how handsome he was. His brown hair was thick and matched his light brown eyes and tanned skin. His smile showed straight, white teeth and a deep dimple on each cheek.

He put his hand out to me and said, "I'm Charles Baker."

"Molly Peale," I said, extending my hand to meet his. His hand was warm and soft, and I felt a tingle throughout my body when we touched. *Get a grip, Molly,* I thought.

He turned to look straight ahead, started rubbing his chin, and then looked back at me. "Molly Peale," he said. "Well, that's a very familiar name. Could it be that you are the famous actress, Molly Peale?" he asked.

"I have done some acting, Mr. Baker. However, I've since retired from the stage and am trying my hand at writing."

"Well, my dear, the stage has suffered a great loss. I don't think I missed one of your plays since you were discovered in the early sixties. I'm honored to meet you. What might the title of your book be?"

"Oh, I don't know yet. I haven't decided. It is a sort of dramatic novel about a woman who marries very young, and through trials and tribulations will eventually become a mother to be admired."

He reached into his pocket, pulled out a business card, and handed it to me, saying, "Please take my card. When you decide on a title, let me know so that I will be sure to get a copy when it's published. Oh, and please call me Charles. My father was Mr. Baker."

I took the card and promised to call him with a title when and if my book was published.

"How long will you be in Norfolk?"

"No longer than necessary," I said. "I'm going to spend a few days with my father, who gets a bit lonely now and then. Today is Saturday and I'll probably stay until Wednesday."

"Maybe we can get together for lunch one day," he said. "Shall we say Tuesday at noon?"

"I'm not sure. Why don't I call you on Monday evening and give a definite answer? I'm not really sure how this time with my dad will go. You know, he may have made plans."

"Okay, then, I'll be expecting your call."

The pilot's voice came over the speaker announcing that we were to fasten our seat belts and prepare for landing.

Dad was waiting when I got off the plane. We hugged and said our hellos, and walked to baggage claim in silence. "Is something wrong, Molly? You seem quiet. Not your normal jovial self."

"I am a little tired, Daddy," I said. "I didn't sleep well last night. I have a lot on my mind."

"Oh, I see. Would you like to talk about it?

I said we could talk at home, and went to the phone to call Rosalie. When she answered, I told her to give us an hour to get my bags and drive home, and then meet us at Dad's house for a powwow. She agreed, and we hung up.

The old house looked the same as it had three months before when I had so frantically left, after the episode with Dad and Martine. I was surprised to see the mess, though. There were dishes in the sink, and Dad had worn two or three different jackets and not hung any of them in the coat closet. "I'll be right down, Dad. After I put my things away, I'll tidy up around here. Haven't you felt well lately?"

"I guess maybe a little tired. My heart condition, you know," he said.

That comment made me want to scream at him. I held my breath and went upstairs. My room was as I had left it. Some of my things were still in the closet. I would remind myself to take them when I left. I hung my dresses and put some other things in the dresser drawers. There was an old sweat suit in the bottom drawer that I had left on purpose. I decided to wear that.

The sound of the doorbell made me hurry to get downstairs. Rosalie's voice drifted up as Dad greeted her. I wondered if they would remain friends after he found out that she had told me about the gossip.

When I reached the living room, Rosalie was sitting on the sofa and waiting for me, as she had so many times over the years. Dad was making coffee. I went into the kitchen and started cleaning up.

"I wish you would let me do this," he said.

"I'll get it, Dad," I said.

"If you insist, dear. The coffee is almost ready. I'll bring it in as soon as it's finished. Go on in and talk with Rosalie."

"Great gobs of goose grease, Molly!" Rosalie said. "I'm a nervous wreck. What are you going to say to him?"

"I don't exactly know yet, but we'll think of a way to start the questioning."

"Shit, you make it sound like an interrogation, Moll!"

"I guess maybe I do. I don't mean to. And please don't say 'shit,' Rosalie. It doesn't become you."

"Sorry, I forgot about your virgin ears. Speaking of virgin, how about all your other parts? Are they still virgin, too?"

"None of your business, girl, but I'll fill you in later."

"Hot damn! I can hardly wait to hear this!"

"Stop cussing! You know we can't let Dad hear us using off-color language."

"Sorry."

Dad came in and put a tray of coffee and tea biscuits on the table in front of the sofa. He poured each of us a cup, and we both said "Thank you" at the same time. Then, in perfect coordination, we picked up our cups and started to sip, like a trio of puppets in a puppet show. I was the first to put my cup down. I picked up a biscuit and started to nibble. Rosalie followed suit. Dad did not touch the biscuits. He looked from me to Rosy and back again.

"Why do I get the feeling that something big is about to occur here?" he asked.

"Well, Dad, I guess you're right. Before I tell you what this is about, I want you to know that Rosalie and I both love you and are concerned about you."

"I don't understand," he said.

"Rosalie, why don't you tell my father what you told me about the things you heard?"

Rosalie looked like she would faint. The color disappeared from her face as she started to speak.

"Mr. Peale, I was in the market and ran into two of your neighbors, and they told me that you are getting a reputation as a player. I don't see you in church anymore, and I must admit that it has me worried."

My father looked shocked. His face drained of color, and he stood up and started to pace around the room. Rosalie and I sat in silence to give him a chance to digest what he had just heard. After five minutes or so of pacing, he spoke.

"I am just appalled at all of this. It sickens me to think that my only living child would come all the way from New York City and team up with her friend to lecture me about my personal life. Did it ever occur to you two that those old busybodies in this neighborhood are lying witches? Do you know that they bring pies and cakes to me, which I throw out to avoid the calories? They are a couple of jealous witches. Just exactly what did they tell you, Rosalie?"

Rosalie looked from me to my father. With tears in her eyes, she said, "Please, Mr. Peale, I'm only trying to help. I'm sure you're right about those women. It's just that you and Molly are like family to me."

"Are you going to answer my question? What did they say?"

I knew it was time to go to her rescue.

"Dad, if you must know what they said, why don't I invite the two of them over tonight and we can ask them? This gossip has to stop. I won't have your good name being drug through the mud."

"Absolutely not," he said. "I won't have those troublemakers in my house. I am taking you out tonight for dinner and I'm inviting Rosalie and Jack to come with us. I would like a man's opinion about all of this."

Rosalie stood and picked up her coat. "I think I'll be going now," she said. "If we are going to dinner tonight, I'll need someone to sit with the boys. I'll call Jack at the office and ask him if it's alright with him."

"That will be great, darling," I said, and walked her to the door. I then left my father sitting in the living room and went upstairs to shower and rest. It was three forty-two in the afternoon, and I figured we would want to go out by seven. I was exhausted, and an hour of rest would do me a world of good.

Dad and I were dressed and in the car by six forty-five. The days were getting longer so we still had plenty of sunlight. It was chilly and windy. The weather man said forty eight degrees, which was a lot milder than I was used to in New York. We decided to go to Duck Inn at the beach, which was my favorite. We picked up Rosalie and Jack at six fifty-five and we were on our way. Jack told my father that it was nice to see him again and thanked him for inviting them along. Dad said he was glad to have both of them, and he was welcome.

"So, Richard, I hear these girls were giving you a hard time about your personal stuff. Wouldn't it be nice if the old bags in your neighborhood would just mind their own fucking business?" Jack never was one to watch his language, which was one of the things his wife constantly corrected him on.

"Come on, Jack, watch your mouth," Rosalie told him.

I could see that nothing had changed in that department. I looked at Rosalie and her face was red. She took the embarrassment of his undesirable choice of words each time he used them, and I got angry every time I witnessed it.

" Jack, let's try to keep this conversation clean. Rosalie and I are trying to help my father understand that a reputation as a whoremonger can be very demeaning to a man's character, and we were hoping for your support."

"Okay, girls, I do apologize, and I promise I will not say another word that isn't edifying this entire evening."

"Thank you, honey," Rosalie said with half a smile.

I said, "Yes, Jack, we appreciate your cooperation on this. Thank you."

"Well, I have figured out what the gossip is about," Dad said. "I guess my secret love life is no secret."

After that, it was small talk about Rosalie and Jack's children, careers, my love life and other things unrelated to my father's problem. By the time we reached the Virginia Beach Expressway, we were tired of talking and remained silent until we reached the restaurant. Everyone ordered wine and crab legs, and I was glad we were on the same wavelength.

Dad spoke first. "Well, I'm sitting here feeling very bad about embarrassing you, Molly. You know I love you more than life and would never intentionally hurt you. I *am* very sorry and I *will* look for other ways to amuse myself. I must admit, though, I have had a lot of fun with all this. Some of those ladies are quite entertaining."

I was mortified at his statement. "Dad, please! This is not a thing to joke about."

"Personally, Molly, I think it is admirable that your dad can find humor in all of this," Jack said. "After all, he has apologized, and now it's time to lighten up. Don't you think?"

Rosalie and I looked at each other and smiled, then all four of us began to laugh hysterically. I said, "Hey, Jack, for once you're right. No sense running Dad into the ground over something that he has shown remorse for. So Dad, since we have decided to see some humor, why don't you tell us how many women you brought home — say, in the last month."

"That will be my little secret, Miss Molly, if you don't mind. There are just some things a father does not share with his not-so-liberal daughter." We laughed again at this remark, and I wondered if maybe I was a bit square in my thinking. The rest of the evening was quite pleasant. Jack told us some of his not-so-censored jokes, and even though I was a bit bashful at some, I laughed and did not let on.

Dad and I stayed up late that night, drinking wine and talking of future plans. He admitted to me that he was actually looking for that special someone and maybe had gone about it in the wrong way. I suggested he go back to church, and he agreed to give it a try.

It was two in the morning when we went upstairs to our rooms. I was exhausted, and glad to crawl under the covers and let the world and everything in it leave me. As I was falling asleep, I thought about Rosalie and how blessed I felt to have such a wonderful friend. Our saying of "Moffitt to forever" might sound childish to some, but to us it was a promise we had kept for twenty-four years. I closed my eyes and my mind drifted off to play hopscotch.

SILVER LININGS

The piercing sound of the telephone ringing startled me from a sound sleep while something crawled under my blanket and grabbed my toe. Opening my eyes, I sat up to see Jeff grinning at me from the foot of my bed. "Damn, Jeff, what are you up to now? Are you going to answer the phone?"

"Nope, let that son of a gun ring," he said. Turning my toe loose, he said, "Hey, time to get up. I have a nice breakfast all ready for you. I thought we would go to an early Mass at church this morning and then take a ride out into the country — maybe have lunch at one of those nice little diners outside of town. The sun is shining and we're wasting time."

"How the hell do you know the sun is shining when it is the middle of the night? I need to sleep another few hours."

"Not so, my beauty. It is seven thirty and you should be up and hitting the shower. I'll get in the kitchen and finish setting up for breakfast."

Grumbling and complaining, I dragged myself out of bed. The warm water felt like a close friend caressing my body. I knew he was right, and it would be nice to dress and go to nine o'clock mass. The church wasn't far from the apartment, and thoughts of a ride in the country seemed like a welcome change from all the concrete in the city.

Wearing my robe, I started for the kitchen. Then I heard the voices. Oh my God! Could it be? It was Martine! I'd know her voice anywhere. Jeff sounded irritated, and I could just imagine why. What was she doing here? I went into the kitchen and there she stood, not looking so well. *She must have gained twenty pounds,* I thought.

"Martine, what are you doing here?"

"Hear me out Molly, please. I need help."

"And just why should we help you?" I asked. She must have felt the sting of the sarcasm in my voice. We stood looking at each other for a few moments. Martine finally turned her face from my gaze and spoke.

"Molly, I am pregnant and it's Richard's child. I don't know what to do. I came here to have an abortion, but I couldn't go through with it. I thought you and Jeff could help me plan what to do. After all, it will be your brother or sister." She sat on a kitchen chair and started to cry.

My heart felt as though it would pound out of my chest. I went over to where she sat and put my arms around her. "Don't cry, Martine. We'll think of something. I don't want my father to know. I'm afraid of what this might do to him."

GIRLFRIENDS

The line for seating at Rosy O'Grady's was long, as usual. It was my favorite place to indulge when I was in the mood for a major food binge. I had grocery shopped for Martine, and had called Cecilia to meet me here for lunch and to share the news of my new brother- or sister-to-be. She showed up late, but that was okay since we would have to wait for a table for at least twenty minutes.

"Spill it, girl," she said. "I've been waiting since last night to hear this marvelous news about whatever it is that's making you sound like a fretting, stuttering fool."

"Wait until we sit down. I can't talk about this on an empty stomach. The subject matter is just too delicate. Anyway, I don't know if you could take this standing up. Here comes a hostess now. We are about to be seated."

After being ushered to a table, we sat down and ordered two glasses of white wine.

"Okay," I said, "are you ready for this? Listen carefully and don't miss a word."

The waitress brought the wine and set it on the table.

"Bring us two corned beef specials," I said. "After that, please leave us alone. We have some very important business to discuss."

The waitress smiled and walked away without a word.

Cecilia lifted her glass and I responded. She said, "Start talking. I can't wait another second." She was staring at me across the table with wide brown eyes and half-parted lips. We took a sip of wine.

"Martine is pregnant by my father."

She had taken a second sip of wine, which ended up across the table and on my black sweater.

"Holy God. Oh shit!" she said. "Give me a fucking moment to pull myself together before you say another word. I do not believe my ears. What the jumping up shit is she going to do? I know; she is having an abortion, right? This whole thing will be a forgotten nightmare. Okay, problem solved, case closed."

The waitress brought the sandwiches and each of us took a huge bite.

"No way, Cel. Little Miss Hot Pants isn't going to murder my sibling. I'm taking charge of this, and I need your help. I want you to help me convince Marty that she should relinquish the baby to me after its birth. This is my only chance of having a family. I feel that I am already too old to have a baby and I do not even have a wedding date yet. I don't think I even want a wedding. I'm too set in my ways now, and fear that I would not make a very good wife to anyone, not even Jeff. I can afford to give the child everything it needs and most of what it might want. I can hire a nanny to care for the child while I continue my work and maybe do a little traveling."

Cecilia looked at me as if I had turned into a grape. Taking a deep breath, she said, "Molly, my capable friend. I'm astounded at your plans in this matter. However, if you insist, I will help you. Hey, it might be fun. This kid will be like a niece or nephew to me. Think of the fun we can have at Christmas and birthdays. I'll do it. I'll help you convince Martine and also help to raise the child. When do I get to see her?"

"I don't know yet, Cel. I think we should wait a while. She may be easier to convince later in the pregnancy. Right now she is still capable of running off. I think we should wait, maybe two more months. We'll talk then." We finished our wine and food in silence and then ordered a cup of coffee.

"You and Jeff need a break. Come over to my place tonight for dinner. I'll make my famous pot roast with potatoes and green beans. We'll have a nice red wine and some sherbet for dessert. I mean, how often does Jeff get a home-cooked meal that he doesn't have to cook himself?"

"Okay, rub it in. I know I'm no cook and have no desire to be. It just isn't my forte. I promise to let you know by three o'clock. I'll call Jeff when I get back. What time is dinner?"

"Come at six thirty. We'll probably eat at seven thirty. That will give us a little time to enjoy the wine before dinner."

"Cecilia, I want you to know that I appreciate your friendship. It means a lot to me. I'll also call Rosalie in Virginia and give her the news. I haven't gotten around to that yet. By the way, tonight at your place is a wonderful idea. Thank you. One other thing though: Please don't mention the baby in front of Jeff. I haven't told him yet that I plan to adopt it."

"My lips are sealed, Mol. I think you should tell him soon, though. Has the thought crossed your mind that adopting this baby could mean the end of your relationship with Jeff?"

"The thought has crossed my mind many times. That is exactly why I'm not going to tell him until the last minute. I am not ready to face losing him. I don't know how I'll handle that just yet." I hadn't exactly given the possibility of losing Jeff as much thought as I let on to Cecilia. I knew I would have to deal with it sooner or later. We left the restaurant at one forty-five. I felt full and relieved that I had shared my thoughts about the baby with a friend.

It was two thirty when I returned to the apartment. I dialed Rosalie's number in Virginia, and she picked up on the fourth ring. "Rosalie, how are you?"

"Hey, Mol, I'm doing well. How are you, my dear? I heard the weather is very cold in New York right now. I hope you are staying warm."

"Yes, I am fine. I hope you and Jack are getting on well. And the children?"

"There're fine, dear."

"Listen Rosalie, I'll get right to the point. Martine is pregnant by my dad and I am planning to adopt the baby. but she doesn't know that yet."

"Blessed Jesus in heaven! Are you out of your mind? I know it's a mortal sin, but why isn't she having an abortion? And what does your dad say about this?"

"My father doesn't know and we're not telling him. I'm not sure his heart could take it. To answer your first question, I will not allow her to kill off my brother or sister. Don't you get it? This is my chance to have a family."

"Does anyone else know about this?"

"I told Cecilia earlier today. She has agreed to help me convince Martine to relinquish the baby at birth. I will need your help also. I know you are experienced at raising children. I need you to advise and teach me how to parent."

"Listen very carefully, my best friend. I think you're taking too much for granted. First of all, no matter how convincing you and Cecilia are, you may not convince a woman to give up her child. I have two, and I would have died before giving them up, even at birth. Do you get it?"

I took a deep breath, and for the first time felt fearful of losing the child to its natural mother. I said, "You have a point. Why else would she change her mind about aborting? She told me she had considered it and came to New York to do it, but couldn't go through with it. I can see where I may have a problem. She came to me for help because she has no job and no possible means of supporting herself and a baby. I am sure there is a way to get this child away from her. If I can convince the courts that she is incapable, I may have a chance of getting custody."

"Molly Face, listen to yourself. You sound like a deviant witch with a diabolical mind. I know Martine and Richard hurt you, but he is your father and she is your friend. Give her the benefit of the doubt. I beseech you, as a mother, please don't do this. I love you and you are my best friend, but I can't be a part of this. I'll honor your request and not tell Richard, but I think you're making a mistake. Where will you tell him this baby came from, after it's born?"

"I'll just tell him that I adopted it."

"It isn't going to work, Molly. Something bad will come from this. I'll pray for you all. I have to go now. The children are coming home from school. Bye." She hung up without giving me a chance to say another word.

"I love you, Rosy," I said to the dial tone.

The clock on the wall showed three o'clock. I pressed the button on the phone to break the connection from my call to Rosalie, and dialed Jeff's work number.

"Jeffrey Wilde here," his voice said. My hands were clammy and my whole body shook from the disappointment I felt from Rosalie's decision. "Jeffrey Wilde, hello!" I tried to speak, but couldn't utter a sound. I hung up.

Fifteen minutes later, I tried again, and that time I told him about Cecilia's invitation. He was pleased to look forward to a nice dinner with friends. I phoned Cel to let her know we would be there at six thirty.

The door opened at around four fifty and Jeff walked in, all smiles. "How is my favorite lady?" he asked.

"Fine, now that my wonderful one is home with me. I have already showered and am enjoying a glass of wine. Would you like one?"

"I would. How about you pour me a glass while I take a quick shower? I think we need not dress up too much for this dinner. I plan on wearing jeans and a sweatshirt. I must say, you are looking very beautiful in that bathrobe, but I think a nice pair of jeans might look a little better outside. Besides, it's cold out there." He kissed me and went off to his bedroom. I poured the wine and went into my room to dress. I felt drained and wasn't sure why.

We arrived at Cecilia's right on time. She answered the door with a big smile on her face and a zing in her voice when she said hello. A woman I had never met stood behind her.

We stepped inside and the woman smiled and said, "Hello, I'm Cel's friend, Debbie. You must be Molly and Jeff. It's such a pleasure to meet you both. I've heard nothing about you. Nothing unpleasant, that is."

Jeff shook her hand and said we were glad to meet her, and we all went into the living room. Cecilia poured us all some wine and we made idle conversation. Debbie was a very attractive woman with strawberry blonde hair, green eyes, and a stature about the same as mine. She had very milky white skin, and I noticed she wore very light or no makeup.

"I understand from Cel that both of you have retired from the theatre and taken up careers as writers."

Jeff and I spoke at the same time. "We have," we said. Debbie told us that she was a social worker for the state, and was looking forward to retirement to also try her talent at writing. We wished her well, and the conversation flowed smoothly and easily. I asked Cecilia to show me the latest dress she had bought. She caught my drift and ushered me into the dressing room.

"So, did you get around to calling Rosalie?"

"I did, and she refuses to get involved. She thinks I should not try to adopt. I understand that she is a mother and feels bad for Martine, but she as much as called me a wicked witch. I guess the best thing to do is leave her out of this. I don't want to lose her friendship."

"That will not happen, Molly. Rosalie loves you and is only thinking of your best interests. You might put yourself through a lot of pain for nothing. I asked around and was told by some folks in the legal system that it is practically impossible to take a child away from its natural mother. Maybe you should rethink this whole thing."

"I won't give up. I want that baby. If you won't help me, then I'll just have to do it alone."

"I'm here for you. I'll do whatever I can. I'm just saying that it may not work, and I would hate to see you hurt. If you leave the baby with Martine, she'll probably love having you in the child's life as its sister. But Molly, if you lose, you may piss Martine off and never be allowed to see the child at all."

"You have a point. I just have to make sure that I have a strong case, or that Martine relinquishes. She has to realize that the child would be better off with me."

"I hope so, for your sake. Now, let's get back in the other room and be sociable."

"Okay, but one more thing. When did you meet Debbie, and what is the nature of your relationship with her?"

"I met her a month ago at a cocktail party at Vinnie's. It's just a friendship right now, but I would like for it to be more. She's very intelligent and I love having her around."

"I wish you the best," I said. We went back into the living room to rejoin Debbie and Jeff.

Meanwhile, Debbie had put dinner on the table, and she called us into the dining room to eat. An evening of wine and delicious food gave us tight waist-bands. Jeff and I went home with our appetites satisfied and feeling caught up on current affairs.

DISAPPEARANCE

Easter Sunday came on a beautiful day in April that year. Jeff and I attended church with Dad at Holy Angels in Craddock. Although Martine had expressed a desire to travel with us for the holiday, I insisted she stay behind in New York and rest. She had complained of fatigue a lot in the past few weeks, and I felt it was best that she didn't travel. Jeff had asked me if I was really concerned about Martine's health, or if maybe I was more afraid that she would spill the beans to Dad about the baby. I admit I was uneasy about getting the two of them together. I was relieved when Marty finally agreed to remain in the city.

After church, we went back to the house to enjoy each other's company for the rest of the day. I started dinner while Dad and Jeff discussed what might happen in baseball that year. We had invited Rosalie and her family over for dinner, but she begged off with a promise to come afterward for dessert and coffee. Dad had cooked the turkey the day before, so all I had to do was the potatoes and vegetables. I put the potatoes on to boil and joined Dad and Jeff in the front room with a glass of wine. We sipped and talked sports and history. It was pleasant. I looked at the two men and thought how blessed I was to have them both. I thought about Martine and the baby, and how wonderful it would be to have a little one in the family. We sat down to dinner at four o'clock. The food was delicious and we all enjoyed more wine.

I was picking up the dishes when Rosalie rang the doorbell. Dad opened the door, and I could hear everyone greeting each other and laughing. "Where is that Molly Face friend of mine?," I heard Rosalie say. I went in to greet them and gave them a big hug. Jack sat down with Dad and Jeff and Rosalie followed me into the kitchen.

"So, have you come to your senses yet about the baby issue?" Rosalie asked.

"My senses tell me to go ahead with plans to adopt. I know you disagree, my friend, but I need to do this . . . for my sake and little Jesse's."

"My God, Molly! I do not believe you have deemed it to be a boy, and even named it after your brother already! What happens if this kid is a girl?"

"Simple solution. I will just go with Plan B and name her after my mother. Don't you see. Rosalie, how important this is to me? I want a family!"

"Fine! Marry Jeff now and have your own kid. I know it is better to have children in your twenties, but some people do have them in their thirties and even forties sometimes."

"Forget it, my friend. I am not even sure that my feelings for Jeff are strong enough for that sort of thing, and I really don't think I would have a baby myself even if I could. I'm not cut out for pregnancy and am fearful of giving birth. Can't you see this is my only chance?"

"Hey girls, how's that coffee coming?" Jeff called out from the living room.

"We're getting there," I yelled back. I put the coffee on and cut slices of an apple pie Dad had bought from a lady down the street who baked for extra money.

Rosalie put her hand on my shoulder and softly said, "Moll, I am not going to mention this baby thing anymore. I'll pray that you make the right decision."

My dad walked in from the living room and asked, "What baby thing?"

I quickly came up with a sensible answer and said, "Oh, Dad, Rosalie is just trying to convince me that now is the time to marry and have a baby."

"Well now, I wouldn't mind having a grandchild before I get too old and feeble to enjoy one. A little girl that looks just like you would suit me just fine."

"Now Daddy, don't hold your breath. I have no intention of having a baby, but I might consider adopting one in the near future. What do you think of that?" I glanced at Jeff, who had a very strange look on his face. I wondered if he had figured out from my comment what I was up to. Oh well, he would have to know sooner or later.

The conversation was light all through coffee and dessert. I barely tasted the pie because I was so full from the great meal we had enjoyed. I noticed that Rosalie was enjoying a large slice of pie and some milk along with the coffee. I hadn't noticed in the kitchen, but now that I looked at her, I could see she had put on some weight. The way she was eating the pie seemed to catch everyone's attention. Dad and Jeff were sort of staring, so I spoke to break the spell. "Jeff, dear, how is your dessert?"

"Oh, it's very good," he answered. He and my dad seemed to have come out of their comas. "The lady up the street really outdid herself with this pie." He went on and on about the pie, as if he were trying to convince us that it was okay to overindulge in it. Jack was quiet throughout the whole episode, and I wondered if he was a wee bit embarrassed by his wife's manners, or the lack of them.

"That was sooo good. I just have this ravenous appetite for sweets lately; I don't know what it is. I could almost eat another piece," Rosalie said, wiping her mouth and then sipping her coffee.

"Go ahead, dear," I said, "but remember your waistline. It doesn't take much to put on weight once we pass that thirty mark. I'm totally stuffed myself and about ready to clean up these dishes. Why don't you forget the pie and come with me into the kitchen? Anyone else care for more pie?" The men all said no and moved into the living room.

"Good idea," Rosalie said, getting up from her chair. "I certainly don't need to eat anymore. I have already gained eleven pounds since Christmas, and just when I am ready to get serious about my diet another holiday comes along."

Once in the kitchen and away from the men, I said rather softly, "Rosalie, what is it with the food? I didn't notice the weight right away so you obviously carry it well, but you have, by your own admission, put on weight. Are you stressed about something?"

Her eyes filled with tears as she said, "I'm lonely, Molly. Jack has been spending a lot more time at the office, and I wonder if there is something going on there besides work. It is so good to see you. To have you home makes all the difference. I can't talk to anyone else about this. You remember Mildred Turner, from school? Well, it's Mildred Crease now, and she just had her third baby. I tried to talk to her and she just made light of the whole situation. She said as long as the children and I are well provided for, I shouldn't worry about Jack's extra curricular activities because boys will be boys. But you know how I am Molly. I can't be that way."

"I know, Rosy Face, and you shouldn't have to be. Boys will be boys is no excuse for men who are supposed to be responsible husbands and fathers. Have you talked to Jack about this?"

She said she had, and he never really gave her a reason that made sense. She said he would shrug his shoulders and tell her to lighten up because he needed to work hard if they were to maintain their lifestyle. "I try to talk to Mother, but she is traveling a great deal these days since Daddy passed away, and I really don't want to give her anything to worry about."

"Rosalie, stop eating. If you gain too much it will give Jack an excuse to stay out more," I said.

"I'll try to do better."

"I promise to call more often."

The airport was very crowded the next day when Jeff and I arrived to catch a plane back to New York. We had offered to let Dad sleep in and take a cab, but as usual he had to be the hero and drive us. We arrived in New York City at 11:15 a.m. I was anxious to get home and go to Martine's to check on her. Once the cab stopped at our building, I felt compelled to go right away.

"Jeff, I'm going to just use this cab and run over to Marty's to see how she's doing. I'll be back very shortly. Please pick up Chinese food for dinner and we will eat around six. I want to have lunch with Marty."

"I won't argue with you, Molly, because I know that my opinion of all this is not going to change your mind. Do what you feel you have to. I guess I'll see you around six."

I told the cabbie that I would wait for him to help Jeff with the bags. By the time we arrived at the building where I had rented the apartment for Martine, it was close to one in the afternoon. I jumped out of the cab, handed the driver the fare plus a ten-dollar tip, and went inside. I knocked on Martine's door, but no one answered. I knocked again, and the door to the apartment next door opened. A very thin, young girl with mousy brown hair came out.

"Hello, you must be Molly," she said. "I have a note for you from Martine." She handed me a white envelope with my name on it and closed her door. My hands were shaking as I tried to open the envelope, fearful of the contents.

"Dear Molly," the note read, "I have thought very seriously about the baby and all of your concern and help. I really do appreciate everything that you and Jeff have done for me, but I feel I should leave New York until after the baby is born, and then I will decide what to do. For some reason, I felt you were too involved in my situation and feared it was interfering in your relationship with Jeff. I do not want to cause anyone any pain, but I must strike out on my own. Wherever I decide to go, I can get help from social services. I have already inquired. I hope you understand. I will contact you sometime in the future. Again, thank you for everything. Love, Marty"

My hands shook and my feet felt cold. I was so shocked that I felt numb. Clutching the note in my hand, I slowly walked outside to the street and hailed another cab. Within minutes I was back in Jeff's apartment, still clutching the note. Jeff was in the kitchen eating a snack of crackers and cheese. I knew he was surprised to see me so soon.

"Molly, what are you doing back so soon? I thought you were having lunch with Martine."

"So did I," I said. My voice was barely a whisper. "She wasn't there, Jeff. She is gone from New York." The tears came as I handed Jeff the note. All I could do was cry and repeat over and over, "She took my baby. She took my baby."

"My God, Molly, get a hold of yourself. That baby is not yours. It's Martine's baby, and maybe — just maybe — your dad's. We can't even be sure of that. It could be anyone's baby. Martine may be lying. Let this thing go, Moll. We have to put this behind us and go on with our lives." He put his arms around me and hugged me tightly. I cried and cried. All the pent-up emotion was finally released in a flood of tears, and I felt relieved for the first time since Martine had showed up at our door and announced that she was pregnant. I clung to Jeff with all my strength. I cried and cried for Jesse, my brother. I missed him so.

WORDS ON THE WIND

The words were flying through the air like autumn leaves in October. Searching for the ones that I needed to make the sentences make sense was like chasing a rainbow through a lightning storm. The last sentence of the ninth chapter of the book I was trying so hard to finish had been an all-day, never-ending ordeal. I was stricken with writer's block and could not seem to overcome it. Reluctantly, I got up from my chair, away from the typewriter, and into the kitchen to start a new task. Not knowing exactly what that might be, I began cleaning out my purse. Tucked inside a side pocket of my wallet were a few business cards. I began to look through them, and in the process I found a forgotten one from a Charles Baker. I remembered the man on the plane during one of my trips to Virginia. The card read "Charles Baker - Consulting Engineer." I hadn't thought about him since that day. I smiled to myself as I walked over to the trash can to throw the card away. For some unknown reason, I changed my mind and went to the phone instead. I picked up the receiver and dialed. The voice on the other end sounded masculine and sexy.

"Charles Baker here."

"Hello, Mr. Baker," I said. "This is Molly Peale. Remember me?"

"Are you serious? How could I forget such an intriguing woman? And please, remember to call me Charles or Charlie. What may I do for you today, Miss Molly?"

"You may start by accepting my apology for not calling you in Virginia as I promised. I do believe we had a tentative date for lunch, which I was supposed to confirm with a phone call."

"Apology accepted. Now, where do we go from here?"

My heart raced and my hands felt cold and clammy. What was I doing? I must be out of my mind.

"Molly, are you there?"

"Yes. I'm here. I came across your card and wanted to apologize, that's all. I did say that I would call you and I don't like to go back on my word. I realize it's a bit late, but if you're in New York in the future I would like to buy you lunch."

"It just so happens that I'll be in New York on Wednesday of next week. How about I meet you in the little coffee shop in the Sheraton near Times Square at, say, noon? No excuses this time. However, I never let a lady buy me lunch, no matter how rich and famous she may be. Understood?"

"Perfectly. Next Wednesday, no excuses."

"See you then. Bye."

"Good-bye, Charles."

I was still shaking when I placed the receiver on its cradle. I was astounded at what I had done, but very excited. I realized that I needed some diversion in my life, and felt certain I was doing nothing inappropriate. I went back to my typewriter, and as easily as I had made that phone call, I began to write. I wrote about a birthday party for one of the children in my story. I called him Ronnie. The party had taken place on January 19 in the little country house where my seven characters lived. The mom struggled hard to care for her six children, but always managed to have a little something for a birthday. I loved my fictional family. Writing about them was therapy for my soul.

LOVE ON THE WING

It was the Fourth of July weekend and I was looking forward to Wednesday. I couldn't seem to keep my mind off Charles Baker, and wondered how our meeting would go. I found it difficult to hold a conversation with Jeff, and spent a lot of time on my typewriter or reading. I was down to the last chapter of my novel and struggling for the proper ending. I remembered Cecilia telling me about the problems she had encountered when looking for ways to end a story. I decided to telephone her and ask her to have lunch. Her secretary answered and said she was out. I left a message for her to return my call.

That Saturday morning passed quickly and it was already lunchtime. I decided to join Jeff and try to give him some of the attention I had withheld from him the last few days. I could hear soft music coming from his study as I approached the doorway. He was standing in front of the window, looking out. I walked up quietly behind him, intending to surprise him. Just as I was about a foot away, he suddenly twirled around, made growling sounds, and grabbed me by the shoulders.

"I am the wolf your grandmother warned you about," he said. "I want to take you to my cave and eat you up."

"I can't believe you heard me come in," I said, startled. "I was so careful not to make a sound."

"Little Blue Riding Hood," he said (I was wearing blue lounging pajamas), "I did not hear you, my dear. I could smell you and feel your presence behind me. Are you ready to go to my cave and be taste-tested for slaughter?"

"Now, Wolf, you know I don't play those kind of games. However, I will allow you a little taste of my lips, if you promise to let me go afterward and return to my grandma. She will be worried about me."

We began laughing hysterically and, still hugging, we went into my room and fell on the bed. Suddenly, Jeff's hands were all over me. He was pulling my shirt down and grabbing at my breasts. The feeling was so wonderful that I allowed him to continue until I was caught up in such ecstasy that I thought there was no turning back. He put his mouth on my breasts and began sucking my nipples. I was lost in the feeling momentarily, then suddenly I remembered the night I walked in on my father and Martine and saw a similar scene. I pushed Jeff away from me and ran out of the room. I went into the bathroom and locked the door, stripped off my clothes, and turned on the shower. The water was warm and felt good to my body. I cried and scrubbed until I felt clean and over the shock of what had almost happened. I was both angry and glad at the same time. I was angry at Jeff — and at myself for allowing it to go so far. I was also glad that I stopped him. I crawled in my bed and began to pray for guidance. I didn't know how to handle a situation like this one.

The next day, I decided to speak with my tenants about moving out of my apartment. I knew I needed to move out of Jeff's place and back into my own. The tenants had already found an apartment in New Jersey and would move the first of August. I was relieved. I knew that I was not in love with Jeff and I needed to end this facade. I went back and told him of my plans. He was understanding, but said he felt sorry for me because of my inhibitions. He thought I should see a therapist. I said I agreed, and we hugged and promised to remain friends. I felt relaxed and at ease, like a weight had been lifted off my shoulders.

Wednesday morning came and I awoke early, remembering my date with Charles. I lay in bed wondering what I would wear, and decided to wear a new basic black sheath that I had purchased recently at a little boutique in the city. I looked over at the clock and it was seven eleven. *Lucky number,* I thought, smiling to myself. I tried to go back to sleep, but after lying there for fifteen minutes I realized it wasn't going to happen, so I got up and hit the shower. I loved the feel of the warm water and the way it soothed both my body and my mind. I thought about my book and what I should do next with my characters. The final chapter was coming to an end and I knew I had to create a fascinating conclusion. After my shower, I threw on a T-shirt and panties and sat down to write.

Ideas came one after the other and the words flowed freely, lifting my spirits like a cool drink on a hot summer day. I lost track of time and before I realized it, it was ten forty-five. I finished the page I had started and got up from the typewriter. My thoughts shifted once again to my date with Charles. I felt like a secret agent on a special mission. I couldn't remember when I had felt so excited. I slipped on my black sheath and a pair of black pumps, called a taxi, put on makeup and brushed my hair. I was satisfied with what I saw in the mirror. When I heard the taxi's horn, I grabbed my purse and ran out. As I slipped into the back seat, I said, "Sheraton, Times Square," and we drove off.

I saw him sitting at a small round table in the back of the shop. He was even more handsome than I remembered. His light brown hair shone under the light, and he smiled when he spotted me, showing those beautiful white teeth. He stood up as I approached the table, bumping it with his knee and spilling his coffee.

"Hello, Charles," I said.

"Hello, Molly," he said, and we began to laugh. "This is sort of like the first time we met," he said, "only this time the laugh is on me."

Remembering our first meeting and the smeared lipstick, I laughed again.

"Yes, like de ja vu."

"Exactly, and it couldn't happen with a nicer person."

"My feeling as well," I said.

We grabbed napkins and wiped up the spill. He pulled out my chair and I sat down. Conversation was easy. Charles told me that he was divorced and had two small children that meant the world to him. I confessed that I had never been married, and had no one except my dad and some friends. I told him how I had lost my mother and my brother, and how I missed having a family. Soon we left the coffee shop and headed to Rosy O'Grady's across the street. Each of us had two glasses of wine and a turkey sandwich. When we were finished eating, he invited me to his suite at the Sheraton for a nightcap. I accepted, thinking how nice it would be to spend more time with him, and besides, it was still early. I had leveled with Jeff about my feelings, so it really didn't matter what time I got home.

We held hands as we crossed the street to the hotel. His hand was warm, and a warm feeling rushed through my body. I wasn't afraid and had no second thoughts about where I might be headed. It was very hot and sticky outside, and I was glad to go back into the air-conditioned hotel. We took the elevator to the sixth floor and walked down the hall to Suite 624. It was roomy and comfortable, and I was impressed with his choice.

"This is very nice," I said.

"Yes, well, thank you. I'm glad you like it. Have a seat and I will pour us both a Gran Marnier."

I sat on a small loveseat near the window. I could see the lights of the city, and suddenly a very strange feeling came over me. It was like nothing I had felt before. Charles walked over and handed me a glass. I took a sip of the liqueur and it warmed me all the way down to my toes. Charles sat down next to me and put his arm around me. We looked into each other's eyes and both of us smiled a knowing smile. We took another sip, then put our glasses down. He pulled me close and began kissing me. Suddenly, I knew that I wanted to make love to this man, and as long as he did not touch my breasts we would be okay. I knew I had to tell him, so I whispered in his ear, "Please don't touch my breasts." He asked why, and I told him I had certain inhibitions connecting my parents to this act. He said he understood and promised not to touch. He led me into the bedroom, and we undressed and got into bed. His lips kissed my stomach and moved down to my clitoris. I was so anxious that I immediately had an orgasm, my first ever. It was so wonderful, and I knew I wanted to have another and another before the night was over. When Charles finally tried to enter me, he was shocked that I was still a virgin, and stopped.

"Molly, have you never made love before?"

I said, "No, but I'm ready to give it a try. I think it's time now."

"Are you sure?"

"Yes, I'm very sure."

"I'll be as gentle as possible," he said.

And so it happened. At the age of thirty-four I gave it away. I gave it to a stranger who meant nothing to me.

Afterward, I cried in Charles' arms. He was kind and sympathetic, telling me he understood how I felt. He told me about his first time. He said he was actually twenty years old and the last of his social group to have sex. It happened with a girl in Atlantic City, under the boardwalk. He said the girl was twenty-four and quite experienced. Afterward, he said he ran down the boardwalk feeling like he had just made the biggest mistake of his life. He confessed that after that night, though, having sex became second nature. It was as natural as eating and sleeping. When he married his wife five years later, he had lost count of the number of women he had been with.

"So, I guess I shouldn't feel so bad then. I suppose I did pretty good to toe the line for thirty-four years."

"What you did is almost unheard of in this day and age. Since the sexual revolution of the sixties, it's almost impossible to find a virgin over fourteen. You are a clean, wonderful girl Molly, and I hope we'll be seeing a lot of each other."

"I would like that," I said. "Now I need to get dressed and go home. My house-mate will be worried about me."

"You live with a girlfriend?"

"Yes," I lied. "I really have to get going."

"Okay. I'll go in the other room and give you some privacy. Feel free to use my shampoo and anything else you may need here. Take your time."

Somehow, I didn't feel so bad after that. I figured Charles was a pretty decent guy, and thought how nice it would be to continue our relationship. I showered, dressed and kissed him goodnight. On my way home in the cab, I had romantic thoughts about our time together. When I arrived at the apartment, I was glad that Jeff was still out. I put on my pajamas, crawled into bed, and fell asleep.

SEPTEMBER 1974

It was 10:00 a.m. and my stomach was gnawing at my backbone, making me realize I hadn't yet eaten. I had been typing cover letters to publishers since I got up at seven fifteen. I had tried to find an agent to handle my novel, which I had finally finished, but after many interviews I realized it wasn't going to work out. I couldn't find one who did not want to make changes to my story and I wasn't going to let that happen. I was happy with the way it was written, and made up my mind it was going to stay that way. In a conversation with Cecilia the day before, she said she felt certain a publisher would jump at the chance to work with a well-known actress. I finished the fourth letter and decided to take a break and have breakfast.

Just as I stepped into the kitchen, the phone rang. I had been back in my own apartment for five weeks and still hadn't put everything away. I turned around to grab the phone, tripped over a box, and came very close to hitting my head on the counter.

"Hello," I said, barely pulling myself up off the floor.

"Hello there, Molly," came the voice on the other end. "How are you today, honey?"

"Hi, Charles. I'm fine, or will be if I can just get some breakfast without breaking my neck."

"Oh, would you rather I called you later?"

"No, I can cook as I talk. Just hold on while I find a pan to fry some eggs in. Okay, got the pan. Now hold on while I crack these eggs and pull a spatula from a box here somewhere. Got it. Now we can talk."

"Okay, I won't keep you long. I just wanted to tell you that I'll be out of town for a while. I'm going to visit my brother in Vermont. I'll call you when I return. Okay, doll?"

"Okay. I didn't know you had a brother in Vermont. Why haven't you mentioned him before?"

"Oh, I don't know. I guess the subject just never came up. I have to go now. I'll call you in a couple of weeks."

"Okay. Have a nice trip."

I couldn't help but think it was very odd that Charles had never mentioned his brother. We had talked about family many times over the two months that we had been dating. I knew he had a mother, a sister, and two children, not to mention his ex-wife, Susan. His father had died when he was very young, so I thought it strange that he hadn't mentioned a brother. I figured maybe there was something about his brother that made him nervous, so I pushed it from my mind and went back to making my breakfast. I had two eggs, toast, juice and coffee. I felt better after eating and decided to go for a walk. I took a shower and put on a pair of jeans and a sweater. Just as I was ready to open the door, the phone rang again.

"Hello?" I said.

"Hi Molly. It's me, Cel. I thought you might want to join me for lunch. I'm going down to the deli on your corner and grab a sandwich. Meet me in fifteen?"

"Okay, but I can't eat a thing. I just had a big breakfast. I will have a coffee, though. I could use another cup."

"See you there."

"Okay."

It was good to sit and talk with Cecilia. I hadn't told her about Charles yet and thought this might be a good time. We were sitting in the deli, sipping coffee and talking about publishers and manuscripts, when a very pretty blonde walked up to our table and said hi to Cel. I figured it was one of her lesbian friends until I was introduced, then my hand shook and I couldn't lift my coffee cup.

"Molly Peale, this is Susan Baker. Susan is starting her first novel and has asked for some feedback from me. Do you mind if she joins us?"

I stared for a moment and then managed to say, "Please do, Susan. It's a pleasure to meet you. How long have you been writing?"

"I just started a year ago," she said. "I recognize you from your pictures. This is such an honor. It isn't every day I meet a famous actress. My husband, Charles, and I adore you. We saw two of your plays. You were fantastic in that Devil and Angel thing," she said.

I admit I was flattered, but needed to get a hold of myself, so I excused myself and went to the ladies' room. Cecilia came in after me.

"Molly, are you alright? My gosh, girl, you're as white as a sheet."

"I'll be fine. Just felt a little woozy. Must be coming down with the flu. If you don't mind, I think I'll just go home and lie down for a while. Please apologize to Susan. She is very attractive. By the way, does she have children?"

"Yes, they have two. She and her family will be leaving sometime today to visit her brother-in-law in Vermont. It seems he is in a mental institution up there, suffering from a manic-depressive disorder. Her husband is afflicted also, but he takes medication. Except for his huge appetite for sex, he seems to stay pretty normal. The brother refuses to take his meds and has attempted suicide for the fifth time. It's very sad."

"I see. Please give her my regards. Call me later."

I felt sick and disgusted with myself at the same time. How could I have been so stupid? I had given my everything to a married man with bi-polar disorder and never suspected that he could be lying to me. Had I fallen in love with him? I had asked myself that question several times over the last two months and couldn't come up with a correct answer. At that point, it didn't matter. I knew I would never see him again. I ran all the way home feeling dirty and betrayed. I telephoned Jeff, but there was no answer. I needed to talk to someone, so I called Rosalie.

"We all make mistakes," she said.

"I know that, but this was a whopper," I said.

"Don't blame yourself, Molly Face. You were deceived and it wasn't your fault. Try to forget about this cheating scoundrel and get on with your life. Concentrate on getting that great book published."

I promised to do just that. I said, "Moffitt to forever."

She said, "Moffitt to forever." We hung up.

Charles telephoned me two days later from Vermont, and told me that Susan had mentioned that she had met me. He swore that they had gotten together for the trip to Vermont only, and that he would be back on his own when he returned to New York. I didn't want to hear any more of his lies and left him with only a few choice words.

"Charles, I have heard enough of your lies. I refuse to be used to satisfy your sinful needs. I want you to forget you ever knew me, and do not ever call me again."

TWO YEARS LATER

If I could take back every bad thing I had ever said about persons that made a major mistake, especially persons that made the mistake of having a sexual affair, I would publicly take it back and do a penalty for every one that I took back. But I know I can't do that because what is done is done. I've had thoughts about people that I should not have had, and they have gone through my head and back out again. In some cases they have even been expressed to others I was talking to. But since my affair with Charles Baker, I have felt differently about people who made those kinds of mistakes. I made the biggest and the worst. Not checking into the background or current status of someone I had gotten too personal with had been my worst mistake. If I had checked, I would have known that Charles was still married to Susan, and that he was committing adultery and I was instigating it. I even made the first phone call. How much worse can you get than that? Even though two years had passed, I was still feeling guilty about it. I had seen Susan a few times in the last two years, and each time wished there was something I could do to make it up to her.

I've heard that something good comes from every bad thing. I'm not sure I agree with that; however, I agree that it is possible. After my affair with Charles, I wrote more. I edited my book, found an agent and a publisher, and by the end of the first year of publication, it had sold over a million copies.

So, two years later, I was standing in the bedroom of my apartment, looking out at a street in New York City, with all these thoughts running through my mind. I wasn't sure where I would go from there. I thought I might write another book, or maybe return to the stage. Unable to make a career decision right then, I thought I would go into the kitchen to make something for dinner. Just as I turned around, the phone by my bed rang. Relief washed over me. Someone to talk to. I had been spending too much time alone lately.

I picked up the receiver and said, "Hello?"

"I'm trying to reach Molly Peale," came the response.

"May I ask who is calling?"

"This is Michael Handson. I'm a friend of Jeffrey Wilde. Is Molly available to speak with me?"

"Yes, this is she," I said. I had not heard from Jeff in over two years and was glad to hear his name mentioned. Then all of a sudden, I realized that something bad might have happened. "Is Jeff well?" I asked.

"Yes, very well. I've been working with him for a year now. We've written a new play that will be produced on Broadway soon. We need a female actress your age, and hoped that you would look at the script and possibly consider accepting the role."

"Tell me about it." My heart was pounding and my blood ran cold. I was afraid and excited at the same time at the thought of going on the stage again.

"The character you would portray is a thirty-five-year-old city girl, a single independent person, who teaches law at a college in Virginia. She is a firm believer in women's lib, and even though pursued by many gents, she refuses to get serious about any of them."

"Well, Michael, that sounds like it's right up my alley, and I am certainly willing to consider it. I'll need a little time, though. Will you give me a week or so to decide?"

"Take two weeks, Molly, but please understand we will need your decision then."

"Of course. Please give my regards to Jeff."

"Will do. We'll talk later. Bye now."

"Bye."

I was so excited, I had to pee. After using the bathroom, I called Cecilia and gave her the news. She was ecstatic.

"That's great news, Molly. I know you have been thinking about going back onstage. This is a great opportunity. But, how do you feel about working with Jeff again?"

"I think I would like it, Cel. I have to admit that I have sort of missed him. I think it will be good to work with him again."

"It sounds like you've already made your decision."

"Yes, I think I have."

Two weeks later, I met Michael Handson and was in Jeff's company for the first time in over two years. I was happy to see Jeff again, and he seemed very pleased to have me back in his life, even though it was strictly business. I loved the script and couldn't wait to start rehearsals. I practiced my lines each night using Cel as the other characters. By the day of first rehearsal, I could recite every line without looking at the script. Michael and Jeff were pleased and did not hesitate to let me know how much. On the second day of rehearsal, I telephoned Dad and Rosalie and told them the wonderful news. They were thrilled and looked forward to opening night.

BREAKING A LEG

The show opened on the fifth of January in 1977. I was so nervous I wanted to chew on something, so I had one of the stagehands go out and buy some licorice. By the time he returned, I was being ushered onto the stage. The introduction was magnificent and I felt like I had never left. The theatre was packed, and I was elated that I was so well received. People were applauding and calling my name. I was ecstatic. The entire first act was too perfect. I was literally performing better than I ever had. The applause was letting me know how well I was doing. When it was over, I was rushed off by Michael and taken to my dressing room. The whole time, he was praising me for my acting ability. At the beginning of the second act, he escorted me on stage again. Before he let go of my hand, he squeezed it and said, "Break a leg, Molly."

Anyone who knows show business knows that term means good luck or knock 'em dead, or anything that pertains to a great performance.

"I'll do my best," I said. And so I went onto the stage and did exactly what he told me to. I broke my leg. I was attempting to climb onto a ladder that was part of a library scene, and I slipped and literally fell and broke my left leg. What a night that turned out to be! The stage manager explained to the audience that I had been injured and they would be using my understudy to finish the performance. I heard loud booing sounds coming from the audience. Very few left the theatre though, and the show went on.

At the hospital, my leg was x-rayed and a cast was placed on it. "This was not exactly the type of casting I had in mind for myself," I said to Jeff, as he waited by my side for the doctor to finish his work.

"My feelings exactly," he said.

"I'm so sorry, Jeff. I really wish I hadn't been so clumsy."

"Not your fault, Moll. I wish I had been there to break your fall." For a moment, I felt an old tenderness for him deep in my chest, but I knew it was just the warmth of the moment.

Before we left the hospital, the doctor said I would be laid up for about eight weeks, and to be very careful about using the crutches. Jeff assured him that I was in good hands. He lifted me onto a wheelchair, and a nurse came and wheeled me to the door. They had given me strong medication so I wasn't in a lot of pain, but suddenly my leg started to throb when I shifted my position. Michael's driver had brought the car to the door, and Jeff picked me up and put me in the back seat, in as comfortable a position as possible. The limo was large, so there was plenty of room for us. Cecilia came running up just as we were ready to drive away.

"Molly, are you feeling okay? I've been worried sick about you. I'll go home and get some things and then I'll be over to stay with you, as long as you need me," she said.

"That won't be necessary; I'm taking her to my place," Jeff said.

"No, please," I said. "I would much rather go home. Thank you so much, Cel. Please come over. Driver, I will be going to my apartment in Manhattan."

"As you wish," Jeff said. He looked hurt, but I knew I couldn't allow this mishap to stir up old feelings between us.

"I really appreciate everything you have done and offered to do for me, Jeff. I just know that I'll be a lot more comfortable in my own apartment."

"I understand, Molly. Please call if there is anything I can do."

We rode the rest of the way in silence.

We arrived at my place an hour ahead of Cecilia. I thought it was taking too long to go home and pick up clothes. Jeff and Michael helped me into the apartment and made three cups of Sanka. The drink felt warm and soothing to my stomach. Finally, Jeff said something about the show.

"You know, Molly, we have to keep this show going. I wish we could hold off until you heal up, but it's impossible. We'll have to use another actress. I hope you understand."

"Of course, I know how these things go," I said. "Please don't concern yourself about me. I'll start another novel. Hell, I'll have plenty of time to write now."

"I think you should write a book about a famous actress who breaks a leg and has to be laid up for a year and becomes a famous writer," Michael said.

"Why, that is a great idea, Michael," Jeff said, laughing. "What will you name your novel? How about, 'Polly Plummets to Success,'" he suggested, still laughing.

The whole joke didn't sit right with me at the moment. The trauma of the whole ordeal had taken a toll on my emotions and I began to cry.

"What is it, Molly? I was just trying to cheer you up. I should have realized you were sensitive after all that has happened. How insensitive of me. I'm sorry, dear. Please forgive me."

"It's okay, Jeff. I guess I'm just not handling this as well as I should. I'll be okay as soon as this medicine wears off and I can make some definite plans."

A kick on the door made us realize that Cel was there and needed help bringing in some stuff. "I'll get it," Michael said, jumping up from the floor where he had been sitting.

"Grab the top box, please, Michael," Cecilia said, as she stormed in from the hallway loaded with packages. "I thought you might be hungry, Molly, so I picked up some Chinese food for the four of us. I also brought enough clothes to last a few days so that I won't have to leave you any time soon."

"I'm so grateful to you, Cel. I'm grateful to all of you for your friendship. I only hope that someday I can repay you all for everything you have done for me since we met."

"I think your mention of our friendship in your book meant a lot to all of us, Molly," Jeff said. "It's good publicity for us that the people know there is more to us than fame and fortune. I might also add that you have been a pretty wonderful friend yourself."

"Thank you, Jeff, I said. "I'm glad you feel that way. Now let's eat some of this wonderful food. I'm starved."

Everyone laughed, and we tore into the bags and devoured the food like a bunch of vultures. After we ate, the men went on their way and Cel helped me into my night clothes. I chose a long cotton gown to save the trouble of pulling pajamas over my cast. After I was washed and ready for bed, I took another pain pill. The next time I opened my eyes, it was morning.

Time passes and bones heal. Old times roll out and new ones come in. I spent the next two and a half years writing another book.

I wrote about my acting career from beginning to end. I wrote it because I knew for sure now that I would never perform again. I titled the book, *Molly Peale — Act One to Curtain*. I decided to publish it myself. It sold nine hundred and seventy copies the first six weeks. A production company wanted to make a movie of my story. I let them. After it was released, I had too much money and too much time on my hands. I was leaving my thirties behind, and feeling older and without a goal in life. I wanted to go home to Virginia, but I wanted to write another book first. I knew I would need to think about it, so I took a walk.

THE BIG 4-0

Looking in the mirror that morning, I wondered if something could have happened to change my appearance overnight. I guess I expected to see more lines on my face than on my notepad. My dreaded fortieth was fast approaching, and I was so down I felt as though I had a one-hundred-pound weight on my head. *Lord, give me strength or something*, I prayed. It seemed that through my thirty-ninth, I had picked up that weird "or something," hook at the end of many sentences; why I did not know. I think I first heard Cecilia use it sometime in February, 1979. Here it was already January 10, 1980 and I was still saying it. "Help me, Lord," I said out loud. Just to make sure he heard me, I screamed it, again and again. "Help me, Lord! Help me, Lord! Help me, Lord!" I thought I had better call someone because I was in dire need of conversation. Evidently, the Lord heard my prayer because my phone rang. "Thank you, Lord!"

I picked up the phone at the same time I looked out the window to see an attractive man in a top coat walking along and carrying a bouquet of flowers. Rosalie's voice came just in time to keep me from feeling even more sorry for myself. Before I could speak, she said, "Hi, Molly Face. How is my good friend?"

"Don't you mean, good *old* friend?" I emphasized "old."

"Oh, come on girl, cheer up. I know you must be feeling bad about turning forty, but don't. I'm right on your tail, you know. Come March, I will be there. Doesn't bother me one bit. It could be a lot worse. We could be dead."

"That's true", I said. "Or worse yet, we could be fifty. It's just so depressing, Rosy Face, that I have done nothing with my personal life in forty years. I don't even have a boyfriend. I should be married, Rosalie. I should have at least one child. I've written books about people with children like I have any idea what I'm talking about, and I am as green in that area as grass. Speaking of grass, I never even tried smoking it. So what about that, or something?"

"You have made wonderful contributions for others to enjoy. The public is still enjoying your books, not to mention a movie made from one of them. Come on, Molly, pull up those boot straps and lift up that chin. Go out and get pregnant; you can still have a baby."

That last comment made me laugh and Rosalie followed suit. "You're right, you know, I have a lot to be grateful for, and yes, I could have a baby. I'm just old-fashioned and think that a baby needs a mother and a father who are married and bonded in everlasting love."

Rosalie paused for a moment and then said, "I have something to tell you, Molly. Jack and I are getting a divorce. We stayed together through the holidays for the kids. They seem to be handling the news pretty well, although John is a little more upset about it than Tammy. I guess they are tired of the fighting, or something."

"Oh mercy, Rosalie! I am sorry you two weren't able to work it out. You were married a long time. What are your plans?"

"Jack is moving out. The kids and I will stay in the house. You know his income has been very high the last few years, so he has to support us to the fullest. I might take a full-time teaching job at the high school, just to keep busy."

"I think that's a good idea, Rosalie. It will give you a chance to become your own person for a change."

"I agree. I'm actually looking forward to it. One of the teachers is retiring in March and they offered me the job. I said I would consider it, but now I'm sure I'll say yes."

"Good for you! I wish you and the children would fly up here for a weekend soon. We could all go to a show and do some shopping. Think maybe?"

"Thanks, Moll. That sounds like a real winner of an idea. We'll do just that. I'll mention it to the kids tonight and we'll start making plans. I'll get back to you tomorrow on this. Meanwhile, stop worrying about your age. Now that I'm going to be single, it will be like our old teenage days. Maybe we can double date."

"Well, this call has certainly cheered me up, Rosy Face, even though you have to go through a divorce to make it happen. If you need to talk, call me, even if it's three in the morning. I'll do the same."

"Good enough. Chat later. Bye now."

"Bye."

On the big day, I stood looking out of the bedroom window onto the street. One thing I liked about my apartment was, I had a nice view of the street from the windows. No disgusting alley for me to block out with heavy drapes. So why did I have heavy drapes on the windows in front of the sheers? It was the style those days.

As I thought of calling Cecilia, it happened. Before I could pick up the phone, the doorbell rang. *Who on earth is here at ten a.m. on a Wednesday morning?* I was hoping for a bouquet from my dad. I looked out the peep-hole and saw no one. I thought someone must have rung the wrong bell, but it rang again. This time, I saw a hand put down a bouquet of flowers in front of my door. They were a mixture of roses and carnations: My favorite. I opened the door and reached for the flowers. A blood-curdling scream escaped from my throat as a hand grabbed my arm. I thought I was being attacked.

"Surprise, little girl," said a familiar voice. "Don't scream or you'll bring the police."

"Jeff, my lord! How good to see you! How long has it been?"

"Much longer than it should. May I come in?" asked the surprise visitor.

"Please do," I said.

Jeff and I had talked on the phone only three or four times since my accident back in 1977. I thought I would never see him again. I was so excited I could hardly speak. "I'm so glad to see you," I croaked. It felt so good to get a bear hug from this wonderful man on my birthday. "I thought I would be spending this horrid fortieth birthday alone," I said. "Thank you so much for coming."

"Thank you so much for having this birthday. It gives me a good excuse to visit. I'm glad you're still here, Molly."

"Yes, and so am I since you came to visit. I'm seriously considering moving in the near future. I spoke to Rosalie a few days ago, and she told me that she and Jack are getting a divorce. I'm really considering relocating before I'm forty-five. I don't think I'll rent my place here, though. I think I'll keep it to return to when I feel like shopping in the city, or seeing old friends."

"I'm glad you're not selling your place, Moll. It makes a nice tax write-off, which I'm sure you need at this point. Am I right?"

"Well, yes, but let me tell you something, Mr. Wilde. If you are after me for my money, you can get in line." We laughed at my silly comment as we moved from the doorway to the kitchen and started coffee. "It's so good to see you. I'm a happy lady right now," I said.

"Well, you will be a lot happier soon. Cecilia and Debbie are coming over, and the three of us are going to get you out of this apartment and out on the town. What do you say we all go to Rosy O'Grady's and start with lunch, and continue on into whatever your little heart desires? Sound good?"

"Sounds great. I'll jump in the shower and start getting ready. I don't think you want me to go in my pajamas."

"Hey, anything goes at this point," he said, with that wide grin I had missed so much. In less than forty-five minutes, I was dressed and waiting for Cel and Debbie.

"Would a glass of white wine be good while we wait?" I asked.

"Wouldn't hurt. Do you have a nice chardonnay?"

"I think so," I said. I found a bottle of Sterling Chardonnay, poured two glasses, and we sat down to relax. I began telling him about Rosalie and her break-up with Jack. He didn't seem very surprised, but why would he? The marriage had been suffering for years. "I think she must be out of it because she didn't call today, to wish me a happy birthday. I guess maybe she forgot."

"The day isn't over yet. Maybe you'll have a message when you come home."

"Oh, I hope."

Cel and Debbie showed up and we grabbed a cab to Rosy

O'Grady's. They insisted I walk in first, so I did. One handsome and one beautiful teenager came out of nowhere, hugged me, and wished me a happy birthday.

"Oh my God! John! Tammy!" I said. "Okay guys, I know your mother has to be here somewhere. Rosalie, where are you?"

"Mom is in the ladies' room, Aunt Moll," Tammy said. "She hoped she would be out before you got here, but it looks like you beat her to the punch."

I ran into the ladies' room calling her name. "Rosy Face, where are you?"

"Oh my God, Molly! I hoped I would be out there before you arrived," she said. "Happy birthday!"

I don't remember when I've had a more perfect night. We ate and drank like a bunch of teens. Burgers and fries, Cokes and beer. What a perfect birthday. Turning forty was the most wonderful thing that ever happened to me.

That night, Rosalie and her kids stayed at my place. The next day we all went shopping. The day after that, we went to see a Broadway play. Unless my memory fails me, the play we saw was *42nd Street.* Rosalie seemed happier than I had ever seen her. She laughed more and seemed more alert. I knew it was because of the alleviation of stress from her marriage to Jack. She had confided in me that he was seeing a girl from the firm and had been for at least a year.

I knew that night that I would leave the city and find a more serene place to write. I needed to get another story out. Maybe a whole series of novels. Who knew?

THE MOVE

It was in the spring of 1982 that I left New York and moved to Cape May, New Jersey. The move had been exciting and sad. My friends had helped me with hauling personal belongings and choosing furniture for the new beach house. It was spring, and we had spent days on the beach and dined at the Lobster House on the water. Cecilia and Jeff had stayed for a week to keep me company until I settled in. I felt like we were on a wonderful vacation together. It was hard to imagine that this would be my new home. I missed them after they went back to New York, but I was also very anxious to get back to my writing. I started a series of romance novels and managed to write one each year. With Cecilia as my mentor and Jeff as my agent, I had been very successful. I was happy that things were going so well.

I was taking a long walk on the beach the day I met Kathy. I heard loud barking behind me and, frightened, I turned around to see where this ear-splitting sound was coming from. A beautiful lady and as gorgeous an animal were running up the water's edge toward me. The long red coat of the Irish setter was blowing softly in the breeze on this beautiful morning in May. I raised my eyes above the dog to witness another vision in red. A red-haired woman clad in a light blue sweatshirt and tan Bermuda shorts was holding onto the dog's leash and trying desperately to keep up with the animal.

I yelled out, as loud as my lungs would allow, "Does he bite?"

"Only if she feels threatened. Her name is Lady, and I think she just wants to say hello."

I held a hand out slowly toward the dog. She knew immediately that I was no threat and began licking my hand. "Hello, Lady. My name is Molly and it's very nice to meet you."

The woman extended a hand to me and introduced herself. "I'm Kathy Lynch. It's nice to meet you. We live up the beach a few blocks from here. I haven't seen you out here before. Are you vacationing?"

"I'm a new resident. Molly Peale is my name. I moved in a few weeks ago. I bought a three-bedroom cottage three blocks up, so I guess we're neighbors."

"Molly Peale, the actress and author? This is exciting!"

"Yes," I said. "I hope we can keep it a secret for a while. I started a new novel, and when it is published I hope to do a signing here. Do you have a family here?"

Kathy's eyelids dropped. She looked down and softly said, "No. I was married for five years until we found out that I couldn't have children. About a year later, my husband showed his disappointment by divorcing me and marrying a younger, more fertile woman. They have three children now. I was devastated at first, but I've managed to forgive and forget."

"I'm sorry," I said. "I've never been married. I've never even had a relationship that lasted very long. Looks like we're in the same boat. What do you do for a living?"

"I teach special ed at the local junior high. Mostly math. I'm forty-five now and already looking forward to retiring. Junior high kids are tough to deal with, especially the special kids. They have learning disabilities so they're frustrated a lot of the time. Since I'm the teacher, they often take those frustrations out on me. They tell me to go get fucked, and there is nothing I can do except complain to parents who are usually as frustrated as their kids."

"It sounds like a career you might want to retire from as soon as possible. I wish you luck."

"Thanks, Molly. My feelings exactly. This is good that we met. Maybe we can get together soon. A morning walk and breakfast would be great. I'd really like to get to know you. Will you be free Saturday morning?"

"I'll make it a point," I said. We exchanged phone numbers, and I walked home feeling good about meeting Kathy and Lady. She seemed nice and I needed a friend in my neighborhood.

BEACH WALK

I was in my third year of residence in Cape May and still as in love with the area as when I first moved there. I was working on the 3rd of a series of romance novels that would take me the next ten years to complete. Looking out at the ocean from my office window made the writing so much easier. My characters were in a hot love scene when a knock came at the door that Saturday morning.

I couldn't believe my eyes. "Rosalie! My God, girl! What a wonderful surprise. Why didn't you call?"

"I figured if I called, we would say everything we had to say on the phone and I'd change my mind about coming. I really wanted to come up this weekend and walk and talk. I have news."

"Great! Go in the kitchen and pour us both a cup of coffee, and I'll wrap up this love scene and be right there."

"Love scene? May I take a peek?"

I turned the screen around on the word processor and Rosalie began to read and squeal. "She let the nightgown drop from her shoulders, revealing her large, firm breasts. He bent down and began sucking her nipples as he held her ass cheeks in his hands? She was moaning and begging for more?" Oh my God! Molly, are you really going to publish this stuff?"

"Most definitely. This is the 3rd of a series of romance novels that I'll write. It's what the public wants. I have plans to write six or eight. There are four women, and all of them have many hot affairs before they realize the consequences. They start out as very attractive young girls and will end up very lonely old women. Sound okay to you, my friend?"

"It sounds like a plan. It just surprises me, that's all. I didn't think you were going to put so much raw sex into your work, especially since you've had so little experience yourself." She laughed and left the room.

I turned off the word processor and went into the kitchen. The aroma of the coffee was very appealing. I sat at the table, poured cream in my cup, and began to stir. I heard the bathroom door open and close, and Rosalie came into the kitchen.

"So, what is all this wonderful news you have for me?" I asked.

"I didn't say it was wonderful," she said. "For starters, I'm dating a real nice guy."

"Great! I can hardly wait to hear the rest. Name, please."

"Do you remember Neil Woods from high school?"

"Yes, but isn't he married to Sandy Bates?"

"Was married to Sandy Bates. They're divorced. It seems she found a lot more pleasure in the arms of a woman. She turned out to be a lesbian. Who would have thought?"

"Holy cow! That has to be terribly embarrassing for poor Neil. It's one thing to be rejected for any reason, but for something like that? Wow! So what else?"

"Why don't we go out and start walking on the beach? This next thing is pretty serious. I think we should walk."

Rosalie had a strange look on her face as she spoke. I knew I had seen that look before. It was there when she had something on her mind that she knew would be upsetting. I began to worry.

The summer was almost over and it was hot, but the ocean breeze felt good as we walked. I figured it was probably hotter in New York City on this day in late August. I was glad to be in South Jersey. This was a day I would always remember. I could see Kathy and Lady running about a quarter mile ahead of us. As always, their red hair was blowing in the breeze.

I waited for Rosalie to speak. I had this eerie feeling in my stomach; that feeling of fear, the one that feels like I have a hole in my stomach and air is blowing through it.

"Molly, honey. There is only one way to break this news to you," Rosalie said. She still had that strange look. "I have heard lately that Martine is back in your father's life."

I thought my heart would stop. I stopped walking and turned to face Rosalie.

"And the child? What about the child? Is it a girl or a boy?"

"I don't know, Moll. All I heard is that they have been in touch and that he has seen her a few times. I don't know for how long or in what capacity. The lady friend of a friend of your dad's mentioned it to me by accident in the market one day. I saw her in the Food Lion and asked if she knew how he was doing, and that's when she told me. She said that they had not seen much of him since Martine had been coming down to visit. She didn't say anything about a kid, and I wasn't about to ask."

"Rosalie, listen, whatever you do, don't tell my dad that we talked about this. I want to wait and see how long it will take him to tell me about it. Know what I mean?"

"I know exactly what you mean. I think it's a good move. He may have blown her off and maybe figures there is no real reason to mention this to you."

"That's true. Maybe he wasn't even told about the kid. Maybe Martine gave the kid up for adoption. Who knows? Anything could have happened."

"Well anyway, it seems Martine has her own modeling school now, supposedly in Minnesota."

"Are you sure?"

"How the hell can I be sure, Moll? I only know what I hear. Anyway, what freaking difference does it make where her business is? We don't know where in Minnesota, and who cares anyway? If the mentally deranged woman has gone out of your father's life, we can just forget about this. Right?"

"Wrong! I do know where in Minnesota. I have her mother's address. I care because that mentally deranged woman probably has my perfectly wonderful half-brother or half-sister, and I would really like to know what he or she is like. Get it?"

"Okay, I get it. How can I help?"

"You can take a trip to Minnesota with me, dear friend, so that I don't have to go alone. Please!"

"Well, okay. When do we leave?"

"Do you mean you'll really go? This is too easy. No nothing else? Just 'okay, when do we leave?'"

"That's right. From Moffitt to forever. Right?"

"Right! Let's do it soon. Let's say, June 10. I'll pay for the airline tickets. I'll call and make the reservations."

"Not so fast. I won't be off for the summer until June 15. I still work for a living, dear friend."

"Okay, then. How about the seventeenth?"

"Okay. That will be just fine."

I was elated. I wanted to grab Rosalie and hug her. I knew she had reservations about this whole thing, so I tried not to show my enthusiasm. I said I would make all of the arrangements for our flight and hotel. We agreed to stay for one week. That should be enough time to complete our mission. I just wanted to meet my sibling; hopefully, Martine would allow me to begin a relationship with him or her.

Walking back to the house, I saw Kathy and Lady again. I called out to them, "Hello there. Stop at my place on your way back and meet my friend. We'll have wine and cheese."

"Okay, great! I'll see you shortly."

Rosalie and I walked back in silence, just enjoying the sound of the sea. I didn't realize how far we had strolled; it must have been a good half-mile or so. We walked faster for exercise. Once we got to the house and inside the door, we laughed and hugged, and at the same time said, "Moffitt to forever."

I put out some brie and cheddar and opened a bottle of chardonnay. Kathy arrived around three o'clock, four hours after Rosalie's surprise morning arrival. As I poured the wine, I thought, *How peculiar things are sometimes.* I expressed this to Rosalie and Kathy.

"You know, girls, this is absolutely grand. Here I was, sitting here alone, working on my book, and bang! The next thing I knew, we are having this great time together."

"Yes, I'm so pleased that you invited me," Kathy said. "What do you say we all go to the Lobster House for dinner? My treat."

"It sounds great to me," Rosalie said. "One more piece of cheese and another glass of vino and we should be ready for a nice lobster tail. Don't you think?"

"I think, yes," I said. We laughed and held up our glasses for a toast. "To lobster tails, the biggest ones in the restaurant. I'll treat the cocktails and appetizers and Rosalie can leave the tip."

"Here, here," Kathy said, moving her glass up and down.

For all the years that Rosalie and I had been friends, we both knew that day that we had found a third. Kathy's personality fit with ours like the missing piece of a puzzle. Did I say third? I meant fourth. Lady, the Irish setter, had to be included. Over the next several years, we became closer, and when we took a trip to Cape Cod, we would only stay in pet-friendly hotels or cottages. In 1990, when Lady died from cancer, Rosalie and I were beside Kathy, holding her as the three of us wept.

OFF TO MINNESOTA

From what I heard about the weather in Minnesota, I was very glad that we went there in the summer. We arrived at 11:00 a.m. on Friday, June 17, 1983. Even though it was June, it was still a bit chilly. We had brought light jackets and worn slacks and long-sleeved shirts. The sun was out and there were some leaves on the trees. We rented a car and drove into Duluth. Rosalie had heard about the beauty of Canal Park, and we agreed to spend our first day there. We were ecstatic.

"Molly, listen to those gulls. I think they have a sound of their own. Isn't this great?"

"Yes, I think you're right, Rosalie. The sounds are quite intriguing. This is a fun place to be. Let's find a place to eat. I'm about to starve."

"Likewise. I feel like I haven't eaten in a week."

I wanted to tell her that she didn't look much like someone who would go long periods of time without food. I made up my mind that I wouldn't bug her about her diet. At least at this point, I knew it had been quite a while since either of us had eaten. We found a little fish house and ordered orange roughy. A small salad and hushpuppies came with the fish. We finished quickly and went on our way.

I was anxious to get started on my mission, and indicated to Rosalie that we should go to our hotel and start making phone calls. We weren't carrying cell phones in those days and needed to get to the room and get busy.

It was approaching nightfall when we arrived at the Holiday Inn just outside Duluth, where we had reservations. We checked in and changed into our night clothes. I found a large phone book and began searching the yellow pages for modeling schools in the area. I saw nothing that indicated one might belong to Martine.

"Okay, Rosy, there are thirty-two schools listed. That gives us sixteen each. You take the last ones and I'll start with the first. Whatever you do, don't speak with Martine. Just say you are an agent and would like to have the owner's name and how to get in touch, in order to scout for models. If Martine's name is given, say thank you and hang up. Try not to speak with your southern accent. Try to sound like you're from New York."

"Gotcha. I think I can handle that. Holy cow, I'm starting to feel like a real detective."

I started punching phone buttons. I made my sixteen calls with no luck, and handed the phone to Rosalie. On Rosalie's fifth call, she said, "Thank you. May I have the number where I might reach her?"

I jumped quickly to Rosalie's side and took the phone. "Hello, this is Joanne Hoffman. I'm another agent and also a scout. The number won't be necessary. We'll just stop in. When will the owner be in the school?"

The voice on the other end was male. He said, "Miss Hamilton will be in tomorrow around ten thirty or eleven. She usually leaves for lunch after her first class, which is at eleven fifteen."

"Thank you. I'll need directions to the school. We are at the Holiday Inn out on the Boulevard." The man gave me directions and I wrote them down, then hung up the phone. Suddenly, I realized I had made a big mistake. Suppose the man at the school or Martine called the hotel and asked for Miss Hoffman? I quickly dressed, went to the front desk, and spoke to the desk clerk.

"I'm registered under Molly Peale," I said. "I am a well-known actress and writer, and would appreciate if you would direct all calls to Joanne Hoffman. She is my associate. Please do not give my name to anyone."

"I understand, Miss Peale. It is such a pleasure to make your acquaintance. All calls will be referred to Miss Hoffman."

I thanked him with a ten-dollar bill and went back to the room to plan for the next day. When I arrived at the room door, I realized I had forgotten my key. I banged on the door. I could hear the phone ringing in the room, and banged even harder. I had told no one about this trip, and panicked that Rosalie would say the wrong thing. I banged on the door again, and could still hear the phone ringing. Rosalie didn't answer the phone or open the door. I ran down to the desk to get an extra key. When I returned, Rosalie was standing in the room with a towel on her head, talking on the phone.

"Rosalie, who are you talking to and who did they ask for?"

"Oh hi, Moll. I'm talking to Tammy. I called her to see how things are going there. Why?"

"Okay, just wondering," I said.

After she hung up, I filled her in on the name thing. I realized she had been in the shower. I didn't bother to tell her about the extra key or the panic I had experienced. How could I not have faith in my best friend to do the smart thing?

"Oh, by the way, Moll, I called room service and I think they called back while I was in the shower. I wasn't sure what you wanted to eat. I'll call now and order. What would you like?"

"Oh, just a salad and half a sandwich will be fine. Would you share a roast beef with me?"

"Sounds good," she said.

I smiled and went to the phone. "I'll call," I said. Why don't you go in and dry your hair?"

"Thanks."

THE FINDING

I woke up in the hotel room early that day. It was the eighteenth day of June, and I was to discover something that would imprint in my mind forever. As I stand here now, after all that has happened in my life in the last thirty-some-odd years since my mother's death, the picture of that day in June is so vivid in my mind. I don't want to get ahead of my story, so I'll start from the beginning.

As I said, I woke up early. It was 7:00 a.m., and I was wide awake and anxious to continue my mission in Duluth, Minnesota. I got up, went in the bathroom, and took a shower. I dressed in jeans and a sweatshirt, and wrote a note to Rosalie that I was going downstairs to get breakfast. Just as I was ready to leave the room, she called out to me.

"Molly, are you dressed already?"

"Yes, I left you a note. I'll be in the dining room."

"Okay, I'll be down in a few."

I hurried down to the dining room, much in need of a cup of coffee. The sign read, "Hostess Will Seat You." I laughed to myself, remembering once in high school when one of the not-so-serious boy students removed the "S" from seat on a sign like that in one of the local restaurants on junior prom night. Go figure.

"Good morning. How are you this morning? One for breakfast?" the hostess said, smiling brightly.

"Good morning. There will be two this morning. My friend will join me shortly. May we have a place by the window?" I asked.

"Certainly. Table or booth?"

"Table, please."

She picked up two menus and led me to a nice table by the window, facing the pool. It was still covered, but I liked the view. The room was cheerful in blue and yellow floral decor. There was a yellow artificial rose in a bud vase on the table. I was feeling good as I thought about my mission and how close I was to finding out. I saw Rosalie enter the doorway as I finished my first cup of coffee. She was looking around. I waved, and she and the waitress approached me at the same time. Rosalie sat down and we ordered coffee and eggs with a fruit cup.

"Hey, girl, I'm glad to see you are ordering healthy. Good fruit instead of potatoes."

"Well, I am trying. I'm single now, so if I'm going to socialize a lot, I need to drop ten pounds and perk up my appearance," she said.

"Good for you. Stay with it. You're going to look great. Speaking of socializing, how were things with you and Neil Woods when you left?"

"I told him I was going to do some fishing up north with a girlfriend. He looked at me a little weird, then ask if I would call him when I return. I certainly will do that because I do like him a lot. I don't want to get serious right now, though. I'd really like to date a few other men before I tie myself down. You know, shop around a bit."

"Very good. I wish you luck. Just don't do anything nutty, like getting married again," I said.

"That isn't going to happen before I'm sixty-five," she said.

We finished our breakfast and went to our room, dressed in professional attire, and got on the road. We decided to park in front of Martine's school and wait for her to walk in. The school was located at 424 Walnut Street. It was nine forty-five when we arrived. There were little shops all around, so we parked and went into a gallery across from the school. We figured we would have an hour's wait, so we busied ourselves looking at paintings and talking to the owner. Most of the work was by local artists and done around Canal Park. I bought a painting and had it shipped home to Cape May. It was a young girl looking up at the seagulls flying in the background. The hour went fast, but we still did not see a sign of Martine. We decided to walk over if she didn't show by eleven o'clock.

"Molly, I think that's her," Rosalie said.

I put down the painting and looked over at the school. It was ten fifty-five, and we knew she had a class very soon. It was definitely Martine. She was thin, and even though her hair was changed from her natural red to a light blonde, I still recognized her. Her hair was long and braided, just like she had worn it in New York a few times. We watched her walk inside the school. We thanked the gallery owner and headed across the street.

Martine was hanging up her sweater when we walked in. There was a man sitting at a desk next to the front door.

"Hello, Marty. Remember me?" I said. She turned and looked at me. A big smile came across her beautiful face.

"Molly! What a wonderful surprise. And Rosalie! So nice to see you both. What brings you two to Duluth?"

"It's wonderful to see you too, Martine. Is there a place where we can talk?"

"There is. Come into my office."

"Would you like me to start the students when they arrive?" the man ask Martine.

"Yes, that would be helpful," she answered. She led us into her office in the back of the room. The area was larger than it appeared from the outside. She said she would show us around after we had a little chat. The office was a nice-sized room. There were black and white photos of young girls and boys wearing stylish outfits on the walls. I asked about them, and Martine told us they were students of hers that were doing professional modeling.

"It appears you have done quite well for yourself," I said.

"We're doing very well, thank you," she said. She went on to say, "Molly, I know why you're here. I'm sure Richard told you about the school and about little Richard. So what can I do for you?"

I froze in my tracks. My father knew about all this and had never told me! I was shocked and disappointed. I looked at Rosalie; she was wide-eyed and calm.

"So Molly, what is it you want?"

"Marty, I had no idea. I heard this from a friend of my father's. I think you know what I want. Where is the boy? I really want to see my brother. Please."

"Okay, I'll send you to him. I can't leave the school, but I will send you to Ritchie's school with a note for the principal. I'll follow up with a phone call. I would appreciate it if you didn't tell him who you are just yet. I'll need a chance to talk with him first."

"It's a deal. Thank you, Martine! This means the world to me." I went to hug her and she backed away. I didn't try to push myself on her. I backed off. She wrote the information about Ritchie's school on a sheet of paper. She also gave us a little map showing how to get there.

"The principal's name is Heddy Carmichael. It's a first-name, hands-on school, so she prefers to be called by her first name only. I will tell her on the phone what I think she needs to know about you. She will introduce you to Ritchie the way that I tell her. Please, for his sake, go along with it."

"I will. I promise," I said. We took the information and left the school.

We drove to the address that she gave us. The building was not very big. The sign over the door read, "Duluth School for Special Children." I was elated! I was sure my brother was an over-achiever. Rosalie looked worried.

"Molly, are you sure you're okay with this?"

"I am very okay. I can hardly wait. Let's go in."

We got out of the car and headed for the door.

AWAKENING

Rosalie put her arm around me as we walked into my little brother's school that day. I wondered why she was so rigid.

"Rosalie, stop holding onto me that way. What is it with you? This is a wonderful day for me."

"Molly, please don't be so positive. This could be devastating for you. You know what 'special' could mean. They refer to all children that are different as 'special.' Your brother may be retarded."

"Rosalie, don't be ridiculous. I'm sure it doesn't mean that kind of 'special.'"

We went into the office just inside the door. It was open, with glass walls just like any normal school. A very attractive woman in her sixties saw us and came out from behind the counter to greet us. We introduced ourselves and she ushered us into a room in the back.

"I am pleased to meet both of you. I had a call from Martine. You understand that this meeting could be difficult for Richard?"

"We were told," I said.

"Okay, Martine would like me to tell Richard that you are good friends and would like to ask him some questions about our school. Will you go along?"

"Absolutely. We'll ask him things about the school," I said.

"Alright. I'll go to his room and bring him out."

I was so excited, I could hardly stand it. "Rosalie, isn't this wonderful? I'm finally going to meet him." She was still holding onto my arm. "Rosalie, you can relax now. Stop being so rigid and let go of my arm."

Rosalie grabbed my shoulders and turned me around to face her. "Molly, look at me. Just promise me that if Ritchie is mentally challenged in any way, you will not be dreadfully shocked — and whatever you do, don't show your disappointment to Miss Carmichael."

"Rosalie, stop worrying. I don't believe for a moment that Ritchie has a serious problem. But okay, I promise not to freak out if things are different than I expect." I began to feel uneasy. Suppose she was right. I began to brace myself for the worst. I had known other children with learning disabilities. I said a silent prayer for Ritchie. I asked God that he would not be mentally ill, and prayed for courage to love him if he was. I was not prepared for what happened next.

Heddy Carmichael came into the room holding the hand of a normal-sized, nine-year-old-boy. He was wearing a pair of navy blue pants, a light blue shirt, and black shoes. I looked at his little face and saw a slight resemblance to my brother, Jesse. I tried not to show my disbelief at the way his forehead and eyes looked. His forehead was wide and his eyes were slanted. My heart went out to my little half-brother as I realized he was a victim of Down's syndrome. I reached out my hand to him as Heddy introduced us.

"Molly and Rosalie, this is Ritchie Hamilton."

"Hello, Ritchie. It's nice to meet you," I said.

"Hello, Miss Molly. It's nice to meet you, too." His voice was normal except for a slightly high pitch.

Rosalie spoke next. "Hello, Ritchie. I'm Rosalie, and I'm a schoolteacher in Virginia. Molly and I are visiting some schools in other states and would like to ask you some questions about your school. Is that okay with you?"

Ritchie looked at Heddy and she nodded her okay. Then the little boy of my heart said, "Yes, it will be fine with me. What would you like to know?"

My heart was pounding and I knew my hands were shaking. I quickly spoke up.

"Rosalie, do you mind if I start the questioning?"

"Not at all," Rosalie said. "I have to use the ladies' room. Would you like to come along, Molly, before we start?"

I went with her into the restroom because I knew she wanted to give me time to regroup. I was so grateful to Rosalie for being such a wonderful friend, and saving me from the horror of total shock.

"Rosalie, thank you so much, my friend. Thank you for being here with me, and for me. What would I do without you?" I leaned against the sink in the restroom. I felt a little nauseated, but it soon passed. "Okay, I'm ready to go back out there and talk with my brother," I said.

"Good! From what I have learned about Down's, Ritchie has a less severe case than a lot of people. He speaks fluently and is well mannered. This school must be one of the best. And you don't have to thank me. You've been there many times for me. It's Moffitt to forever, no matter what the issue. Remember that. Now let's go back in there."

"Okay, let's go," I said.

Before we left that day, we talked with Ritchie about his school. He gave us very positive feedback and appeared to be happy there. We talked privately with Heddy after Ritchie went back to class. I gave her my address and told her to let me know if there was anything I could do to help the school.

Driving back to the hotel, Rosalie brought up another good point. "Molly, I hope you realize that Martine deserves a lot of credit for the way she has provided for Ritchie. Maybe we should stop by her studio and tell her that before we leave."

"You are right that she deserves credit, but stopping by her studio is not a good idea. I think she would just as soon not see too much of me. I'll call her. I really don't think she needs my help."

Back at the hotel, I made the phone call to Martine and told her what a wonderful mother she had turned out to be. She said, "Thank you, Molly. I want you to know the reason I ran away when I was pregnant. The doctor told me there was a strong chance that my child would have Down's because of Richard's age. I wasn't sure if I would keep the baby. Once he was born, there was no way I could let him go. I'm glad you like the school. Heddy told me of your offer and I do appreciate your thoughtfulness. We'll keep you posted on Ritchie's progress."

"That will be great, Marty. I have one more request, though. May I please have his actual birth date, so that I might send him a card from his new friend?"

"Okay, Molly. He was born a month early. His actual birthday is August 24. If you would like, you may sign his card 'Aunt Molly.' He calls some of my other friends 'Aunt.'"

"Thank you, Marty. I'll do that. Take care now, and don't be a stranger. I'll look forward to hearing from you."

Rosalie and I took an early flight out the next day. Our mission had been accomplished much sooner than we had expected, and neither of us cared to hang out in Duluth. On the plane, I confessed to Rosalie how thankful I was that I had not succeeded in my quest to steal Martine's baby from her nine years ago.

THE RECKONING

Flying home on the plane from Minnesota was a time of reckoning in my mind. I knew that I would not have been the kind of mother that Ritchie would need, had I won a custody suit against Martine. That day, I realized something very real about myself. I loved perfection. I realized that throughout my life I had had nothing much less. The loss of my brother had been the most devastating event I had ever had to deal with. I said, "Rosalie, I am a selfish, self-centered person."

She turned in her seat next to me and said, "Molly, you are the best friend a person could have. How could you say that about yourself?"

"Because I know that if I had gained custody of Ritchie, I would have given him back to her or found a home for him or something. I wouldn't have wanted a less than perfect child."

"Okay, so maybe you are a bit of a perfectionist. But Molly, you are not selfish. You have the opportunity now to do something for Ritchie and children like him by contributing to that school. You can also join an organization that supports research to improve the lives of people who are afflicted with Down's."

"Sure, but doesn't that still sort of glorify my own name? I mean, something like that will just make me look good while it is helping someone."

"Only if you broadcast it, my friend. Be an anonymous donor. Don't tell them that you are the great Molly Peale. You can do that by working something out with your accountant. Get my drift?"

"I certainly do. That's a wonderful idea. Would you be part of it?"

"I would love it. We'll plan it when we get back."

Heaven help me, Rosalie and I never made those plans. I did, however, send donations to the school over the years. I remembered to send a birthday card to Ritchie every year from his Aunt Molly. I was furious with my father for not sharing with me his knowledge and the part he took in my brother's life. Our relationship was never the same after my trip to Minnesota.

THE PLAN

The sound of the phone ringing in the hallway woke me from a sound sleep. It was Nick again. "Hi, Molly," he said. I looked at the clock on the nightstand. It was eight forty-five. I must have slept for a couple of hours. "Hello?" he said again. "Are you there?"

"Yes. Hello, Nick. I must have fallen asleep. Lunch is at noon tomorrow. The house is still in the same place and I am looking forward to seeing you. To what do I owe the honor of a second call this evening?"

"I wanted to hear your voice again and just talk a minute, I guess," he said. The tone of his voice was much like the way I remembered it from my youth. He had a certain way of speaking when he was trying to be exceptionally convincing. "I wish we could see each other tonight, but I understand that you have been through a terrible ordeal. I didn't say much earlier about your dad, but I am so very sorry. I know how close you were."

"Thank you. You are right about the terrible ordeal. But my dad and I were not quite as close during the last ten years as we had been when you knew me. It isn't something that I want to talk about tonight. I guess you know that my friend, Rosalie, has been married and divorced, and has two beautiful children and four grandchildren. We have managed to stay friends all these years."

"I didn't know all that," he said, breathing a kind of sigh. I realized he was not really interested in my friend and her family situation. I knew I had to end the conversation.

"Nick, I really am very weary tonight and need some time to myself. Lunch is at noon tomorrow and there is plenty of food here, so we'll have our choice of a lot of different things to nibble on. I must say goodnight for now. See you tomorrow?"

"Tomorrow," he said. "Sweet dreams."

Then I was wide awake. I picked up the phone in my bedroom and punched Rosalie's number. She answered on the second ring. I said, "Hi, Rosy Face. I hope I didn't wake you. I need to talk."

"By all means. I was just thinking about you. Feeling down?"

"Not exactly. I had a very interesting phone call. Are you sitting down?"

She was silent for a moment and then said, "Martine?"

"No, a ghost from my past. Would you believe, Nick Graziano?"

"Jesus, Mary and Joseph!" she screeched. "How the hell did he know you are here? What's his story? Is he married? What did he say?"

"Rosalie, hold on to your bloomers. He knows I'm here because he has family here and my dad's obituary was in the newspaper. I didn't ask him if he is married or what his story is. I invited him over for lunch tomorrow. He hinted that he wanted to come over tonight, but I couldn't handle that," I said.

"Well, holy shit, I guess you couldn't," she said. "Am I invited to lunch? I wouldn't mind checking out the old boy."

"Why don't you just drop by nonchalantly around two or so? Act surprised to see him. How do you like that idea?"

"Great idea, my friend. Looking forward to it. I can hardly wait. See you tomorrow around two."

PARENT PEOPLE

It was 9:00 a.m. when I awoke the day after my father's funeral. I realized I had not dreamt the night before. I dragged myself out of bed and went downstairs to make coffee. I sat in the kitchen and looked out of the same window I had so happily looked of out as a child. The realization of where life had taken me slapped me hard in the face. I said to myself, "Self, you are an orphan. You have no family. Little Ritchie is your only living relative, and God help you, you don't want him or his mother in your life." I put my head on the table and began to sob. I was still sobbing when the doorbell rang. I wiped my eyes and looked out the peep-hole, and saw Rosalie and two other women standing outside the door. I slowly opened the door and fell into Rosalie's arms before she had a chance to say hello. "What am I going to do?" I said.

"You are going to do just fine. We are all here to be with you, through thick and thin. Look who's here! I brought you some parent people. It's my mom, and do you remember Connie?"

I looked up and saw the two women smiling at me. I was so surprised to see Connie. I could hardly believe it. She looked wonderful. She had hardly aged.

"Hello, Molly dear. I am so sorry about your father," she said.

"Come in and have a seat, please," I said. "I just made some coffee. Please sit here in the front room and I'll bring some out. Connie, it is so nice to see you. You too, Mother Callahan."

"I'll help you get the cups, Molly," Rosalie said. "It's good that you can grieve," she said as we got cups and a tray for coffee. "You can't always be strong. You have to be human as well, you know."

"Yes, I know. I don't know what I'm crying about. That is the problem. I think it's about me more than my father. It's about me being alone in the world, Rosalie. Remember the time on the plane coming back from Minnesota a few years ago?"

"Yes, very well. I remember the conversation, too. You proclaimed yourself as a selfish person. We were going to start a program for donating to Down's and we never did. But Molly, you are not selfish. I have said to you before that you have worked hard to contribute to society. Your books have provided much reading pleasure to many folks. You are a wonderful friend."

"Then why am I thinking about myself this way again?"

"Because you are not perfect, Moll. No human being is perfect. It's okay to not be perfect. Please get yourself together. Mom and Connie are waiting to spend some time with you. Let's get in there."

"Okay. I do want you to know, though, that I have had my accountant send a check each year to the Down's Syndrome Foundation."

"There! Now that proves you're not selfish. Grab that tray with the coffee pot. I'll bring the cups."

"Hey, you two. What is the hold-up out there? We need some coffee in here. Do you need more help?" It was Mother Callahan calling out from the front room.

We walked into the room laughing and I said, "No, thank you, Mother Callahan. Here is the coffee, and I'll run right back out to the kitchen and bring in some of that wonderful danish you made."

We sat quietly, sipping coffee and munching on danish. Rosalie broke the silence by saying, "Moll, may I tell Mom and Connie about your expected visit from you-know-who today?"

"Yes, I suppose so. I hadn't thought about it all morning. Go ahead, Rosy Face. You may be the bearer of boring news."

"This news is hardly boring, so listen up, ladies. Miss Molly had a phone call from her childhood sweetheart yesterday. He is coming for lunch today. Isn't it exciting? They haven't seen each other since 1955."

"My heavens, Molly! Do you mean that Italian boy from New Jersey?" Mrs. Callahan asked. "This really is exciting news. What time will he arrive?"

"Well, he is due at noon. I don't have to do much preparation, though. There's plenty of food here for sandwiches, so all I need to do is fix myself up a little."

"Don't forget, I have your permission to drop in," Rosalie said. "I just can't wait to see how Mr. G. is looking these days. Did he talk about his line of work at all?"

"Yes. I know that he is a real estate developer. I'm not sure how successful, but will certainly find out today. That is, if he shows up. And speaking of how folks are doing these days, how are you, Miss Connie?"

"I'm doing well, my dear. My husband, John, is retired from the military, as you probably know, and in fairly good health for eighty-one years old."

"No, I didn't know. I'm glad to hear."

"Oh, your dad didn't tell you that we talked now and then at the market?"

"No, he didn't. Actually, my dad and I were not as close the last few years as we used to be."

"I'm sorry to hear that, Molly. In all of our conversations, he never mentioned there was a distance between you, other than geographical. I don't want to pry dear, so if you're not sharing information, I understand."

"I don't mind sharing with you, Connie," I said. "It had something to do with the relationship between him and Martine. Did you know there is a child?"

Connie dropped her head and said, "Yes, I knew. Richard told me that he was sending money to her for the child. I knew he took a small mortgage on this house to buy the modeling school she has in Minnesota."

My heart felt as though it would turn over. I don't know who looked more shocked, Rosalie or me. Mrs. Callahan looked rather pale, and at almost exactly at the same time, the three of us screeched, "Oh my dear God!"

Connie turned beet red as she said, "Molly, I'm so sorry. I thought you knew. I didn't mean to let the cat out of the bag. I'm sorry, dear."

I felt the blood coming back into my face. "That's alright, Connie. I would have found out anyway when I went to settle his estate. This house on Channing Street will have to be sold if there is a mortgage. I refuse to pay it so that little wench can get richer."

Rosalie said, "I am so shocked at you, Molly. Think about what you're saying. The modeling business has put Ritchie in a very good school. I don't think your dad bought the modeling school for Martine. She needed a good source of income for the boy. Anyway, didn't you agree to help out with the child's expenses?"

"Yes, of course," I said. "I realize my father did what he thought was right for his son. It's just that he hurt me so by keeping the news of Ritchie from me. If only he would have been honest with me about everything. He knew all along that he had a son who was a Down's victim. Why wouldn't he tell me?"

Mother Callahan had tears in her eyes. She fingered nervously at her short salt and pepper hair, then said, "Your father loved you, Molly. He probably wanted to spare you the worry and disappointment that he had to deal with."

Suddenly, I felt ashamed for having shunned my father the last few years of his life. I wished I had been more understanding while he was alive. Now it was too late. Our conversations had been strained each time he called. I had found out he knew about Ritchie two years after my visit to Minnesota. I was so angry with him for not telling me that I had stopped communicating with him. I would talk with him when he called, but it wasn't the same between us. My father had known about Ritchie since the child had been two. He had known about him for seven years before Rosalie found out, through gossip, and told me. I was furious with him. I was beginning to feel angry at Dad again just thinking about it. Had I known my dad had contributed to Martine's business, I would have had a discussion with him before I sent those donations. I was at my wit's end. I just wanted to stop thinking about it.

I looked at the clock on the mantle. It was ten forty-five. "Ladies," I said, "I really need to start getting ready for my other company. You are welcome to stay a while longer and converse, but I must go up and get into the shower."

"Molly," Rosalie said, "before we go, let's talk for five more minutes about your anger at your dad. I can tell by the look on your face that you are avoiding the issue, and it isn't good for your emotional health. Forgive him, Molly, and mean it in your heart. After that, you won't have to think about it again."

"It's too late now. The man is dead. I can't tell him that I forgive him."

"No. But you can tell yourself and let the anger go."

"Rosalie is right, dear," Connie said. "Holding a grudge isn't good for you. I can tell you something else that might help. Since I have already spilled the beans, I may as well tell you everything. In one of our conversations, Richard mentioned that you had known about Martine's pregnancy and he was surprised you had not told him. He seemed disappointed, but not really angry. Let the anger go, dear. Please, before it continues to ruin your good memories."

I was shocked beyond belief. All that time, my father knew that I knew Martine was pregnant. Connie was right. I had to forgive all in my heart. I was just as wrong as he had been. The anger left me at that moment. I felt as if a log had been lifted off my chest. I didn't laugh or cry. I just sat there, staring at Connie for I don't remember how many seconds, until I finally said, "Thank you. Thank you, Parent Person, for sharing that. I do forgive him. I forgive my father, and for all I know, he may know that I do."

Rosalie touched my hand, and when I looked over she was smiling at me. She said, "Molly Face, for all you know, he very well may know."

The three women stood up. "Time to go," Mother Callahan said. "Lock the door behind us and up in the shower with you. It's almost time for your date." Each gave me a hug and assured me of their fondness for me. They said I could call on them anytime and I knew they meant it. They left, and I locked the door and bounded up the stairs two at a time. It was forty-five minutes till lunch.

THE MEETING

I felt good about the way I looked. I thought about what I would wear while I was in the shower. I looked in the mirror and liked what I saw. The white slacks and light green top complimented my new tan. I put on some white summer beads, little white bead earrings, and white sandals. It was a nice outfit for a Friday afternoon in mid-June. I was thinking how strange it seemed to be in that house and know that my dad would never walk through the door again. I was wondering about the mortgage I might have to pay when the doorbell rang. It was eleven forty-seven.

I opened the door expecting to see Nick. It was Sally who stood there. Her face was swollen, and I knew she must be taking Dad's death very hard.

"Hello, Molly. May I come in?" she asked.

"I'm sorry, Sally. I have to say no. I'm expecting company, and I need to be alone with him. Can you come back tomorrow?"

"Well, okay. What will be a good time? I have the whole day, and I really want to talk with you."

"Around this same time will be fine. I'll make us some lunch."

"See you then," she said and turned to go. I watched her walk off the porch. I thought, *She must be very attractive when she's feeling well. Without the swollen eyes, and everything.* I called out to her just as she got to her car.

"Sally, thank you for coming."

She smiled a big smile, nodded and got into her car.

I was glad that she had stopped by. How nice it would be to talk with someone who had a personal interest in my late father.

I was still standing at the door when I saw the green Lincoln pull up in front. My heart began to pound and my hands were sweating. I closed the door so as not to seem too anxious. I stood back in the front room and looked out the window through the open blinds. I watched him walk up the walk to the porch. The shoulders were broad, and the body was slender, tall and tanned. The hair was still black, but the temples had some gray. He was even more handsome having aged. I was fifteen again and my hormones were going wild. I didn't answer the bell on the first ring, again not wanting to appear too anxious. Finally, on the third ring, I opened the door.

"Hello, Nick. You're looking well."

"And you Molly, are looking even prettier than you did at fifteen. It's good to see you. May I come in?"

"Oh yes, of course. I'm sorry. I didn't mean to stand here like a bump. Please come in and have a seat."

He stepped inside and looked around the front room. "Can we sit in the kitchen? There is something special about the kitchen that makes me feel welcome in a home. This is a very nice house. I used to wonder what it was like inside. I was never invited here before."

As I ushered him into the kitchen, I said, "Well, now that you are, I want you to feel totally comfortable here. Have a seat at the table and I'll start the coffee. Unless, of course, you would like something else instead."

"No. Coffee will be fine. I take cream and sweetener. May I help you with something?"

"No thanks. Relax. I'll have coffee and cold cuts out in no time. Are sandwiches alright with you?"

"Wonderful. Seeing you and having this conversation is the best thing that's happened to me in a while. I know a lot about you because I've read your books and seen your plays. I read the celebrity magazines, so I know you were involved with your director for a few years. Are you still?"

"Jeff and I are very good friends. There was a time when we were romantically involved, even engaged. I was going through a bad time and Jeff rescued me, sort of. Emotionally anyway. Now it's just a friendship. And you?"

"I got married when I was thirty-five. We stayed married for three years. I have a son, Michael. He owns a ski lodge in northern Vermont. He has a lady friend, but they chose not to marry, so I guess I will never have grandchildren. I used to think that was okay, but I feel differently now. Making my fortune was the most important thing in my life for so many years, but now that I am self-made and, for the most part, retired, the money doesn't seem so important. I really wish I'd had a bigger family."

"So what happened to your marriage? Did she die?"

"No. She divorced me because I was never home. I was so busy making money and trying other things. I was a poor excuse for a husband. I probably wouldn't have married, except she became pregnant with Mike. I felt I should give the baby a name. It was never much of a marriage, and I don't blame her for leaving. We had a friendly separation. Mike lived with her until he turned sixteen, and then he came to me. We lived mostly in Vermont in the warmer months and Florida in the winter."

"So where is she now, Nick? Your wife, I mean."

"Her name is Anna," he said. There was a sadness in his eyes when he said her name. I wondered about his feelings for her, but didn't ask. "She lives in Freehold, New Jersey. She remarried when Michael was seventeen. Married a nice guy named Ed. He treats her well. Gets along well with Michael, too. They visit quite often."

"That's very positive influence for your son. So many divorced people are full of hostility toward each other. So what does Anna's husband do?"

"Ed is a pediatrician. Darn good one too. That's how Anna met him. She became a nurse after the divorce and they met at a hospital."

"I see. That's quite impressive. Both of them in the medical profession, I mean."

"I suppose so, to an extent. But doctors and nurses are a dime a dozen, Molly. I'm much more impressed with you. You made a name for yourself. That's saying a lot." Nick smiled his old familiar smile, and I felt a warm sensation throughout my body. We sat quietly and made our sandwiches. After we ate, I offered more coffee and dessert.

"I don't think so," Nick said, holding his hand on his stomach. "I need to watch my figure. Maybe a little more coffee, but no dessert."

"Very well," I said. "Maybe you'll have a small shot of Tia Maria in your coffee. I hear you Italians like that sort of thing."

"Now that's a horse of a different color. Will you join me?"

"Yes. We Brits like it also." Both of us laughed, and I went into my dad's liquor cabinet and brought out the liqueur. "Why don't we pick up our coffee and go into the living room? We might be a little more comfortable there now."

We sipped our coffee and talked about everything and anything. I filled him in as best I could on the last forty years of my life. As the liqueur took effect, I found myself confessing to this first love of mine how I had thought about him so much over the years.

"I wondered how you were and what you were doing. I didn't have the guts to call your uncle and ask questions," I said.

"Well, you see, that is where I had the advantage." He pointed a finger at me as he spoke. "You were so famous that all I had to do was pick up a paper and read about you."

"You can't believe everything you read in the papers," I said. "And even if it were true, you could not know my thoughts and feelings. Why didn't you call me through the years, Nick? I often wished you would."

"And likewise," he said, "I often wished I would hear from you, Miss Molly. I used to ask my uncle about you. I even asked about your silly friend. How is Rosalie?"

"She's doing just fine. We're still very close. Like sisters." As I spoke, I began to wonder about her. It was getting close to two o'clock and she hadn't shown for her surprise visit.

"I really should be going, Moll. If I stay much longer I might want another drink, and I have to drive back to Uncle Sal's. I would like to take you out to dinner tomorrow night, though. Are you free?"

"Well, yes. Is five thirty okay with you? I'd like to eat by seven."

"I'd like to go early also. Five thirty will be fine. We'll go to Duck Inn at the beach."

"Perfect. I'll be ready."

Just as Nick stood up, the doorbell rang. "Excuse me." I opened the door, and there stood Rosalie.

"Hi, Moll," she said. "I was on my way to the store and thought you might take a ride with me." She looked across the room at Nick. "I'm sorry. I didn't know you had company."

Oh boy, I thought, *I didn't know she could act that well.*

"I was just leaving, Rosalie. You're looking well," Nick said, smiling.

"Oh, my God in heaven! Aren't you Nicky from forever long ago? You've grown more handsome with age. Why is that? Men get better and we women just seem to get older."

"I think you both look fantastic. Now if you wonderful ladies will excuse me, I must be going. Molly dear, I'll see you tomorrow at five thirty sharp."

"Five thirty. I'm looking forward to it," I said. I walked him to the door and he gave me a wink as he left.

"Jesus, Mary and Joseph, Molly! Is he gorgeous or what?"

"Yes, he is quite handsome," I said, laughing. "What took you so long? You almost missed him."

"I thought I'd give you two some time alone. So, did you get caught up? Is he rich and still single? I heard him say he will see you tomorrow, so I'm assuming things went well."

"Rosy Face, which question would you like me to answer first?"

"Take your pick, Moll, but for God's sake, tell me!"

I answered in the order that my overzealous friend had asked. "Yes, we got caught up. Yes, he is rich and single. And yes, things went very well. We are going out tomorrow night to the beach for dinner."

"This is so freaking exciting, Moll! I can hardly stand it. Aren't you just thrilled to the gills?"

"Yes, there is a certain amount of excitement to this whole scenario. Just so I don't leave anything out, I will tell you all about his previous marriage and his son, Michael, as we're driving. Now, let's really go to the store. I need a new outfit for tomorrow's date."

Rosalie was staring at me with her mouth open. "Former marriage? Son, Michael? Oh, shit. I can't wait to hear! Your car or mine?"

"We'll take mine, girlfriend. We can put the top down and cat around a bit. Is that okay with you?" I had bought a new Cadillac convertible that spring and driven down from New Jersey.

"That's great! I have the haircut for it. Cut it especially for your car."

"Get real, Rosy Face. You've worn your hair short since the fifth grade, so who do you think you're kidding? Come on, let's get out of here. This house is starting to give me the creeps."

"So grab your pajamas and stay over at my place tonight. Why should either of us be alone?"

"Good idea. Give me a second. I'll just run upstairs and get a couple of things to wear. Be right down," I said.

As I passed my dad's room, I couldn't help but look in and my heart began to ache once more. I tried not to cry as I gathered some clothes, but the tears came anyway. I sat on my bed and gave myself a moment to grieve. Then I picked up my overnight bag and went on my way.

SALLY'S VISIT

I woke up on Saturday morning much earlier than I had hoped. I looked at the clock on the table in Rosalie's guest room where I had slept the night before. Seven forty-four. I heard a familiar noise outside. Thunder, I thought. I could hear the raindrops starting to fall on the roof and beating softly against the window. "Oh, great!" I said out loud. "Just what I need. I'm already looking forward to a fairly depressing afternoon with Sally crying on my shoulder. Now it's complicated by the rain."

A light tap came on the door. "You okay, Molly?" Rosalie's voice came from outside the door. "I thought I heard you talking."

"You heard right. I was just saying how this rain will complicate an already depressing day."

"Come on, Moll. What is it? You seemed perfectly fine last night. You purchased an absolutely gorgeous outfit for your date with Nick. So what are you depressed about?"

"I might answer that if you will come in and stop talking through the door. It's hard to tell if it's your voice I hear or the muffled sound of the rain."

She came into the room and plopped down on the bed. "Okay, I'm here. So tell me."

"I forgot to tell you last night. Sally, Dad's fiancée, stopped by yesterday just as I was expecting Nick. I told her to come back today for lunch. She looked as though she had been crying for days. I have to feel sorry for her. After all, she was expecting to marry and her fiancé dropped dead only a few weeks before her wedding day."

"Don't feel too sorry for her, Moll. I hear old Sal was more interested in a meal ticket than a wonderful companion. I wouldn't be surprised if she tries to hit you up for money."

"When did you hear this? You mean you knew my dad was engaged and didn't tell me?"

"Don't go getting your panties in a knot. I didn't know. My mom mentioned it yesterday. She heard it from a friend of a friend."

"Blessed Jesus! These old women around here are certainly a bunch of know-it-alls. With people like them, who needs the media? I'm not going to draw conclusions about Sal until I've had a little time with her myself. What does Mother Callahan think?"

"Mom doesn't know what to think. She feels pretty much the same way you do about the old hens around here. I must say I agree. But then on the other hand, where there's smoke, there's sometimes fire. Know what I mean, girlfriend?"

"I certainly do. I will be on my toes with the lady. Now I think I'd better get dressed and get started. Is there coffee in this establishment?"

"I'll make a pot right away. If you want me to, I'll come home with you and help with this lunch thing. I need to get my car from your house anyway."

"That will be great. I think it might help to have my best friend present. I hope Sally won't feel uncomfortable with that. If she does, then something is in the wind."

"Bingo!" Rosalie said, holding up a forefinger. "Let's get that coffee."

We had two cups of very strong coffee, poured another for the road, then went over to my house. The newspaper was on the driveway, soaked with rain. I picked it up and threw it into the trash can, spilling half of my coffee. "Who needs to read this shit, anyway? Probably just more nonsense about debates on political issues," I said.

"Right! Since the first British one was aired ten years ago, you never know what you will see on television or in the paper."

"Rosalie, what on God's green earth does something that happened ten years ago have to do with anything?"

"It has a lot to do. I have to teach this stuff at school. The more they show us in foreign countries, the more things go wrong. Just think about the war. The most current one."

"For Pete's sake! Desert Storm? Are you for real? You're comparing the desert and England. What is your point?"

"I don't know exactly. I just think that the whole thing ties in and that it's not over till it's over. Get my drift?"

"No, Rosalie, I don't. Let's not talk about it. Shall we get some food in the works here? It's already ten thirty and Sally will be here at twelve."

The bell rang at twelve noon. I opened the door to a much more attractive Sally than I had seen the day before. The puffiness was mostly gone from her eyes and she had a new hairdo. The light bleached blonde was toned down just a little, and she wore a beautiful summer dress with white and orange flowers on it.

"Hello, Sally. Won't you come in?" I introduced her to Rosalie and offered something to drink. We all agreed on iced tea with lemon and a little sugar.

"Thank you, Molly. It means a lot to me to spend this time with Richard's daughter. I've heard so much about you from your father that I feel I have known you for years. You were your dad's heart-throb, you know. He loved you very much."

"I'm sure he did. I loved him very much also. However, we were not as close the last few years as we had been in previous times. I never even knew you existed, Sally. My dad, nor anyone else, bothered to tell me about your engagement. Why do you suppose that was?"

Sally had a rather sad look as she began to speak again. "That's why I wanted to see you before you leave, Molly. To explain that to you. You see, dear, Richard knew that you had heard some not-so-nice things about some of the women he dated. He didn't want you to get that impression of me. We were planning a surprise visit to Cape May sometimes this month. We felt we should meet face-to-face. I have to admit, I was a little worried about how you would receive us. I knew that you and he had had some problems with your relationship because of the child that Richard fathered with your friend."

"I see. I wasn't sure if you were aware of that. I want you to know that when someone comes to my door, I receive them kindly. I would have listened to you and Dad. I am truly sorry that we never had the opportunity. Now, let's go into the dining room and have something to eat."

Rosalie had not spoken a word the whole time. She sat there sipping her iced tea. Suddenly, at the dining room table, she said, "You know, Sally, we all loved Richard very much. We were all just a little disappointed that he didn't share with Molly some of the most important issues of his life. His knowledge of young Richard's existence, for example."

"Thank you, Rosalie," I said. "I understand now, though, why he didn't. It was because he didn't want me to worry."

"You're right, Molly. That's what he told me," Sally said. "However, I convinced him that that was a cop-out, and that was why we were planning to visit with you. He realized he was wrong and wanted to beg your forgiveness. We wanted to be a family; to include both you and your little brother."

"I think I could have accepted that, Sally. I'm sorry he died before it materialized. My next question may surprise you, and it may not," I said, staring directly into Sally's eyes. "Did you know that my father took out a mortgage on this house to finance Martine's business?"

Sally took a bite of her salad. When she finished it, she looked at me and said, "Yes, I knew. That's one of the things that I want to talk to you about. He borrowed ten thousand for the down payment. Three months later, he expressed worry over doing that because of not sharing the information with you. I loved him so much, I could not stand to see him so worried. I took money from my savings account and we paid off the loan on the house. The house is yours, Molly, free and clear. However, I will need you to pay the money back to me, since it was all that I had. I won't ask for interest. I just need the ten thousand dollars back."

I was shocked out of my wits. I looked at Rosalie; her mouth was open and she had stopped chewing her food. For a moment, I couldn't speak. When I regained my composure, I said, "Do you happen to have any paperwork to that effect, Sally?"

"No. I trusted Richard. We were to be married in the very near future. Why would I have paperwork?" she asked.

I thought for a moment, and then stood up. "Sally," I said, "when you can provide proof that my father's estate owes you ten thousand dollars, then I will gladly pay you. Until then, there is nothing I can do for you. Now, if you will excuse me, I have things to do. Good day."

She put down her sandwich, took a sip of her tea, and walked to the door. Her face was flushed and her hands were shaking. She said, "Goodbye, Molly. It was nice meeting you. Thank you for lunch."

After Sally walked out the door, Rosalie and I looked at each other and burst into a fit of hysterical laughter. "My God, Rosalie! You were right. Ten thousand dollars! I don't believe this."

"I heard she is a real gold digger. But do you suppose it's true? Maybe she did give Richard the money."

"I'll look into it tomorrow. Right now, I want to get ready for my date. I'm just grateful it's no more than that. I thought he would have mortgaged for a much higher figure. I won't lose sleep over ten grand," I said.

"My thinking exactly," Rosalie said. "Go up and start getting ready. That light blue outfit is going to look great on you. I'll just finish these dishes and slip out. Have a wonderful evening."

NICK'S STORY
AS TOLD BY NICK

I had lunch with Molly the day after her father's funeral. It was the first time I'd had an invitation to her house. I've seen her so many times over the years. Watched her walk home from school in her younger days. I saw her change from a girl into a beautiful woman. Suffered silently with her and her family when her brother was killed in 1959 in a surfing accident. Forty years had gone by since we were teenage sweethearts. Now there I was, an old man of fifty-seven, feeling like a teenager again at the sight of her. I had seen her father's obituary in the newspaper and called to pay my respects. As a result, she invited me to lunch. We actually held hands, kissed, and made a real date. I remember thinking, *Oh, Molly, if you only knew.*

I was staying at my Uncle Sal's house that week. I headed over there as soon as I left Molly's place, to spill my guts about how I was feeling. I needed someone to talk to.

I decided to stop in a deli on Route 17 and pick up some cold cuts and bread. I had wanted another sandwich at Molly's, but didn't want to appear piggish. I bought the food and was on my way to Virginia Beach from Craddock. It was four o'clock when I pulled up in front of my uncle's home. I had always loved his big white house with its huge porch and giant white columns. I grabbed my bag, got out of the car, and quickly walked to the porch. The sound of the ocean from behind the house was music to my ears. I walked around back just to get a glimpse of the surf gently touching the beach on this warm, clear day in June. I enjoyed the view for just a minute, then walked around to the front, tapped on the front door twice, opened it and went inside.

"Uncle Sal, are you here?" I called out as I walked through the large foyer toward the back of the house, to the movie room. "I have sandwich food. Are you hungry?"

"Hey-a-Nicky," he answered in his broken English. "Meet-a-me in-a the kitchen. I'm in-a-the bath-a-room." I went into the kitchen and put the food down on the servant's table by the window. I put the meat on a plate that my Aunt Grace had purchased in the old country. Both Sal and Grace had come here from Sicily sixty years ago. Uncle was now seventy-nine and still very much in control of his senses. Grace had passed away two years ago. They had worked very hard as cooks in the beginning, and then managed to purchase a restaurant of their own. Eventually, they bought three more in the heart of Virginia Beach. Uncle Sal made and marketed the best Italian sauce in the area and acquired millions as a result.

"So tell-a-me Nick. How is-a Molly? Still a faccia-bella?"

"She is just great, Unc. She's even more beautiful than she was as a girl. She's fifty-five now. Her blue eyes still sparkle, and she wears her blonde hair in a short style that sort of circles her face. She has that same old smile showing those beautiful teeth. You know, her teeth always protruded just a hair, but it never detracted from her beauty. We're going out to dinner tomorrow night, and I just can't wait to see her again. I've never stopped loving her, Uncle Sal. I don't think I ever will."

"Don't-a-count-a your a-chickens a-before they a-hatch-a, Nick. You and-a Molly were just-a bambinos when-a you a-knew each other. She is-a very famous. Maybe-a set in-a her ways. Caparie."

"Yeah, I understand, Uncle Sal. I won't count my chickens before they hatch."

"Does-a she know that a-you a-stalked a-her for forty-a years, Nicky?"

"No, Unc. I think I'll keep that to myself. I wasn't really stalking her, anyway. I used to sit on the street and watch because I wanted to see how she was doing. I never meant any harm. I sent her roses every Valentine's Day, with an anonymous card. I wonder if she ever figured it out. I'll tell her someday. Just not anytime soon."

"Okay a-Nicky. I made-a some-a good-a pasta-fogiolo. I'll a-heat-a some up-a. We'll a-have-a some-a soup and-a sandwich. Let's-a mangia."

Soup and sandwich with Uncle was enjoyable enough, but my mind was constantly on Molly. It was hard to have a conversation about anything else. After we ate, I managed to watch a movie on television, but didn't hear much of what the actors were saying. I went to bed at ten o'clock, but didn't fall asleep until the wee hours of the morning.

When I awoke Saturday, it was almost noon. Uncle was knocking on my door, saying something about having a pepper omelet. I yelled through the door, "I'll be there in fifteen minutes, Uncle Sal." I dragged myself out of bed and hit the shower. I felt pretty good afterward. I decided to dress in a pair of tan shorts and a cream-colored pullover.

"Good-a afternoon, a-sleepy head. You-a have-a sex in-a your-a sleep with-a Molly?"

"No. I just had sweet dreams of holding hands and walking the beach," I lied. In reality, I had not dreamed at all. I was glad it was morning and I could start planning for the evening.

We ate at the servant's table again, my favorite place in the house. There were no longer servants on a full-time basis. Minerva, a woman Uncle Sal had hired to do household chores, came in every day at noon and left at five. I often wondered if she serviced Uncle in other ways, but was too ashamed to ask. I had a reason to be suspicious. There was a certain way they looked at each other. Uncle would raise an eyebrow and she would smile a knowing smile. To top it off, Minerva drove a Jaguar. That's a pretty classy car for a cleaning lady.

"Nick, what-a time will-a you be-a going out-a?"

"I'll be leaving here at four thirty. Remind me to call the florist when I'm finished eating, Uncle Sal. I'll want them to have a couple dozen roses ready for me to pick up. I think I'll bring a nice bottle of red wine to my favorite lady also. It's good for the heart."

"I'll do-a one-a better. I'll call-a my guy down-a town. Have-a the flowers a-delivered here. He can-a pick up-a the nice-a wine on-a the way. I'll a-give a nice-a tip."

"Thanks Unc, you're a gem." I finished eating and read the newspaper. I went downtown and got a haircut and had my nails manicured. I wanted to look my best for Molly. I took a long walk on the beach that afternoon. At three thirty, I took another shower, shaved, and dressed in casual khaki slacks, a short-sleeved cream shirt, and a tan blazer. I looked in the mirror and gave myself two thumbs up. The flowers and wine were delivered at four twenty-five, and I was out the door on schedule.

As I drove over the Virginia Beach Expressway, "I've Got You Under My Skin" was playing on the radio. I thought, *How appropriate,* and sang along. I was deliriously happy. This was a special day. Brunch with Uncle Sal, his help with the flowers and wine, a nice walk on the beach and, within the hour, I would once again hold the hand of my teenage sweetheart.

THE DATE

I was dressed and anxious to go when Nick arrived at five thirty-five. The light blue sundress stopped just above my knee and I thought I didn't look half bad for fifty-five. I had purchased a pair of matching sandals and wore the same white beads I had worn the day before. When the doorbell rang, I didn't play the game of trying not to appear anxious. I immediately opened the door and my eyes drank in this handsome man. He wore a tan and cream outfit that emphasized his dark brown eyes.

"Hello, Nick. You look handsome."

"Thank you, my dear. You're absolutely breathtaking. That dress brings out the blue in your eyes. Let's go. I can't wait to show you off. Grab a sweater in case it gets chilly at the beach."

"I have it covered," I said, picking up a white sweater from the back of the couch. My heart sang and I felt as light as a feather. When he opened the car door to let me in, he bent down and kissed me lightly on the lips. I felt shivers run through my body. As we drove off, I wondered how many of the busybodies on Channing Street had seen us.

"Well Nick," I said, "we may have given my nosy neighbors enough gossip to keep them busy for the next six months."

"Let them talk," he said. "I'm happy to oblige. I'd hate for the poor old things to be bored to death for the next few months."

"I have no problem with it," I said.

"Good. Let's listen to some music. Are you a Mozart fan?"

"I enjoy it," I said. "*The Magic Flute* is my favorite by that composer."

"Maybe the sound from that is on this tape. we'll see," Nick said, as he slipped a cassette into the player.

"That sounds delightful," I said, as we drove onto Highway 17 and off toward the beach. As we rode along, enjoying the music, I looked out of the corner of my eye and saw Nick glancing over at me. I remained silent, feeling as though I was living a dream and hoping that I wouldn't wake up.

The traffic was heavy and it took us an hour to reach the beach. "Well, my lady, here we are. Sit tight. I'm coming around to your side to let you out. You are much too delicate to open a car door."

"I won't argue, suh," I said, showing off my best southern accent. "I hate these big ol' doors. One could break a lady's arm."

We laughed as he opened the door and I stepped out. Suddenly the laughter stopped as we looked in each other's eyes. He put his arms around me and pulled me close to him. I raised my arms and put them around his neck.

"Molly, I've waited forty years for this. I knew it had to happen eventually. We were destined."

"Yes," I said. "It's serendipity."

"Seren-what?"

"It means exactly what you just said. It was destined to happen. All these years we were bound to get together. It's fate."

"That ain't no lie, girl. I'm glad we both realize it."

He pulled me close and kissed me hard on the lips. I thought I would explode. My heart raced. "Shall we go and eat? I'm a little hungry, and all this excitement is making me dizzy."

"By all means. I'm hungry myself. I had soup and a sandwich with Uncle Sal, but that was hours ago."

We were told by the hostess that we would have to wait about forty minutes for dinner, but we could go out to the bar on the dock and have drinks and hors d'oeuvres. We ordered two Southern Comfort Manhattans and some crab claws.

As we sipped our drinks, Nick gave me a loving look and said, "I think we can have a nice future, Molly. What do you say we start seeing more of each other? I'll be staying at Uncle Sal's place a lot this summer. Maybe next winter we can take a trip to Hawaii. I was there last year and it was so beautiful. I would love to go back."

"I would like that. It's been a while since I've done any serious traveling. I stay so busy most of the time. I plan to retire soon, though. As far as seeing a lot of each other, with you staying at your uncle's, I don't think that will work, with me living in Cape May, New Jersey. Did you know that I moved there?"

"I had no idea. I just assumed that you would be living here, in your father's house. It won't be a problem though, since I live up that way anyway. I have a condo on the beach in Ocean City. It's less than thirty miles from Cape May. That would work out fine."

"It's certainly a possibility," I said. I was beginning to feel uneasy and I didn't know why. "Nick, what do you say we take it slow? After all, we haven't seen each other in forty years. I mean, it's like we just met. People change, so we really don't know each other."

"Okay, slow it is. I didn't mean to sound pushy. We'll give it some time. I just want to see you more. Isn't that how people get to know each other?"

"Yes. I don't want you to think I'm giving you the brush-off. I would like to see you also. Let's wait on reservations to the islands, though. I don't think we should plan a trip like that until we're better acquainted. Agree?"

"Agree. I don't want to do anything that makes you uncomfortable."

"Thank you. I'm glad you understand. I've lived alone since college, except for those few months with Jeff. It might be difficult for me to rush into a serious relationship right now."

"I understand completely. I guess both of us are set in our ways. I have no problem waiting, Moll. I've waited for forty years. That's damn near a lifetime. Know what I mean, girl?"

"Nick, please don't call me 'girl.' I haven't been a girl in years. And yes, I do know what you mean. And again, thank you."

The hostess approached us carrying menus and we followed her to the table. Only twenty minutes had passed, so I figured Nick must have slipped her a few bucks. She seated us at a nice candlelit spot inside, by a window facing the ocean. The candle's flame flickered in Nick's brown eyes, and I couldn't help thinking again how handsome he was. We ordered two more Manhattans and asked the waiter to give us a few minutes.

"You know, this is a beautiful moment," I said.

"Yes, it is. I just love sitting here, holding hands with you and watching the candlelight in your eyes," he said.

We sat there for about five minutes, sipping our drinks and scanning the menus. This restaurant was my favorite in Virginia Beach, so I already knew that I would have: Lobster tail, preceded by a cup of she-crab soup and a light salad. No bread or potato.

The waiter returned, and Nick placed my order and ordered the broiled flounder for himself, with the same appetizers. The soup was served quickly. We were hungry after two Manhattans, so we enjoyed the food. We chatted only between courses, and our conversation was mostly about the food. When we were finished, we ordered coffee with Tia Maria. No dessert.

"Do you like to cook, Molly?" he asked.

"Well, nothing gourmet. Living on the beach, I often steam shrimp, clams or mussels for myself and a friend or two. I love making an omelet for breakfast now and then. Egg whites only, of course. I might add one yolk to three whites sometimes. But I'm very good at making reservations," I laughed. "My lifestyle has been too hectic to get into a cooking mode. I really don't think I'd like to spend a lot of time on it."

"Well, maybe soon, after you return to New Jersey, you could spare me a weekend and I'll cook for you. Do you like Italian food?"

"Love it. And that sounds great. I'm glad you said New Jersey. I think for the next few days here, I'll be busy with the business of my father's estate. I'm a little tired now, so if you don't mind, I would like to go home."

"Okay. Let's finish our coffee and go."

Driving home, we didn't talk much. We held hands and listened to the music. In front of my door on Channing Street, Nick began kissing me passionately and I didn't want to let him go. I felt a need and wanted desperately to fill it, so I invited him in.

The lovemaking was better than I had dreamed. Afterward, we fell asleep, exhausted. I had a dream about my father. He told me to be careful of this Italian man.

The next morning I made omelets for breakfast. Nick left around 10:00 a.m., and I went for the phone to call Rosalie. It rang before I could pick it up.

"Well, how did it go?" It was Kathy, calling from Cape May. "I just got off the phone with Rosalie. We're dying to get the scoop. She's on her way over your house. She asked me to call and warn you. So tell me."

"My heavens! You two won't give me a break, will you?" I said, laughing.

"Nope. Now, spill it!"

"Okay. It was wonderful. We had a great dinner at the beach."

"And the sex?"

"That's where I draw the line. I'm hanging up now. Bye!"

As I hung up, the doorbell began ringing non-stop. I was beginning to feel a little annoyed with my friends. "What the hell is going on here? I'm coming, damn it!"

I opened the door to a grinning girlfriend with her hand on her hip. She was wearing a pair of jeans, a T-shirt, and a pair of multicolored sandals with wide straps. I had a feeling she was ready for the beach after she was finished prying into my personal business. I was pretty good at reading Rosalie's mind by the way she looked.

"Hello, Molly. I don't want to pry. I just want details about your date last night. I'm all ears."

"Okay. I'll tell you just like I told Kathy on the phone. We had a nice dinner at the Duck Inn. The rest is nobody's beeswax. And stop standing there with your hand on your hip. Come on in and have coffee with me. Heaven knows, I won't be much good for anything else today." We went to the kitchen and I poured the coffee.

"Okay, my friend. For starters, how many drinks did you have?"

"We had coffee with liqueur."

"Before or after dinner?"

"After, of course."

"And what before?"

"Oh, just a couple of Southern Comfort Manhattans."

"Did you have the liqueur at the restaurant or here?"

"Why do I feel as though I'm being interrogated?"

"Because you are?"

"That must be it."

"Come on, Molly Face. I'm your best friend. I promise I won't tell Kathy or anyone else. I told you about Neil and me. Did it happen?"

As usual, with Rosalie, I got tickled and couldn't stop laughing. I must have turned a dozen different colors. "Okay, damn it all. Yes, it happened, and it was just great. Better than I ever dreamed. The oral was the best part. I had three orgasms in an hour. Now, are you satisfied?"

"Yeah. I am. And, evidently, so are you."

"More than you can imagine," I said. I lied about the three orgasms and the hour. In truth, we were both so hot that it lasted twenty minutes at most. We each had one big one and passed out from exhaustion.

"Whadda ya say we ride down to Chesapeake Beach and walk a while? It's a beautiful day and we could use the exercise," Rosalie said.

"I'd love to, except I need to call Kathleen back first to apologize. I was sort of rude to her when she called."

"Oh, really? How rude?"

"Well, I hung up on her, more or less. I hope she isn't angry with me."

"Oh, Moll, that's not good. Kathy's pretty sensitive. Why don't I call her and see how she feels before you speak with her? I'll go out and call from my car phone. Be right back."

"Okay. I'll go jump in the shower."

When I had finished my shower, I dressed in a pair of light jeans, a tank top, and brown sandals. I grabbed a light blue parka in case it was cold on the beach. When I got downstairs, Rosalie was sitting on the couch and looking a bit forlorn.

"Did you get a hold of Kathy?"

"Yeah, and she's pretty hurt. Said you hung up on her as if you were really pissed at her. Were you?"

"Well, I have to admit, I was annoyed. I was annoyed with you, too. The difference was, I was looking at your face. I'll call Kathy and apologize."

"Okay. We'll take my car. I feel like driving. You can use my mobile phone. Ready?"

"Ready!" We got into Rosalie's car and headed for Chesapeake Beach. I telephoned Kathy as we were driving along the Military Highway. She was quick to forgive me for hanging up and apologized to me for prying. Then we both cried and said how we missed each other.

I think Rosalie and I must have walked three miles that day. There was a breeze on the beach, the sun was bright, and for a while I forgot what lay in store for me during the coming week.

THE READING

The days that followed were filled with meetings with Dad's attorney and the banks in the area. I found out through Reggie Barfield, the lawyer, that Dad had accounts with two banks; one in Portsmouth and one in Norfolk. Mr. Barfield gave me a list of the accounts and set up a date to read the will. I thought I would be the only person needed at the reading. I was surprised that he wanted Martine and Sally there also. The reading was scheduled for Thursday morning, almost two weeks after the funeral. I was nervous. I called Kathy in Cape May a few days ahead of time, and she agreed to come to Craddock to lend moral support.

Nick had returned to New Jersey and called me every day. I promised to call him and give him the lowdown after the reading. He asked if he should fly down to Virginia and ride back with me, but I said no. Rosalie and Kathy had already made plans to help me drive. I thought I would have to decide if I would leave my dad's car in Virginia to sell, or take it back to Cape May and sell it there. I would soon find out that that would not be an issue.

My father's bank accounts contained very little money, only a few thousand in each one. His pension stopped at the time of his death, and I was told by Reggie Barfield that he had informed Martine to apply for his Social Security, on behalf of their disabled son. I cried more those days before the reading than I had at the funeral. I was told not to take anything out of my father's house until after the reading — not even a cup and saucer that had belonged to my mother. I was devastated; however, I understood there were legalities we had to follow. Rosalie and Kathy walked the beach with me every day unless it rained. They stayed at the house on Channing Street every night, and I wondered what I had ever done to deserve such wonderful friends.

On the day of the reading, we got up at seven. Mr. Barfield had asked us to be there at nine. Rosalie and Kathy went with me to Reggie Barfield's office. It was located on the third floor in an old building on High Street in Portsmouth. I was the first to arrive.

"Molly, it's so nice to see you again. I'm glad you came before the others. I want you to know that your father and I did not agree on everything that you will see and hear today. He was my dear friend, but we didn't always see eye to eye." Dad and Mr. Barfield had served in the navy together. I was surprised that Barfield was still practicing law at seventy-seven years old.

"I understand. I know how strongly opinionated my father was. Whatever happens here will be taken with a grain of salt. I'm really not too interested in my father's money. I have more than enough."

"I admire you so much, Molly, for what you have accomplished. The city of Portsmouth, and especially the small community of Craddock, are very proud of you. You've made quite a name."

"Thank you, sir."

"And please call me Reg. I think you are grown up enough and we have known each other long enough to be on a first-name basis."

"Thank you, but I still prefer Mr. Barfield."

"Whatever you are comfortable with, my dear."

Martine and Sally showed up at exactly nine twenty-four. Martine spoke first.

"Molly", she said, holding her arms out. I went over to her and we embraced.

"How are you and Ritchie?" I asked.

"Just fine. I was so sorry to hear about Richard. I truly loved him at one time, Molly. I really did. I hope you believe me."

"It doesn't matter now, Martine."

"It does to me. Believe it or not, I care what you think. I hope you are well."

"I'm doing fine. I've been working very hard."

"I know. I've read all of your novels. Enjoyed every one."

"Thank you."

"Ladies, we should get started," Reggie Barfield said. "Please take your seats in front of the television. Richard left a video."

Sally was already seated, not saying a word. We sat down. Barfield turned on the set and put the tape in. My father was sitting at his desk, writing. My heart started to pound at the sight of his image and the sound of his voice, which I listened to intently.

"Hello, my loved ones. I am writing my last will and testament. I want each of you to know that I love you all. Molly, my daughter, you have always been my most beloved. I want you to know that I regret anything I ever did to hurt you."

I began to sob. Martine reached over and squeezed my hand. I held onto her hand and dried my eyes.

Barfield had stopped the tape. "We'll resume when you feel better, Molly. Take your time. Let me know when you are ready."

I continued to hold Martine's hand. Sally handed me some tissues and I dried my eyes again.

"I'm ready," I said. "I'll be okay now. Please continue."

The video was restarted and the image of my father began to speak again.

"Even though I love you, Molly, more than anything or anyone, you are not a needy person. Because of your talent and efforts, you are a wealthy lady. I want you to have our house on Channing Street, free and clear. Do as you wish with it. Also, everything in the Channing Street house is to go to Molly, to dispose of as she sees fit. My 1992 Lincoln car will go to my fiancée, Sally Winston. It will more than make up for any money I may owe her. I hope this isn't seen by y'all until after our wedding. Many years after. In that case, you will have no need to view it. The last thing on my gift list is any monies that are in my existing accounts. I would like the money to be deposited into a trust fund for my son, Richard Hamilton, with his mother, Martine Hamilton, in control. That is the extent of my estate. I hope you will all understand, and carry out my wishes without ill feelings toward one another — especially you, Molly, and Martine. Please patch up your friendship, for Little Ritchie's sake. I love you all very much. Bye-bye. I have gone to rest."

The tape ended. We all stood up, and Martine and I hugged each other and cried. Sally was the first to speak. "Molly, when may I pick up the car?"

"Tomorrow morning around ten," I said.

"Fine. See you then."

Martine and I were still standing close together. Reggie Barfield walked over to us and invited us to lunch. "My wife won't take no for an answer," he said. I grabbed Martine's arm and held on tight.

"I would love to have lunch at your home," I said. "The only thing is, I have two girlfriends waiting outside for me. I really don't want to impose on Mrs. Barfield by asking to bring two extra people."

"Now, Molly, you know Mrs. Barfield. The more, the merrier. She would gladly welcome a party of ten and enjoy every minute of it. Like I said, we won't take no for an answer."

"Okay. I just need a few minutes to inform the others. I'll go out and tell them. Martine, are you okay with this?"

"I'm delighted. It will give us a chance to spend some time together. Thank you, Mr. Barfield."

"You are very welcome. I'll wait here for you to talk with the other girls."

Martine and I went down on the elevator. Rosalie and Kathy were sipping coffee in a little coffee shop and news-stand on the first floor. The old building had the same old-time black and white tile that I remembered. When I was growing up, my dentist's office had been in the same building. My mother and I used to go to the coffee shop after having our teeth cleaned and enjoy a treat. When we approached the girls, they jumped up from their seats and smiled.

"How did it go?" Rosalie asked. Kathy looked on in anticipation, waiting for an answer.

"It went very well," I said. I introduced Kathy and Martine, then said, "Reggie Barfield, Dad's attorney, has invited us to his home for lunch. Martine and I agreed to go, provided it is alright with you two."

"Do we have a choice?" Rosalie asked. "I'm surprised those two old geezers are still kicking. If I remember from some of the gatherings I've been to, Mrs. Barfield is a good cook and the price is right." She looked at Kathy and said, "Let's do it."

The Barfields lived in an upscale neighborhood in Churchland, a few miles away. The four of us chatted most of the way there. We filled Martine in on our current status, including our recent love experiences.

"I'm happy for you all," Martine said. "I want you all to know how great it is to be with you. Molly, you must be so excited about hooking up with your old boyfriend. It's wonderful that you and Kathy found each other and you all have this wonderful friendship. I've been seeing a nice guy myself. We may be getting married soon. He is one of my agents. Helps me a lot with my business."

We congratulated Martine and made plans to get together that night at my house on Channing Street. "We'll eat a lot at the Barfield's," I said. "That way, we can just have a snack at my place and drink a lot of wine. I have a great red, and we can pick up a nice chardonnay."

Martine said, "That will be great, Molly. I'm staying at the beach, though, so I can't be late. It's a long drive."

"Cancel the room at the hotel. I insist you stay at the house with us. How long will you be in Virginia?"

"I'm scheduled to fly out tomorrow at three. I'll take you up on your offer, but I won't cancel the room. I'll need to go there tomorrow and pick up my things. I have a rental car back at the lawyer's office, too. I'll need to pick it up tonight and drive to the house."

Lunch at the Barfield's was enough to tempt even the most weight-conscious person. There was tons of fruit, cold cuts, chips of every variety, four different kinds of bread, and cake and frozen yogurt for dessert. Mrs. Barfield welcomed us with open arms and insisted we call her Anne. We indulged in food and delightful conversation. Martine seemed relaxed and happy to be back. Deep down, I was happy to have her back as a friend. She ate well and seemed to have overcome the bulimia from her younger days.

We left Churchland around two thirty that afternoon and drove back to Craddock. Rosalie dropped us off, went home to change, and promised to pick up the white wine.

When we went inside, Martine looked around the house. "It's good to be here, Moll. I feel as if I never left. Richard didn't make a lot of changes."

"No, he didn't," I said. "Go on upstairs and look around. You'll find shorts and shirts in my room. Help yourself to something comfortable."

"Thank you. I'll be glad to get out of these dress clothes. Kathy, why don't you come up with me?"

"Go on up, Kathy. I'll be up in a few. I just want to get out some wine glasses and take an Alka-Seltzer. I feel like I'm about to pop. I think when Rosalie comes back, we should all go out for a long walk. Whadda ya say?"

"Good idea," Kathy said. "I need to walk off some of these calories."

"Me, too."

Rosalie arrived with the wine within the hour. She was wearing her beach clothes and was ready to walk. Kathy, Martine and I had changed into shorts and shirts and were all set to walk off the huge lunch. We left the red wine on the counter and put the white in the fridge to chill.

We drove to the beach in Chesapeake and walked about three miles again. There was major bonding and re-bonding that day. Four women with different histories; yet we had similar stories to share. Martine talked about the abuse she had endured from Jason Carter. Rosalie sounded off about her unhappy years with Jack. Kathy told her story of her broken marriage and how it had affected her life. Of course, I brought up old hurt feelings about the betrayal by Charles Baker. Another dear friend, Cecilia, was not able to be with us because of a series of book signings. If she had been there, perhaps she would have shared her horror story of a rape that took place in New York City a long time ago. Back at the house on Channing Street that evening, we raised our glasses; some filled with red and some with white. We made a toast to Cecilia and to each other, and then we drank the wine.

REUNION

Sally was ringing the doorbell at ten o'clock on the dot the morning after the reading. She had wasted no time in coming for the car. I had been up since eight thirty, but Martine and Kathy were still sleeping. Rosalie had decided to go home the night before, after dropping Martine off at Mr. Barfield's building to pick up her car. I opened the door and invited Sally in for coffee.

"Thank you, Molly. I would love a cup."

"I'm glad you're joining us, Sal," I said. "I just put another pot on. It will be ready in a few. Have a seat in the kitchen. I'll be there in a sec." I was honest when I told Sally that I was glad she was staying. I really wanted to be friendly with everyone that had been named in my father's will. I wanted to love the people he had loved. Maybe then, I could make up for some of the time I had lost with him.

I was pouring the coffee when Rosalie arrived. "Good morning, sunshine," I said. "I didn't think you would be up this soon. Kathy and Marty are still asleep. Grab a cup and I'll pour you some java."

"Good morning, Moll. Oh, morning to you too, Miss Sally. It's nice to see you again. How are you today?"

"I'm doing okay, Roe. How are you?"

"Very well. I'm wondering where I've seen you. Have we ever met before?"

"I was wondering when someone would remember me. You must remember my daughter, Sarah Winston. Molly's brother, Jesse, dated her before he died. My husband and I were divorced five years ago. I left town for a while and went to live with a sister in Atlanta. I came back last year. Richard and I ran into each other at the Food Lion. He invited me to lunch and we started dating. One thing led to another, and here I am."

I was stunned. I had only met her once while Sarah and Jesse dated. I thought she looked familiar when I first met her, but didn't mention it. "Sally, why didn't you say something about this before? I would love to know how Sarah is doing."

"I intended to mention it, Molly. I wanted to wait for the right time. Now that we're relaxed and socializing, I'm glad it came up. Sarah is doing just fine. She went to school in Boston and earned her law degree. She still lives there. Comes home sometimes in the summer to visit. She's married and has one child; a daughter, Linda. The girl is twenty-two now and following her mother. She also wants to be a lawyer."

"That's wonderful. I'm glad she's doing well."

"Thank you. I spoke to her last night and she asked me to give you a big hug, and to let you know she is very sorry about Richard. If it's okay with you, I'd like to give you that hug before I leave here today."

"That will be quite alright with me. I'd like you to give it right back to Sarah when you see her. I'm feeling very blessed right now. I'm in the midst of so many people who loved my father. We're all so different, yet bonded."

"I'm delighted you feel that way, dear. I consider myself blessed, too. I've made some new friends and have reunited with old ones. It's wonderful. I know you have a lot to do, so I'll gulp down my coffee and be on my way." Sally stood up, drank her coffee, and said, "Now, about that hug and those car keys." I delivered the hug, keys, and title to my father's car. Sally went on her way. Little did I know that I would never hear from her again.

We sat around the house and chatted until time for Martine to leave. We followed behind her rental car to the airport, to see her off. I made her promise to visit me in Cape May as soon as she had the time.

"It would be nice if we could spend a week together before my wedding. I hope you will consider being a part of my big day. Ritchie is giving me away. I think it's time we told him the truth about his big sister."

I was so touched by her words that I took her in my arms and cried.

"Take it easy, Molly. People are giving us funny looks."

"I don't give a hoot. Let them look. I just feel so good now. When is the wedding?"

"I don't know yet. Probably in the fall. Let's figure on September. Gotta go. Bye, Molly. Bye, girls." Kathy and Rosalie were sitting in the car, waving and crying. They yelled out their good-byes. I got in the car and we headed back to Channing Street.

Three days later, Kathy and I were on our way back to New Jersey. I had given Barfield the power to handle any estate problems I might have in Virginia. I was glad to be on my way home and getting my life back. We decided to stop in Rehoboth Beach, Delaware to shop the boutiques. We were coming out of Diane's around four thirty when a thunderstorm started. I looked at Kathy and said, "Boardwalk Plaza?"

"Right on!" We went to the hotel and booked a room. We decided on dinner and some jazz music at Sidneys. A tall, handsome man came over to Kathy and started going on about how he loved redheads. Before the evening was over, he had her phone number and address. I danced a few times with different fellows and was relieved that no one recognized me. My mind was on Nick and I was anxious to see him. I knew I would call him as soon as we left the next morning.

HOMEWARD BOUND

I woke up just a few minutes before Kathy the next morning. The sun shone between the blinds and I knew the storms were gone. I rolled out of bed and onto the floor, and started doing some stretching exercises. Arms and legs stretched out and waist twisting, I called out to Kathy. "Coffee time, Kathleen. Up and at 'em. Room service, or dress and head to the restaurant?"

"I hear you, for Christ's sake! I woke up five minutes ago when you started pulling covers — not to mention that I woke up several times during the night. Anybody ever tell you that you snore?"

"Never! You were probably hearing the leftover thunder from last night's storm. Now pull yourself up out of that bed and let's roll."

"I'm coming! I'm just as anxious to get back to Cape May as you are. This guy I met last night is supposed to come up next week and take me out. Maybe the four of us can double. You know; you and Nick, and Ron and me."

"Sounds like a plan," I said, and headed for the shower.

Forty minutes later, we were in the restaurant having coffee and pancakes. Kathy chatted away about this Ron that she had met the night before. "He sounds great, Kath," I said. "I hope he doesn't disappoint you. Don't get too excited until you get to know him. Did I tell you what happened to me with Charles? Just make sure he isn't married before you get too involved."

"Don't worry. I'll do a complete check on him. If I decide to have him overnight, I'll check his wallet for a Social Security number and a driver's license while he's in the shower."

"Oh! You deviant little witch. I didn't know you had the guts. I love it!"

"Well, darling, after all the abuse I took from my husband? Jekyll and Hyde? Believe me when I tell you, I trust no man on earth."

"Likewise. I'm crazy about Nick, yet there is something very different about him that I can't quite put my finger on. We really don't know each other, Kath. Forty years is a long time, and when we knew each other, we were so young. Life changes people. Nick has been a dream of mine. But will the dream become a reality? Who knows?"

"Time will tell. Ready?"

"All set. I'll pay for this. You get the next one."

"Okay. I'll go up and grab the bags. Meet me at the car."

We didn't talk much from Rehoboth to Lewes, and mainly listened to the music on the radio. We got in line for the noon ferry boat to Cape May. It was eleven fifteen.

"This is just ducky. I could have slept another thirty minutes," Kathy said.

"Better to be a little early than miss the boat."

"Wouldn't be the first time. I was just wondering, Moll. What if Nick turns out not to be the Mr. Right you dreamed about? What will you do?"

"I don't know, Kath. I haven't thought that far ahead."

"Personally, I think Jeff is more your type. I mean, what do you and Nick really have in common?"

"That's a good question. But you know the old saying: Opposites attract. Maybe we are just what the doc ordered for each other. You know, a difference in lifestyles. We can learn from each other."

"Point taken. But ask yourself this question: If something really devastating happened right now — like, say, Ritchie died — who would you want to comfort you? Jeff or Nick? Don't try to answer me. Just think about it."

I thought about Kathy's words for days that followed. The question haunted me. I thought about that Valentine's Day back in New York, and all the fun we had with the clues that led me to the ring on the window sill. Then I remembered the time that Jeff tried to make love to me and I freaked out. I wanted to continue to dream about Nick, and now, I was living my dream. Real or surreal? Kathy hit it on the head. Time would tell.

I had called Nick the day that we returned to Cape May and left a message on his voice mail. I didn't get a call back until three days later. I sat at my desk and let the phone ring four times before I answered.

"Hello."

"Hi, Molly. It's me, Nick. How are you?"

"Oh, hi there. I'm doing just fine, Nick. And you?"

"I'm good. Sorry I didn't call sooner. I was up north with Michael. He needed help with his business, so I went up to give him a hand. I'm terrible with numbers and I had forgotten my little black book in Ocean City. How did things go for you in Virginia? Get everything settled?"

"Everything is pretty well taken care of. I left all the unfinished business in my attorney's hands. Kathy and I returned on Tuesday, and I've have been really swamped with catching up on things here."

"Yes. I arrived late last night, and didn't call because I thought you'd be asleep. Are you free tonight?"

"I could be. What did you have in mind?"

"I thought I'd pick you up and we could have a fun dinner at the Ugly Mugg. I'm hoping to spend the night and tomorrow go shopping for something nice for you, and maybe have dinner at the Pelican Club."

"It sounds great, Nick. It's eleven now and I have some writing to do and thank-you notes to send out to people who sent flowers for my dad. I can be ready by seven with no problem."

"Wonderful. I thought about you a lot while we were apart. I'm looking forward to tonight. I can hardly wait."

"I'm so looking forward to seeing you, Nick. I could be ready earlier, if you like."

"Well, I have a meeting at four with a business associate. I probably can't get there much sooner than seven, but I'll do the best I can."

We said good-bye and hung up. My heart was doing flip-flops and my hands were damp and shaky. I lost interest in what I was doing and ran to the bedroom to look for something to wear. The Ugly

Mugg was a very casual Irish pub in the shopping area in town. It was a fun place to eat and I already knew what I would order: a burger with fries and a large mug of light beer. I hoped to get Nick out on the beach for a walk before we came back to the house. I went to the phone and called Kathleen to tell her the news.

"That's good, Molly. I'm glad he finally called and you're happy. I have a date with Ron tomorrow night. If you and Nick don't mind, how about having dinner with us? I'll have him here for a glass of wine first, and then maybe we could meet at Lobster House."

"It's fine with me, Kath. I'm sure it will be okay with Nick as well. Let's chat tomorrow. I need to get back to my writing."

I took my thank-you notes out and sat on the seawall. I looked out at the ocean and thought about Nick, and wondered what the weekend would bring.

NICK'S THOUGHTS

Talking to Molly gave me a lift. I was tired from my trip to Vermont, but felt better after she agreed to see me. I jumped in the shower and dressed for my meeting with a buyer. I had a sale agreement on a small piece of land located on Somers Point Mays Landing Road, about three miles past the Ocean City bridge. I was meeting the buyer in the Point Diner, so I figured I would leave early and grab a bite to eat before the meeting.

It was 2:30 p.m. then, so I needed to get moving. I stopped in the Crab Trap Restaurant for some of their great clam chowder. I thought about Molly and how wonderful it would be after we were married and I could take her to Uncle Sal's for cooking lessons. No more of this restaurant food.

The meeting with the buyer went smoothly. I was finished by five thirty and on my way to Cape May. The song actually came on the radio as I was driving, and I hummed along. "On the way to Cape May, I fell in love with you. On the way to Cape May, dee, dee, da, dum, dee, dee." I thought about all the women I could have married over the years. So many, but none so sweet or challenging as my Molly. Okay, I had loved Anna, Michael's mom, at first. She was just too easy from the beginning, and not the least bit interesting. I knew it would take some scheming to get Molly to marry me, and I was ready for the challenge.

I was at her door by six fifteen. She answered, looking radiant. Her hair was just so and those blue eyes were shining. I drew her into my arms, kissed her, and caressed her body. I couldn't help but ask, "Why don't we go to the bedroom? I could have you for my appetizer."

"Put me down, Nick. This feels wonderful, but first things first. I'm very hungry and I'm afraid making love with you is not what I need at the moment."

It was pretty close to what I expected from her, and I loved her all the more.

She changed from her cover-up to a cute pair of shorts and a polo shirt, and we were off to the Ugly Mugg. I will never forget that evening. We went home early, had a nightcap, and made love. She wasn't the best lover I'd ever had, but I knew she could learn. I wasn't real worried about the lovemaking problem. I wanted a smart, honest wife. Anyway, the little brunette that I had met in Vermont had fulfilled my hottest sexual fantasies, and I knew she would be around. After all, sex was just sex.

CAPE MAY MADNESS

I showered and was almost ready for my date with Nick by six o'clock. I decided to hang out in a cover-up until he arrived, since he wasn't officially due until seven. To my surprise, he rang the bell at six fifteen. As soon as I opened the door, I was scooped up and kissed and caressed. As I suspected, the first thing on his mind was a quick roll in the hay. Wanting to be coy, I begged off, using hunger as my excuse. I changed into a pair of shorts and a top and we were off to the Ugly Mugg.

I loved the little shops in the Cape May Center. While we waited for our table, we went across the street and browsed through an art shop. Time passed quickly and we heard them call Nick's name from a speaker.

"Let's go, Molly. Time to fill that cute belly of yours."

We ran across the street to meet the hostess. She was a nice redhead whom I had met before. "Good evening, Miss Molly. Evening, sir." I was impressed that she remembered. I had gotten used to living without the notoriety I had experienced in previous years. This hostess had recognized me from the cover photo on one of my novels. I had signed two books for her when I first moved here, and she and I had been on first-name basis ever since. I remembered her name was Colleen and she was from Scotland.

"Hi there, Colleen. This is my friend, Nick."

"Hello," she said. "It's nice to meet you, Nick."

"It's Graziano," Nick said. "Mr. Graziano. May we have a server, please?"

"Of course," she said. She put two menus on the table and walked away.

I was fuming. "Nick, why were you rude to that girl? I think you hurt her feelings. She referred to you the way I introduced you. We've been acquainted for some time now. I'm the one who made the error. My apologies. Now, if you will excuse me while I go to the ladies' room?"

I went through the restaurant to the back by the ladies' room and found Colleen talking to a server. After she sent the server away, I said, "Colleen, I must apologize for Nick. He's an old friend from my younger days and I didn't realize he was so formal."

"It's okay. I'm used to insults. Working in a restaurant, it happens all the time. People look down their noses, and half the time I'm better off than they are. It doesn't really bother me."

I knew she didn't mean that. She was bothered very much. From a previous conversation with Colleen, I knew that she was a medical student and probably only a year away from her internship. I was hurt and disappointed by Nick's attitude and hoped it wouldn't cloud our evening. When I returned to the table, Nick stood up and smiled.

"I'm sorry if I hurt the girl's feelings. It's just that I'm not used to people younger than my son calling me by my first name."

"Yes, okay. Let's forget about it. I'm glad it was her age and not her position here that prompted you to correct her. Colleen is a medical student only a year away from an internship. She is thirty years old and a brilliant lady."

"I ordered Southern Comfort Manhattans for both of us. I hope that's okay with you. I remember how we enjoyed them on our first date."

"It's fine."

When the waitress brought the drinks, Nick asked her to send Colleen to our table. She came over to us smiling her bright Scottish smile. "May I help you?"

"I would like to apologize if I insulted you," Nick said. "It's just that I have a son in his thirties, and for a lady as young as you — probably not a day over twenty-three — to call me by my first name is something I'm not used to."

"Apology accepted, Mr. Graziano. Actually, I'm thirty. Thank you for the compliment."

"Please call me Nick. Molly tells me you're in med school. I'm impressed."

"Thank you. I would love to stand and talk, but I have customers waiting to be seated. Please excuse me."

"That was sweet, Nick. Thank you for smoothing it over."

"No problem. I'm really not a monster, Moll. I truly thought she was younger. It's a matter of respect. I hope you understand my reasoning."

"I do. Perfectly." When I really thought about it, I guess I did understand.

After a dinner of burgers and fries, and another Manhattan, we took a short walk on the beach. It was a beautiful starlit night.

Later, back at my place, we were both anxious to be in each other's arms. Our lovemaking didn't last long because of our strong desire. Afterward though, I sensed something different in Nick's actions toward me.

"You're a wonderful lover," I said.

"Thank you," he said. "I'm really very tired. Let's get some sleep."

I fell asleep almost instantly. I woke to the sound of pans banging together and the smell of breakfast. I got out of bed, threw on a wrap, and wandered out to the kitchen.

"Good morning. It smells good in here. What's cooking?"

"I found some pancake mix in the cupboard. I hope you don't mind my starting breakfast. How many can you eat?"

"Just one, thank you. It's rather overcast outside. I was hoping we could get on the beach for an hour before we go out, but it doesn't look promising."

"You're right. It is a little cloudy out. Well, maybe it'll clear before long."

"I hope so. Oh, by the way Nick — my friend Kathleen, who lives up the street, would like to double with us for dinner tonight. She has a date with a new friend and would like us to get together. Okay with you?"

"Sure thing. I'm looking forward to meeting your friend. I feel like I know her already. Where did she meet this guy?"

"The other night in Rehoboth. We had dinner at Sidney's, and afterward went to listen to some jazz. They got to talking and one thing led to another, and bingo. Of course, she doesn't know much about him. Time will tell."

"That's nice. And how many dates did you make?"

"Not even one. I had you on my mind the whole time."

"Did you dance with anyone?"

"One or two. Light conversation and that was it. Why would you ask me if I made a date?"

"Isn't that why women go alone to clubs? To pick up men?"

"I guess it depends on the women and what their needs are at the time. I went there because I like jazz. Frankly, Nick, I'm a little uncomfortable with your insinuations. Do you mind if we change the subject?"

"No, of course not. I'm sorry if I was out of line. Anyway, your pancake is getting cold."

We ate in silence. I enjoyed the pancake even though it was a little cold. I poured a second cup of coffee for both of us. After coffee, I excused myself to take a shower and get dressed. By then, the windows were spattered with rain, and I felt a little depressed and uneasy from the conversation. I knew before the weekend was over, we would have to talk about certain issues. I was worried that our relationship was at stake, if we even had a relationship. Kathleen's words came back to me again. Time would tell. I called her to make arrangements for dinner, but there was no answer. I left a message for her to call me back.

The town was buzzing with the sounds of summer. It was complete madness, with tourists and party people heading for the beach and the shops. The sky stayed overcast the whole day, but it didn't rain. Nick held my hand as we crossed the street to the beach.

"It's two o'clock now, Molly. We have a reservation at the Pelican for seven. Let's not forget about the time. Will Kathy and her friend meet us, or will we pick them up?"

"I don't know yet. She hasn't called me back. I left a message. I expect she will have phoned by the time we leave the beach. I guess we should leave by four thirty. Is that okay with you?"

"Fine."

There was a message from Kathy when we got back to the house. She said she and Ron would meet us at the bar at six thirty for cocktails. Nick and I agreed. We got dressed quickly and were at the restaurant a little early. We ordered Manhattans, and had just started to sip them when Kathy and Ron walked in. We got through the introductions, and Kathy and Ron ordered drinks. The conversation between the men was the beginning of the end for Nick and me, and I think I knew it that night.

"So, tell me Ron, what do you do for a living?" Nick asked.

"I work for a computer company, Nick," Ron answered.

"I understand you travel a bit in your work. Is that right?"

"Yes, that's right."

"Then I guess you're used to people asking questions. Is that true?"

"That certainly is, Nick," Ron laughed. "What do you need to know about computers? Are you looking for a new system for your work? I understand you're quite the investor."

"Yes, I guess I am. My question isn't about computers though, Ron. It's really about the night you met these two ladies. I wondered if you got on well with Molly's date."

"Excuse me?"

"The guy that Molly picked up that night. Was he a friend of yours?"

My face must have turned scarlet. I was furious. I tried to be calm and pass it off as a joke. "Ron, Nick likes to kid. Don't you, Nick?," I said.

"Molly, let the man answer the question. You have nothing to hide. right?"

I started to speak, but Ron interrupted.

"Nick is right, Molly. Let me answer his question. The night that I met these two ladies, no one picked anyone up. Kathy and I danced well together, and since we're adults and have a right to do as we please, we decided to see each other again. As for Molly, she talked about you a lot. We talked about getting together, and here we are."

The hostess came over to the bar and told us our table was ready. We followed her to the table in silence. We were seated at a nice table by the window, overlooking the ocean. The conversation between the men had certainly strained the atmosphere. I looked over at Kathy and she smiled shyly at me. She sort of cocked her head, the way someone does when they are trying to say, "It's okay, we understand." I was glad if they understood, because I certainly didn't. I had never been more humiliated. I wanted to go home alone and crawl under the covers. I wanted to get as far away from Nick Graziano as I possibly could, and I wasn't sure if I ever wanted to see him again. But I didn't run. I picked up the menu and said, "Well, everyone, the food is really good here. Meanwhile, shall we order a bottle of wine?"

Somehow, we struggled through dinner, making light conversation. When everyone was finished, I picked up the check. I insisted on paying. The men gave me an argument at first, but relented. I paid the bill and we went outside.

"Why don't we go dancing down in Avalon?" It was Nick who made the suggestion.

"I don't think so. I have a headache. I'd like to just go home and nurse it. I really enjoyed dinner. Kathy, I'll call you tomorrow," I said.

Nick and I got into his car and drove to my house. When we pulled up out front, I said, "I really need to be by myself now, Nick. I think you should go on home to Ocean City. I'm not feeling well."

"Okay, Molly, if you really want me to. I'll call you tomorrow."

"That will be fine. We'll talk then."

DAYS OF GLOOM

The morning after dinner at the Pelican, I awoke with a major hangover. I was surprised that the clock on the wall said nine fifteen. It was unusual for me to sleep that late. I stumbled out of bed and threw on a summer cover-up. My head was pounding and I felt shaky. I could see the sunlight through the closed shutters in the room. I went to the medicine cabinet in the bathroom and took two Bufferin. I went into the kitchen and made coffee. I opened shutters in all the rooms. I looked out at the ocean and watched the whitecaps glisten in the sunlight as they gently touched the shore. I smiled to myself as I realized my headache was starting to subside. I was feeling better. I picked up the phone to call Kathleen to invite her over for breakfast. The phone rang only twice before she picked up.

"Hello?"

"Good morning, Kath. It's me."

"I know it's you. Do you think I'm stupid or something?" Kathy always knew how to get a laugh from me.

"Have you eaten?"

"No. I was going to call you, but I wasn't sure if Nick was there."

"He didn't stay over. I sent him home last night. I'm not planning to see him anymore."

"You sound like you need to talk, Moll. Let's hang up. I'll throw on some shorts and walk over."

I took a quick shower and put on shorts and a T-shirt. I had two cups filled with hot coffee when Kathleen knocked on the door. I let her in, and she immediately put her arms out. I fell into her arms and we stood there, hugging while I cried. The crying lasted only about three seconds before we started to laugh. We were two friends filled with emotion. Me, because I had been hurt by Nick. Kathy, because she was feeling my pain.

"Our coffee is out there getting cold," I said. "I poured it, not expecting to have a five-minute emotional outburst. Let's go in and get some breakfast. I'm starved."

"Me, too. The brisk walk over gave me a big appetite. What are we having?"

"Oh, the usual. Two eggs, Canadian bacon, and of course our favorite wheat toast. Let's drink our coffee first. I still have a slight headache. It may be caffeine withdrawal."

"Sounds great."

We sat down with our coffee and started sipping. In about five minutes, my headache had completely disappeared. Amazing stuff, caffeine.

"So tell me, Molly. What's the scoop with you and Nick?"

"What would you do, Kathy? The way he questions me and then interrogates my friends? Don't you think that's a bit inappropriate?"

"It doesn't matter what I think. I'm here to listen and offer support, not to pass judgment. So what do you intend to do?"

"I intend to end this forty-year fiasco in dreamland. Also, I've been thinking about my religion lately. I need to start going to church again. I don't know if I can handle all of this without some spiritual assistance."

The phone rang and we ignored it. I think we both knew who was calling, and knew I wasn't ready to take that call.

"I'm glad you didn't answer that. Whoever it was will leave a message. I agree with what you are saying. I don't talk about it much, but I often get up and go to early Mass. It helps me get through the week. Even if I had told you, I don't think you were ready to listen. Maybe God is speaking to you now, Moll."

"I think you're right. I need to sort all this out. Know something else? I miss Jeff at times like this. Maybe I'll call him. What do you think?"

"I think I would wait a while. Like you said, you need time to sort things out. That means spending time alone. Alone with God."

"I know Kathy. But even though I know how wrong Nick is for me, it still hurts a lot."

"Of course it hurts. You're taking a loss. Losing a dream. You need to grieve. Now, can we have breakfast?"

"Oh, gosh! Of course. Let's cook."

After breakfast, we took a short walk on the beach. When we returned, we agreed to leave me to myself until I was ready to socialize again.

"I might call you in a week or so just to let you know that I'm thinking about you. If you need me for anything, Molly, please call or come over."

"I will," I said. "Don't worry about me. I'll be fine. Bye, Kath."

"Bye," she said, and walked away. I knew it would be a while before I saw her again. I went into my house and called Nick.

"Hi, Nick. Did you try to call me earlier?"

"Yes. Where were you?"

"It doesn't matter where I was. I called you back to tell you that I can't see you anymore. Our meeting again has been a mistake. We have nothing in common. I'm sorry."

"Molly, you can't mean that. I've loved you for all these years. If I seem a little possessive it's because I love you so much. Can't you understand that?"

"Nick, we were little more than kids when we met. This whole thing has been a fantasy. It can never become a reality. I'm not really in love with you. I don't want you to contact me, ever again."

There was a long pause and I could hear him breathing. I felt better already because I knew I had handled this the best possible way. Nick finally spoke.

"Can't we at least discuss this?"

"No. There's nothing left to say. Good-bye, Nick."

I hung the phone up and went into my room to grieve. I remembered I had to call Rosalie and inform her of my decision. I did that in sort of a daze. I felt like a robot. No emotion. I seemed to have fallen into a pit of depression. I stayed that way for a long time, unable to cry or laugh. All I could do was think. I crawled inside myself. I was in a dark vacuum for weeks. Gloomy days were ahead — many days of gloom.

FLAWLESS

I found upon a riverbed,
A charming little stone
Polished like a marble
And colored gray in tone.
I found a plant not far away
Blooming on that cool spring Day

I found a leaf shaped perfect
Spade
Resting on the pond,
Where chance had laid.

I found myself in wondrous
Cheer
For the charming beauty here.

I found again, a love I lost
Stolen by the winter's frost.

I found the spring to bring
me joy
Thanks to flawless beauty's
Ploy.

I found myself lost in
Dreams
Where only love exist it
seems.

By: Ryan Zachary Ricciardi

A TIME TO DREAM

Most of my life I had dreamed a dream. Dreams are what they are. Just dreams. As a child, I had fallen in love with a boy I hardly knew. Forty years later, the dream died. It died because dreams always do. They don't come true. If they come true, they become realities. I remember reading that somewhere once. We make things happen. We can't simply dream and bingo! Everything we dreamed becomes a reality? Not so. My dream had kept me from happiness. My love life suffered because I was a dreamer. I wish I had gotten to know Nick when we were young. I don't think I would have wasted so many years dreaming about him. When I let him walk out of my life at fifteen, I should have let him go forever. I allowed his memory to interfere with my real life. My dream had stolen true love from me. At fifty-five, I finally knew that. I found out when I got to know him. I felt I had sacrificed my only true love. The one man I could have been happy with. My best friend. My confidant. I could have married, had children, been fulfilled. I let it slip. Now it was too late. I had lost everything.

A month had passed since I had seen Nick. I hardly spoke to my friends. I don't remember how many times Kathleen had called. She knocked on my door; I didn't answer. Rosalie called me several times and left messages of encouragement. She said she had spoken to Kathy and knew I was hurting and needed to be alone. She understood. She said to call her when I felt like talking.

I was sitting on a chair in my beach house the day I felt like talking. I looked up and saw the sun shining through the window. I felt like talking, but not to friends just yet. I dressed myself in a nice sundress and packed a suitcase. I got into my car and drove to the ferry. It was 11:00 a.m. when I got there. I had to wait twenty minutes for a ferry. I went to the gift shop and got a cup of coffee. I got back in my car and turned on the radio. I felt very good and free. I looked up at the sun again. It was shining through a beautiful white cloud. I thought about my parents and brother. I wondered if they could see me. I thought about Jesus. I knew he had spoken to my heart.

The ride on the ferry across the Delaware was pleasant. I had gotten my mother's bible out of the closet where I had kept it for much too long. I took it with me on my trip. I read it on the ferry boat. I was on my way to Channing Street.

I arrived at the house on Channing Street at five o'clock. I hadn't noticed before that the place looked so old. The whole neighborhood had changed over the years. I was just now seeing things in their true light. I took my bag in the house, but I didn't stay. I drove uptown to Holy Angels Church. I went to the rectory and rang the doorbell. A lady answered the door and I told her I wanted to see a priest.

"Come in, dear. Have a seat in Father's office and I will get him." She showed me to the office. I sat down.

"Hello, miss. I'm Father Carl. How can I help you this evening?" He looked at me again and said, "My Lord, it's Molly."

"Hello, Father. I just need to talk. I have so much on my mind. I've made so many mistakes and I need to talk to you about them. Will you listen?"

He sat at his desk across from me. He nodded his head and said, "Go on and talk, my dear."

I talked for two hours about all of the things I had anguished over the past month. I went back to my fifteenth year and told about Nick and how I had deceived my parents. I told him about Jeff and how I had been unable to love him the way I should. I told him about my affair with Charles and others that I had not mentioned to my friends. I told him my life up until that very moment. I told him how I wanted to stop dreaming and start living. I asked him if he thought I should become a nun. I broke down and cried. I cried and cried. Father Carl gave me some tissues, and I dried my eyes.

"Molly, I have heard many stories like yours throughout my life as a priest. Your actions are not so different from those of many other women. I cannot tell you if you should become a nun. Only you will know if the Good Lord has called you to such a vocation. Here and now, I can tell you that we must ask the Lord to forgive you your sins, and if you are truly sorry, he will grant you absolution. Please bow your head."

I bowed my head and Father began to pray. "In the name of the Father, Son and Holy Spirit. Your child, Molly Peale, has come here tonight, Lord, to ask your forgiveness for her sins. She said she is truly sorry and must repent. Please forgive her."

I looked up and made the sign of the cross and said, "Thank you, Lord. I feel as though I am forgiven. Thank you, Father Carl, for listening to my confession. I feel like a new person."

"And you are, my dear. You are washed in the blessed blood of Jesus. Now, may I make a suggestion?"

"Yes, of course."

"Call Jeff. Talk with him about your feelings. You could be wrong. Maybe it isn't too late for you to be happy with the one you truly love."

"Okay. I'll think about it. Thanks again, Father."

"Okay, Molly. But don't thank me. Thank your Father in heaven. He sent you here."

GOOD NEWS AND MEMORIES

I drove home from Holy Angels not knowing what I would do. I wanted to call Jeff, but wasn't sure if all of this would make sense to him. I went to Rosalie's to give her the lowdown on what was happening. It was eight o'clock on a Thursday night. She answered the door dressed to kill.

"Molly! When did you get here? Why didn't you call?" We hugged and cried.

"I got in at five. I needed to talk to Father Carl, so I went to the rectory at Holy Angels. You're all dressed up. Are you going out?"

"I'm expecting Neil in fifteen minutes or so, but that's okay. Please come in and sit down. I'll get us a glass of wine."

"Thank you, Rosalie, but I'll pass on the wine. I won't stay long. I don't want to interfere with your evening. How's Neil?"

"He's just fine. Check this out." She held out her left hand and showed me a beautiful diamond engagement ring. I grabbed her and hugged her again.

"This is wonderful. When did you get it?"

"Last week. I didn't want to tell you because I knew you were dealing with a lot at the time. I'm so happy to see you. You look thin. Are you eating properly?"

"Probably not. Actually, I'm about to starve right now. I'm going to go home now and eat. I have food in the pantry. I just wanted you to know I was here and feeling okay. Can we get together tomorrow?"

"Positively! Come over first thing in the morning. Be here by nine and I'll make us a nice breakfast. Wear your swimsuit — I had a pool put in. We'll have a great day, just the two of us."

"A pool? That's wonderful. I'll see you then. Don't worry, I really am okay."

"I know you are. You're a strong woman, Molly. See you in the morning."

I was disappointed, but couldn't let Rosalie know. I was hoping for time with her that night. I was very happy for her and Neil. We had known Neil since grade school and I knew he would be good to her. I drove back to Channing Street and opened a can of chicken soup. I found some bread in the freezer and tuna fish in the cabinet. I ate the soup and a tuna sandwich. I was hungrier than I had realized. When I was finished, I went upstairs to shower and change for bed.

I got into bed, but couldn't get to sleep. I had so many decisions to make. I wondered what I would do with the old house. I knew I didn't want to live there. The people on the street had let their homes become run-down. I had spent a lot of happy years there, but many sad things had happened there also. I was bothered by thoughts of the night I had seen my father and Martine together. My father's death had occurred in the room across the hall. I relived my brother's and my mother's funeral receptions and decided the bad memories outweighed the good. The old house couldn't be my home anymore. I wanted a bright and happy life. I didn't want to dwell on the sad times. I wanted to call Jeff, but decided to wait another day, at least. I must have fallen asleep around 2:00 a.m.

My alarm went off at 8:00 a.m. I was glad it was morning and time to go to Rosalie's. I quickly got up and put on a swimsuit and a cover-up. I was at her door at eight forty-five. She greeted me looking like something the cat had dragged in.

"Rough night?" I asked.

"Rough as a porky-pine. Neil brought over this great champagne. I think I overdid it. The coffee is brewing. Come on, I'll show you the new pool." I followed her to the back of the house and out the back door. Where the yard had been, there was now a deck and a pool the size of the house.

"My God, girl! You didn't tell me you could float the Titanic out here."

"Like it?"

"I love it. It's absolutely marvelous. When did you do this?"

"Last week. I had this whim. I want to start staying home more and enjoying it, so — presto! I figured a nice pool would do the trick. It has a heater for when the weather gets a little too cool. We can use it through part of the fall. Neil and I have decided we like water sports, so we're even planning to spend the coldest part of the winter in Marco Island, Florida."

"This is all so fantastic, Rosalie. I'm so happy for you. Do you think that coffee's done yet?"

"Ought to be. Let's go sip some java."

"I'm ready. I'm really hungry, too. We can't fix breakfast too soon."

"Two cups of coffee and we're breakfast bound."

We sipped the coffee and started breakfast. There wasn't much conversation until we sat down to eat.

"Okay, Moll. I'm ready to listen, because I know you are more than ready to talk. How did it go with Mr. G.?"

"Well, he wasn't happy about my decision. The good part is, he hasn't called and bugged me about it. I'm grateful for that."

"So, are you talking to Jeff yet?"

"I haven't called him yet, but I plan to very soon. I just wonder how much of this is going to make sense to him. It's been a long time since we talked. I think I'll invite him to come to Cape May for a visit. That way, we can talk in person."

"I'm sure he'll understand. Nothing makes any sense when it comes to romance, Moll. You know that. Heaven knows you've written enough books about it."

I had to laugh at that comment. "That's true. However, there's a big difference between reality and fiction. In the novels, the girl usually gets the right guy. This is reality, Rosalie."

"I think that what you just mentioned is about to happen in reality — the part about the girl getting the right guy. I certainly never thought Nick was right for you. Even when we were kids, I had a bad feeling about him. It's a shame you wasted so much of your life thinking about him."

"I agree. I'll call Jeff tonight. I hope it isn't too late."

Rosalie didn't say anything after that. We ate our breakfast without a lot of conversation. I helped with the dishes and we went out to the pool. We swam and sunbathed all day. We didn't think about food again until around five. Rosalie stood up and started drying herself off.

"I'm not going to see Neil tonight," she said. "I told him that I wanted to leave this time open for girl stuff. Shall we dress and go to dinner?"

"I'd love it. Are you sure this is okay with Neil? After all, you are newly engaged."

"He's fine with it. Neil always liked you, Molly. He wants me to be there for you now. He made me promise to call him if he can help in any way."

"Neil is a kind person. You're very blessed to have him, Rosalie. I know you'll be good to each other. There is something else that I wanted to tell you. I'm planning to do something with my home on Channing Street. I don't know what yet. I don't want to sell it, because I don't need the money. I think I would like to donate it to some worthy cause. Any suggestions?"

"I must have read your mind. I was thinking about that last night. I even mentioned it to Neil. We both agreed that you should probably sell. There are so many memories connected to that house. It must be hard for you sometimes. You need to move forward. I think the idea of donating it is very kind of you, Moll. I can't think right now of what or whom would benefit most from it, but it's something to kick around and look into. Between the four of us, I'm sure we'll come up with something."

"Four?"

"Yes. You, Jeff, Neil and me. You are going to tell Jeff, aren't you?"

"Well, yes. I am going to tell him. That is, if he's willing to listen."

"I think he'll listen. I think Jeffrey Wilde will be more than glad to listen to Miss Molly."

"I hope you're right. Are you driving to dinner? I'm going home now to change. What time will you pick me up?"

"You get exactly one hour. So, not too much primping. We'll go to the beach; probably eat at Driftwood, unless you have other ideas."

"Anyplace is fine as long as it isn't Duck Inn. I'm not ready for that yet. Talk about memories!"

"Okay, get going. One hour."

As always, Rosalie and I had a great evening. We ate light and were careful not to drink too much wine. We made it home around midnight, full of shrimp and veggies. We were both exhausted and ready to hit the sack. She dropped me off and went on home.

When I walked in, I noticed the message light on my phone was blinking. I called in to voice mail and listened to the message twice in disbelief. It was Nick.

"Hey there, Molly darling. I'm just calling to see if you've changed your mind about us. I haven't been able to think about anything else. Please call me back. I love you."

My knees felt weak and my heart raced. I quickly called Rosalie.

"I don't know what to do."

"Of course you know what to do! You do nothing. Don't call him back. Ignore the whole thing and get some sleep. I'll see you tomorrow."

"Yes. You're right. See you tomorrow." It always amazed me how the voice of my friend could calm me down. There was nothing to worry about. I would simply ignore Nick's call. I fell asleep that night thinking about Jeff and that I would call him the next day. I thought about the good news of Rosalie's engagement, and all the good memories I could think of.

FOREVER FRIENDS

The breeze felt cool against my face and body. I held out my hands and stood facing the sun. Then I lay down and reached my hands out to touch the vines where I thought the strawberries might be. I ran my hands along the ground very slowly, but it was too smooth for a strawberry field. The breeze gave me a delightful sensation as I slowly opened my eyes. I started to laugh hysterically as the ceiling fan took shape above my bed. The dream had been pleasant.

The day before with Rosalie had been emotionally and psychologically rewarding for me. Then there I was, alone in my own nescience, not totally sure what I would do next. I got up and took a shower. I could think better if I was clean. I thought about the phone message I had gotten the night before from Nick, and how pathetic it seemed. I decided to call Jeff. I let the phone ring several times before I decided to hang up. Just as I was moving the receiver from my ear, I heard a click on the other end of the line.

"Hello. Whoever you are, whatever you are, have you any idea what time it is?"

"Hello, Jeff. It's Molly. I didn't realize how early it was. Sorry. Would you call me later? I'm at my home in Virginia."

"Molly? It's okay. I had no idea. Please stay on the line. I'll put some coffee on while we're talking. It's so great to hear from you. How are you?"

"I'm fine, Jeff. And you?"

"I'm just fine. I've been thinking about calling, but I wasn't sure if it was okay since you're all involved with Nick. How are things in that area?"

"Things in that area didn't work out. Anyway, even if they had, you could still call. Friends forever, remember?"

"Yes, I do. Thank you for saying that. I guess I should say I'm sorry that your relationship with Nick didn't work out, but to be perfectly honest, I'm not sure that I am sorry. I was never really sure about that relationship. I was afraid you were rushing into something."

"Well, it's over. So what about you? Are you seeing anyone?"

"Well, yes. Actually, I'm seeing a nice lady from this area. We seem to have a lot in common. I met her through Cel. Her name is Jocelyn. It's just a friendship at this point. I'd love for you to meet her, Moll. When will you be coming to the big city again? Maybe we can do lunch."

My heart sank to my knees. "Serves you right," I said to myself. "What did you expect?"

"Speak up, Molly. Did you say something? I didn't hear you."

"I said it's wonderful that you met someone. I'm sure she's very nice."

"Yes, she is. But like you said, friends forever. Right?"

"Absolutely! How is Cecilia, by the way? I haven't spoken to her lately."

"She's well. Still seeing Debbie. You should give her a call."

"I'll do that. To answer your question, I don't know when I'll be coming to the city again. No time soon. I have a lot going on here. I wanted to touch base with you, though. I'm glad you're doing well."

"Likewise. Thanks for calling, Moll. Don't be a stranger."

"Of course. Call me sometime. Bye, Jeff."

"Bye Molly, my love. Take care."

After we hung up, I felt numb all over. I picked up the phone and called Rosalie. She sounded surprised when I gave her the news.

"What a shock. Well, don't let it get the best of you, Molly. His relationship with this woman is fairly new, so anything could happen. Give it time. Call Cecilia. Maybe she can shed some light on the subject. If she introduced them, she must know her pretty well. Get the lowdown. Do it now and call me back."

I called Cecilia, but got her voice-mail. I left a message and called Rosalie back.

"So, did you tell her why you were calling?"

"No. I just asked her to call me back. I've decided to leave tomorrow for New Jersey. I miss my home, and there isn't much I can do here until I decide what I'm going to do with the house here on Channing Street."

"Anything I can do?"

"Nothing I can think of at the moment. I told Cel to call me on my cell phone, so it won't make any difference where I am when she calls me back. I'm leaving early tomorrow. I'll say bye now, and I'll keep you posted."

"Bye, Moll. Moffitt to forever?"

"Moffitt to forever."

CALLS ALONG THE WAY

I was in the car at seven the next morning. As I drove away from the old neighborhood, I started thinking how much it had changed since my mother's death. I drove around Craddock, remembering how it was when I was a girl. The only thing that had improved in looks on most streets were the old trees. They were huge and beautiful. I drove past Holy Angels, made the sign of the cross, and said a prayer of thanks to God for my visit with Father Carl. It had been a turning point for me in my outlook on life. I knew the decisions I was making now were more mature and realistic than before. I was in touch with the Lord and could handle anything.

I drove out onto Route 17, made my way to George Washington Highway, and took Route 64 East to Virginia Beach and on to the Chesapeake Bay Bridge Tunnel. I was on my way home. The eighteen-mile drive across the bridge and through the tunnels helped me unwind and allowed me to think clearly. I dug my phone out of my purse and called Kathleen. She answered on the second ring.

I said, "Hey, girl. It's Sunday morning. I hope I didn't wake you."

"Molly, how are you?"

"I'm fine. I'm on my way home. I should be home by three o'clock. I'll call you when I get there. If it's nice, I plan to drop my bags in the bedroom and head for the beach. Can you meet me there?"

"Is my hair red?"

"It was, the last time I looked."

"See you on the beach around three if it doesn't rain. If it rains, I'll meet you at your house. I'll bring a bottle of white wine and order a pizza. Sound like a plan?"

"Is my hair blonde?"

"Yes! And sitting on the head of one of the nuttiest women I know."

We began laughing like a couple of fools. I knew right then that I didn't have to have a man to be validated. I had girlfriends and a great guy friend in Jeff. I was blessed with a talent for acting and writing, and I felt happy and at ease with that. I was thinking about calling Rosalie when she beat me to the punch. I answered her ring as I was leaving the toll gate at the end of the bridge.

"Hey, girl. It's me, Rosalie. How's it going?"

"Going great. I'm over the bridge and out on route thirteen already. I should be home by three or so. Kathleen will be out on the beach or at my house, waiting for me. It's so pleasing to have such good friends to bounce me back and forth."

"I was thinking about your house on Channing. I think if it were me, I would use it to do something for the Down's kids."

"You must have read my mind. I was thinking that maybe I would sell it and give the money to the Down's Foundation. That way, I wouldn't have to bother with rentals and such. Could you ask Neil if he would find a good agent to list it, and send me the paperwork to sign? He can use his judgment about price."

"I'll ask him tonight. Safe trip."

"Thanks, Rosalie. Chat later. Bye."

By noon I was feeling hungry, so I stopped at a small restaurant in Maryland and had a salad. I was opening the car door to leave when I heard the phone ring. I answered without looking at the number. Jeff's voice was music to my ears.

"Molly, it's me, Jeff. Ever since you called yesterday, I've been thinking how nice it would be if we could get together."

"I would love that. Can you come to New Jersey?"

"Yes, I can do that. I want to say tomorrow. Will you be busy?"

"I won't be busy. Come early. We'll hang out on the beach."

"I'll try to be there by ten. See you then."

I was so excited I must have lost track of my speed. I was rounding a curve when I saw the trooper behind me and the flashing lights. I pulled over to the side of the road and put the window down.

"Good afternoon, madam. Do you know how fast you were driving back there?"

"If I was speeding Officer, I'm truly at fault. It's just that I'm heading home to New Jersey and I'm in a very big hurry."

"Well, you were doing seventy-five back there in a sixty-mile-per-hour zone. May I see your license and car registration?"

I pulled out my documents and handed them over. At the same time, I looked at his face. He was young; I figured about twenty-five years old. The name on his pin was C. Johnson. He looked at my license and back at my face. He backed away from my car and looked at me again, then started to laugh.

"Gosh darn! I mean, holy cow! Are you? No! It can't be. Molly Peale? The writer of all those romance novels?"

"Well, yes, Officer Johnson. I've written a few. Have you read them?"

"No, ma'am. I can't say I have, but my wife sure has. I can't wait to tell her about this. Say, listen, I wonder if I could have your autograph? It's for her, you know. My wife. She'll just be so dang pleased." He handed me a slip of paper and I signed my name and returned it. "Well, thank you ma'am. I sure do appreciate this. I'm going to let you go with a warning this time. Just be careful the rest of the way. I wouldn't want you to have a wreck and kill yourself."

"Thank you, sir. I appreciate your concern. And you're certainly welcome to the autograph. Give my regards to your wife."

I drove the rest of the way to the ferry thinking what a nice young guy he was. I felt a sudden ache in my heart that I didn't have a son. I thought how proud I would be of a son like that nice policeman. I was careful not to speed. Once on the ferry, I took out my pen and pad and wrote the first few lines of a novel entitled "Trooper."

Once off the boat, I was home in minutes. My beach house was a disaster. I hadn't realized how messy I had made things during my days of depression. I wondered how I had let myself get in such a state. "Never again," I said to myself. The sun was out and only a few scattered clouds were in the sky. I threw on my swimsuit, grabbed my bag, and headed for the beach to meet Kathleen.

We hugged and cried. I told her about Jeff. I told her everything that had happened in Virginia. Our time on the beach was glorious, as usual. Later, back at my house, we had wine and pizza. I slept like a log that night, dreaming of Jeff.

WEDDING IN MINNESOTA

I had always loved the month of July, only this year, I hadn't paid much attention to my calendar. I had made my plans for the house, and my love life was pretty much on hold. It was early Monday morning and I was having coffee and reading the news when Jeff arrived. I opened the door wearing my best smile. I was more than excited to see him. He had gained a few pounds and was growing a beard. The hair in front of his head was starting to recede. I couldn't care less if he had a third eye and a hump on his back. He was Jeff, and I would welcome him, warts and all. I opened the door wide, and we hugged each other and danced around the living room.

"You look absolutely wonderful, Miss Molly. Skinny, but nice."

"And you! Look at you with that beard. Hey, now I know where my ten pounds went. You may give me back five, but no more."

We laughed and kidded each other on the way to the kitchen. Jeff sat down without an invitation. I poured coffee for both of us. We sipped it and chatted for about thirty minutes before I popped the question. I knew I had to ask, even though I dreaded the answer.

"So, tell me about Jocelyn. What's she like?"

"Oh, shit! I brought her. I hope you don't mind. I'll get her. I told her to wait in the car while we had a few minutes to catch up."

"Oh, Jeff! How rude! Get that lady in here right away."

He stood up and straightened his shorts. I thought how unlike Jeff it was for him to dress in shabby clothes when he was escorting a lady. Those shorts had to be the worst pair he owned. I cleared the table and put the cups in the dishwasher. I heard Jeff come back into the house and turned to greet them, smiling. I was surprised at what I saw. He was holding her with one arm and she was beautiful. Her hair was black and shiny and she had big brown eyes.

"Molly Peale, this is Jocelyn."

"Hello, Jocelyn! You are the most beautiful girl I've ever seen. You have no idea how pleased I am to meet you." I held out my hand to her and she licked my fingers. "Oh, Jeff. She's so pretty. What kind of puppy is she?"

"She's a King Charles spaniel. Cecilia found her at a pet shop near her apartment. She felt sorry for me because I spend so much time alone, carrying a torch for an old love of mine. An old love whose initials are M.P. Do you know who that might be?"

I stood there staring at them. I knew that tears were streaming down my face, but I didn't care. I was so relieved and happy that I began laughing and crying at the same time. Jeff did, too. We were hugging and laughing, and Jocelyn was whining as if she knew what was going on. I took her in my arms and stroked her head and neck.

"Young lady, if you only knew the anxiety you caused me the last three days. I was so worried about meeting you. Now that I have, I'm so happy to find out you're a dog." She let out a big bark at my last remark.

"Careful, Moll," Jeff whispered. "Jocelyn doesn't know she's a dog. I think she might have a hard time accepting it."

"Oops! Sorry, Jocelyn. Strike that statement. What was I thinking?"

I put her down and she peed on the floor. I didn't care. I was just so happy she was a dog, even though she didn't know it. Jeff cleaned up the pee and went to the car to get her crate. He came back in with a grim look on his face.

"I don't know about the beach. There's a black cloud on the horizon and I thought I saw lightning. Looks like we might have to stay inside."

"That's okay. We can do that. I'll put a movie on and make some popcorn. We can cuddle on the couch with the d- . . ., I mean, with Jocelyn."

"I would much rather put Jocelyn in the crate for a nap and cuddle with you, if that's okay."

"Sounds fine. Let's watch an old classic. How about *Singin' in the Rain*?"

"Perfect movie for a perfect rainy day. I'll put it on. You start the popcorn."

Singin' in the Rain was one of my favorites, but my mind stayed on other things during the movie, like the realization that Jeff was sitting there beside me. I couldn't take my eyes off him for a second. He was almost sixty-five years old, a whole ten years older than me. Even so, he was handsome and, I knew, so much wiser. I reached over and touched his hand. He turned and kissed me, and the way I felt was beyond anything I had imagined. We made love that day for the first time in all the years we had known each other. I couldn't help but cry afterward.

"Oh, Jeff, my wonderful friend, I wish this could have happened years ago. I love you so very much. I was so foolish not to realize what we had."

"Don't talk that way, Molly. Love is a very strange thing. It's a feeling, and our feelings aren't always true to us. So many times our thoughts interfere, and vice versa. Let's just go from here. I still have your old ring. So, will you marry me?"

"Yes, I will marry you. Yes! Yes, I will. We may have to get the ring sized. Will that be a problem?"

"Anybody ever tell you that you're a silly shit?"

We laughed to beat the band. There we were, two old farts, acting like young folks again. Only this time, with all of our theatre experience, it wasn't a play or a romance novel. This was the real thing. We got up and started calling friends. Cecilia first; then Rosalie and Martine. Last, but not least, Kathleen. Jeff called a few of his friends in New York. They were elated. Martine offered to make it a double wedding, but we wanted to have our own ceremony at the little church in Manhattan where we used to go when we were house-mates. We sat in the kitchen and started making plans. We decided to do something in red, since Jeff had originally proposed on Valentine's day.

Two months later, we were on our way to Minnesota to attend Martine and John's wedding. Jeff had not left my house in Jersey, except to fly home to pick up a few belongings. We arrived in Duluth on Friday, September 15, at 3:30 p.m., one day before the wedding. Kathleen and Ron flew out with us. Their relationship had developed into true love and they, too, were talking marriage. Rosalie and Neil were due the next morning. Cecilia was committed and not free to leave New York.

The forecast for the weekend was pleasing; sunny and not too cold. The temperature was in the high sixties. Martine lived outside of town, in a restored Victorian home, with her mother. Ritchie lived at the school in town, but was home for the wedding. I was thankful that they were doing so well.

"I don't believe how beautiful it is here," Jeff said, as we drove from the airport to the house.

"Isn't it, though. Sunday, before we leave, we'll go to Canal Park. It's very nice and there are fine restaurants where we can have dinner."

"Sounds great. I'm looking forward to that. The whole weekend is almost like a fairy tale. Being here with you. Everyone friends again. It's a shame Cecilia wasn't able to make it. I just wonder if she held back because she was worried that her relationship with Debbie might not be accepted here."

"I doubt that, Jeff. I know it's fine with Marty. Ritchie doesn't know the difference, and Mrs. Hamilton is too old to care."

"And you, Molly? We've never really talked about this. How do you really feel about it?"

"My spirit disagrees. However, I love Cel and really believe she was hurt so deeply by men that she saw homosexuality as the only way to have love in her life. So, what about you, Jeff. Agree or disagree?"

"I think you're right. Whatever the reason, I wish her happiness. As the old song goes, I wish her love."

We made it to the house just in time to shower and dress for the rehearsal dinner. I was a bridesmaid and Jeff an usher. Martine insisted we stay at the house rather than in a hotel. The house was huge, and she put us in a large room with a nice bathroom and windows on the side, where we had plenty of light. It was decorated in mahogany colonial with blue and white accessories.

I had not seen Ritchie when we first arrived. Martine said he was upstairs with his caretaker, being dressed. He came down right after me. He tapped me on the back, and as I turned he reached up for a hug. I took him in my arms and held him tightly. I said, "I love you, Ritchie."

"I love you too. I love my sister, Molly."

I can't explain the joy that I felt at that moment. I said, "Thank you, little brother." And we laughed together. How else could I have hidden the tears?

The dinner was exquisite. It was cooked and served at the house by Martine's house staff. Martine was gorgeous in a beautiful mauve tea-length dress. Her long hair was pulled back and clasped with a diamond barrette that sparkled under the lights from the crystal chandelier in her dining room. John was dressed in a white tux, and the other men wore dark suits with white shirts and matching ties. I wore a black gown, as did most of the women. It was like something out of a fairy tale. There we were, all princes and Cinderellas. The best part? No one would turn into a pumpkin at midnight.

We stayed up late that night, celebrating. The next day we had plenty of time to rest before the candlelight wedding at five. We all cried as Martine and John said their vows. The ceremony and reception were both over by nine. We stood outside and waved as the newlyweds left for the airport. They were flying to Hawaii for a honeymoon.

We spent the rest of our time in Duluth having fun at Canal Park. Jeff was mesmerized by the beauty of it all. The sound of the seagulls intrigued us as we walked and took it all in. We boarded our plane at ten fifteen on Monday morning. We had had a great time, but were glad to be returning home to make plans for our own wedding. The trip back was pleasant, and before we made it all the way home, Kathy and Ron were officially engaged. How much better could it get?

BIG NEWS IN A SMALL TOWN

I wanted a small, but elegant wedding. Jeff agreed, and we started making plans. We decided on a sacred heart wedding in July, 1996. Colors would be red and white and we would invite one hundred and fifty guests.

Jeff had relatives I had never heard of, and friends and associates from Massachusetts to California. My list was small. My grandparents died before I was born, and neither of my parents had brothers or sisters, so I had no aunts, uncles or cousins. Ritchie was my only living relative. So my list totaled forty-eight. That left Jeff space for one hundred and two guests. We planned to mail the invitations three months before the wedding.

It was two weeks before Christmas when Rosalie, Kathleen and I planned to shop for my gown. I wanted to find something that my parents would have approved of. I made appointments at bridal shops in Cape May and Somers Point, but never made it to the first one. I didn't see or hear the commotion until Kathleen rang the doorbell the day we were supposed to shop. I heard the bell and was heading for the door when I heard Kathleen yelling.

"Molly, don't open the door! It's a jungle out here!"

I peeked out of the window and saw at least thirty reporters with cameras and microphones. The word was out. It must have leaked by way of the bridal shops. I was mortified. I had managed to live in this town with little or no attention from the media. Until now. Kathleen yelled out to them that I wasn't in the house.

"Who are you?" one woman yelled out to Kathleen.

"I'm just a friend. Now go away."

"Just tell us if it's true. Is Molly Peale marrying Jeffrey Wilde, the former Broadway director?"

"Just go away! Molly isn't here. I only came by to feed the dog. They're both in New York. I'll ask them about giving you a story when I meet with them tomorrow. Now, please leave," Kathleen yelled out to them as she was squeezing herself through a tiny opening in the door. I sat on the floor, holding Jocelyn. There was nothing left to do but get a flight to the Big Apple.

I called Rosalie and gave her a heads-up on what to expect. I didn't see anyone outside at that point, but I knew they could be hiding around the corner, waiting for me to try and sneak out. Rosalie said to make a plane reservation for her also. She and Kathleen were both determined to help me choose a gown. We called all of the airlines that flew into the city and could not book a single flight for three. "Too close to Christmas, no seats available," they said.

Rosalie arrived in Cape May with no problem. No one followed her to the house. There appeared to be no one outside. It was one o'clock in the afternoon, and I had a solution. We could take my car straight up the Garden State Parkway and be in New York by six, if the traffic wasn't too bad. Jeff had gone the day before to tie up some loose ends at his apartment. I called and told him what we were doing.

"Good thinking, darling. Drive carefully, and I'll see you when you get here. I'll make a reservation for dinner. I love you."

"I love you, too, sweetheart."

Kathleen and Rosalie went to the car and got in the front seat. They left the back door open facing the house. I ran out and slid in the back, lay down in the seat, and we were on our way. We brought no clothes or extra shoes. I had thrown some underwear and nightgowns in a bag for the three of us, and some cosmetics. Kathleen and Rosalie liked the idea of a shopping spree in the big city. I stayed down on the seat until we made it out of town. It was Tuesday, so except for a few afternoon Christmas shoppers, the traffic was light.

Kathleen drove most of the way while I relaxed in the back seat with Jocelyn. She was such a good dog. She loved to ride in the car. She loved Jeff and me, and we loved her. I thought about Jeff as we rode along the Parkway. I wondered if — had we married when we were younger — we would have had children. I was so happy then, and yet a little sad when I thought about the time I had wasted dreaming a childish dream.

"You're awfully quiet back there, Molly Face. Are you dreaming about your big day?" Rosalie was evidently getting bored.

"I am so dreaming about my big day, as well as how old and fat I'm going to look in that wedding gown, if I ever get it," I said. Everyone laughed at that remark. I had, however, gained five pounds since my engagement. My face was showing a few lines, but not too bad for my nearly fifty-six years. We laughed, sang songs, and talked silly the rest of the way. I couldn't have been happier.

We arrived at Jeff's apartment at half past seven. Not bad timing, since the traffic in the city had been a little heavier than on the Parkway. As soon as we arrived, Jeff called a cab and was ready to whisk us off to Vinnie D's for dinner.

"You girls are late. I guess you must have hit a little traffic."

"Yes, more here in the city than on the road," I said.

"Well, you lovelies are here now, and I am ready to wine and dine. Shall we?"

The cabbie was blowing the horn as we came out the door. On the way to the restaurant, we talked about the problem with the reporters and agreed that we would have to select a place to marry that wouldn't be accessible to the public.

"We could have it at my house. My living room is huge, and the staircase would make a perfect spot for bridal entrance and pictures," Rosalie said.

"Thank you so much for the offer, Rosy Face, but I would rather marry in New Jersey or New York. The way it looks now, it will be new York. Jeff and I are just two rusty spokes in a big wheel here in the city. In Cape May, I think the reporters would find a way to get past security. Big celebrity weddings in small towns make big stories for small papers, even if the celebs are past-tense."

"That makes sense, Molly," Kathleen said. "The less you have to deal with, the better. And anyway, it will be easier for Martine and Ritchie to fly here to the city."

"Yes," I said. "I'm going to have Ritchie give me away."

"That's a great idea, Molly. I'll bet he's excited," Jeff said.

"I don't know yet. I haven't talked to him about it. I did talk to Martine, though, and she seemed excited. She wants to hold off telling Ritchie until the week of the event. If we tell him now, he will ask her about it every single day for months."

We arrived at the restaurant and everyone stopped talking. We were all so hungry that all we could think about was food.

AND THEN WE WERE ONE?

St. Paul's Church on Fifty-Ninth seemed like a perfect place for a wedding. We could hire good security people to keep out the photographers. The invitations had gone out in May. We planned a five o'clock candlelight service on Saturday, July 20, 1996, with a reception immediately following at Vinnie's in the "Garden Room." Rosalie was to be my maid of honor. Kathy, Cecilia and Martine were chosen as bridesmaids. An old friend of Jeff's was the best man, and Martine's husband, John, Rosalie's fiancé, Neil,Kathy's fiancé, Ron, and another friend of Jeff's were ushers.

Time had passed quickly, and we were one day away from the wedding. I had cold feet just a little, but every time I looked at Jeff, the fear vanished.

Martine and Ritchie had arrived on Thursday afternoon and we had the rehearsal on Friday night. Following the rehearsal, we had an informal dinner at Vinnie's. We separated after dinner; Jeff went to his apartment and I was holed up in mine. I rested and gave myself up to my best friends and bridesmaids. They pampered me with a facial and a massage. I felt like I had back in high school when I landed the part of Abby Brewster. So special, like a princess. There would be no bachelor party for either of us. We felt we were much too old and too much in love to bother with all that hullabaloo. So that night, July 19,1996, at ten thirty, after a light dinner and one glass of wine, I went to sleep.

I awoke the next morning at seven. I could hear Kathy, Cecilia, and Rosalie talking in the kitchen. Martine was still asleep in the guest room. Ritchie had spent the night at Jeff's. I was so grateful to

Jeff for taking time with Ritchie. I knew he must have asked a million questions.

Oh, that morning. I remember looking out the window that beautiful, hot, summer morning in New York City and feeling like nothing in my life or the world could go wrong again. Life would always be beautiful and love would always rule.

"Morning everyone," I yelled out as I walked into the kitchen. "Isn't this the most wonderful morning?"

"Well, the sleeping beauty has arisen. How are you feeling this morning, Queen Molly?" It was Kathleen who spoke.

"We have to get breakfast now," Rosalie said. "The hairdressers will be here at noon. As I see it, they have a big job on their hands." We looked around at each other and laughed. Everyone's hair looked a fright.

Martine came out of the bedroom just as Kathleen started making strawberry crepes. "Something smells great," she said. "Is it breakfast?"

"Almost. Kathy and Betty Crocker are hard at work. Sit down and have some of the delicious coffee that Cecilia made," I said. "Where is Cel, anyway?"

"Bathroom, I think. She left the room a few minutes ago," Rosalie said.

"Personally, I think she's upset about something," Rosalie whispered. "She left the room without saying a word. That isn't like her. Molly, maybe you should check her out."

I went to the bathroom and knocked on the door. "Hey, Cel, it's me, Molly. Are you okay in there?"

"I'll be out in a sec. I was just having myself a good cry. Know what I mean?"

"I know exactly what you mean. Anything I can do?"

"We'll talk when I come out Molly. Okay?"

"Okay. Take your time. Breakfast is almost ready."

I told the others what she had said. I had told Cecilia that I knew what she meant, but in all honesty, I didn't have a clue. Why would she cry on this, the most important day of my life? I had hoped no one would do anything to put a damper on my happiness. Cel was crying and I didn't know why. She came out with red eyes and a big smile.

"Stop looking at me like that," she said. "I was thinking about Calvin and how he would have loved to be here. I was also crying out of sheer joy that I have such wonderful friends in all of you. I know other gay people that are so lonely and unaccepted. I know how lucky I am, that's all. Now where are those crepes?"

Kathy was standing there with her mouth open and a dripping spatula in her hand. The rest of us started to laugh, pounding the table and chanting, "Crepes! Crepes! Crepes!" Kathy moved with a start.

"Crepes coming up," she said. She went around the table serving crepes and strawberry sauce. When she got to Cel, she kissed her on the cheek and told her we would always be friends. "Your sexual preference couldn't matter less. If they ever legalize gay marriage, we'll all come to your wedding and give you our blessing. Right, gang?"

I raised my coffee cup and said I agreed, but in my heart I felt differently. I had always hoped that Cecilia would all of a sudden realize that she wasn't gay, and find a wonderful man. I finally accepted that it wasn't going to happen. She was still my friend and I loved her anyway.

Shortly after breakfast, the housecleaner came. The hairdressers showed up right on time. Kathy had already showered, so she issued instructions to the cleaner and entertained the hair guys. By noon, we were clean and well groomed. My hairdresser, Michael, had turned my blonde head into a thing of beauty. It was crowned with red roses, and a short off-white veil was attached and fell over the back of my neck. I chose to do my own make-up since I was used to a certain way. So did the others.

The wedding was scheduled to start at five thirty. The limousine came at four to take us to the church. There were some photographers outside the church taking pictures, but no problems arose. There were no reporters that I could see. I learned later that the police had threatened to arrest anyone who interfered in our private affair. I felt blessed and happy.

Once in the special room upstairs in the church, it really dawned on me what was about to happen. What usually happened to women in their twenties was finally happening to me at fifty-six. "Better late than never," I whispered to myself. I heard a noise in the room, and when I looked around I saw the sweetest sight ever. My little brother was coming out of a side section of the huge room. He was dressed in his white tux, with a red cummerbund and white shoes. His arms were stretched out to hug me, and my heart ached with love for this very special child. I briefed him on the walk and we patiently waited. Rosalie must have checked my headdress a dozen times or more.

Before I knew what was happening, I was walking with Ritchie to the stairs, behind Martine. She was beautiful in her red and white dress. Ritchie was holding my arm, just as he had been instructed. Rosalie was close behind me. Her dress was mostly red, with just some white trim, and she looked radiant. I was nervous. My mind was going a mile a minute when the wedding march started. I thought about my parents and my brother, Jesse. I pictured their smiling faces. All of a sudden I lost the nervousness. I was getting married! This is my big moment. I was elated. Ritchie did just fine. We walked slowly down the stairs without missing a beat. I remember smiling the whole way.

When we reached the bottom and made the turn into the aisle, I saw Jeff. I thought my heart would burst. I glanced at the red and white roses on the altar and the red bows on the ends of the pews. I looked at Jeff. Again. He was smiling and then suddenly, a strange look came over his face. As I approached him, I noticed he was rather red in the face and was perspiring. I smiled, wondering why he looked so hot when it was so very cool in the church. Then it happened. Jeff fell to the floor, holding his chest.

VOWS

Jeff was lying on the floor, holding his chest. The church became a place of total chaos. Everyone was gasping at what they saw. Martine and Rosalie were screaming, "Call Nine-One-One!" I ran to Jeff and knelt beside him. He was gasping for breath.

"Oh, darling, I'm so sorry. I think I'm having a heart attack. I've ruined our wedding."

"I love you, darling. Please hold on. It's okay. You'll be alright. I promise you. You have to be okay. Everything will be okay. Help is coming soon. I love you. I love you."

It seemed like forever before the ambulance came. A friend of Jeff's family came to his side. "Jeff, it's me, Bill Hoffman. Remember me? I'm a doctor. Stay awake, Jeff. Don't pass out. It's very important to stay awake and breath as deeply as you can. Don't talk or do anything to use oxygen." He told me and everyone else to stand back. I started to feel faint, but I knew I had to be strong. Dr. Hoffman was still talking to Jeff with words of encouragement. "You will be fine, Jeff. They can fix this at the hospital. It's probably just a little blockage. Nothing to worry about."

I don't remember when I've felt such fear. I thought I was losing the most important person in my life. "Dear God," I prayed. "What did I ever do that was so terrible? Why are you punishing me this way? Is it because of my rejection of Martine and my father? Please Lord, give me strength and wisdom. Help me, please."

Rosalie had her arms around me, trying to comfort me. "Molly dear, don't give up. Jeff is not going to die. The ambulance is here now. It's only been seven minutes. He is getting help now."

I looked up and saw the paramedics putting a mask on Jeff's face. It looked like they were starting an IV. "Rosalie, what are they doing? Why don't they go to the hospital? Tell them to please hurry. Don't let him die." I saw Neil leaning over him and talking. I began to feel faint. I held on as long as I could. I felt weak, and everything turned white, then black.

When I came to, Dr. Hoffman was kneeling next to me. He was putting an oxygen mask on my face.

"Breathe, Molly. Breathe deeply," the doctor was saying. I started to take deep breaths. I began to feel better. I knew I had to be strong for Jeff. "They are on their way to the hospital with Jeff. I think he will be okay. He had a good heart rate and his blood pressure was only slightly elevated. He may need surgery and he may not. Try not to worry. Do you want to change your clothes?"

"No, please. I just want to be where Jeff is. Please take me to the hospital."

Dr. Hoffman held my arm and pulled me up off the floor. We walked outside. The limo driver was still standing by the white limousine. We climbed in and headed for the hospital. When we got there, we rushed to the emergency room and inquired about Jeff. People were all around, looking at us. I must have drawn a lot of attention in my wedding gown. There was a sudden commotion in the hallway. I could hear the security guards telling everyone to go outside and remain calm. I knew the reporters must have followed us, but I didn't care. All I wanted was for Jeff to survive.

After what seemed like forever, the doctor came out. He smiled at us and I began to feel better. "Hello. I'm Dr. Walker. You must be Molly."

"Yes, Doctor," I said, "and this is Dr. William Hoffman. He was a guest at our wedding." Dr. Hoffman extended his hand to Dr. Walker.

"Please call me Bill," he said.

"Nice to meet you both. I like first names as well. I'm Alan."

"What can you tell us about our groom?" Bill asked.

"We think Jeff has a blockage in a coronary artery. He may need surgery. If so, we will keep him on nitro for tonight and take him to the operating room at seven tomorrow morning. Of course, if the arteries are severely blocked and he is in immediate danger, we'll do it right away. But don't worry. I think he'll be fine. We have him stabilized and pain-free."

"Oh, thank God," was all I could manage at that moment.

"Doctor, may we see him when he returns from the lab? Molly has suffered quite a shock. Maybe you could give her a Valium to ease the stress a little."

"No. No drugs. I'll be fine as long as I know Jeff is going to be okay," I said. "I just need a few minutes to get myself together. I would love a cup of tea, though."

Bill asked Alan for a private place for me to sit. He led us to an office down the hall. Alan went back to his duties and Bill went for the tea. I sat in the little office and prayed for Jeff. I began to relax and feel better. When Bill returned with the tea, I ask for Kathy, Rosalie,

Martine and Cecilia. He went to fetch them, and I sat and sipped. The tea was warm and soothing. I wondered what to do next. When Rosalie came in, she said she had sent all of the guests on to the reception and asked Vinnie to go ahead and feed them. She promised to keep everyone informed.

It was seven o'clock that evening when Alan came back and gave us the news about Jeff.

"He has two arteries that are eighty percent closed. It could be a lot worse. There will be no problem with waiting until morning to perform his surgery. Molly, you may see him now. I'm afraid the rest of you will have to wait a little longer."

I followed Alan to the elevator and then to Jeff's room on the second floor. I was warned to try to remain calm in his presence. We could not allow anything to upset him at this point. I knew I could do that. I was elated to see how well Jeff looked when I walked in his room. He was sitting up in bed with an IV in his arm. He held his arms out and I rushed to him, smiling. I kissed him and told him that I loved him.

"You frightened me half to death, but thank God you are going to be okay. I will be right here to take care of you when you come out of surgery tomorrow. I love you so much."

"Oh, Molly Girl. My sweet angel. You bring me so much joy. I'm sorry that I spoiled our wedding day. We'll be married eventually."

"It's alright, darling. Please don't worry. This wedding will take place sooner than you think."

Jeff closed his eyes for a moment and I motioned to Alan to step outside. "Alan," I said, "I would like for Jeff and I to be married tonight. If I can arrange it with the priest, would it be okay with you?

For more reasons than one, I want to be his wife when he goes into surgery tomorrow."

"I don't know Molly. There are so many risks to any surgery. We don't expect any problem, but there are no guarantees. He could die, or worse yet, have brain damage. Are you sure you want to take a chance like that?"

"That's just my point, Alan. I need legal rights as his wife. In case anything goes wrong, I want to be authorized to care for him and make decisions for him. It means a lot to me."

"I'll see what I can do. I certainly don't think it will affect Jeff at this point, health-wise, as long as he agrees to it. Of course I'll have to clear it with the surgeon. You go in and talk to Jeff and call the priest, and I'll try to locate Dr. Sinke, the heart surgeon."

"Thank you so much. You have no idea what this means to me."

When I got back to Jeff, he was wide awake and happy to see me.

"Where were you, my love? I missed you. Stay awhile longer?"

"Of course I will, darling. I have something to talk to you about. Please listen and don't interrupt until I have finished what I have to say. Alright?"

"Do I have a choice in the matter?"

"No, not really. Now listen: I want us to be married tonight. I want to be your wife when you go into surgery tomorrow. I want to be legally responsible so that I can make decisions about your care, in case you need more than we feel necessary at this time. I can call the priest now and clear it with him. Alan is clearing it with the heart surgeon. Please darling, it means a lot to me."

The look on Jeff's face was very serious at first, then suddenly, he began to laugh. "Molly, darling, you never cease to amaze me. Well, what are you waiting for? Call Father O'Malley and let's get this show on the road."

I kissed him at least ten times on the face and lips and threw my arms around him, being careful not to pull on the IV tube. I grabbed the phone and called the priest.

"Father, can you come to the hospital and perform a wedding ceremony? Jeff and I want to marry before his heart surgery tomorrow."

"Are you sure? Did his doctor say it was okay?"

Just then, Alan walked in the room with another doctor that I hadn't met. "Molly, Jeff, this is Dr. Sinke. He will be performing the surgery tomorrow."

We smiled and nodded. He stood there looking at us. "I have no problem with this wedding taking place here tonight. There is just one condition though."

I was still holding the phone, with the priest on the other end of the line. I said, "Stay on the line, Father, the surgeon is here. We're about to get an answer. So tell us your condition, Dr. Sinke. We will comply with anything as long as you allow this wedding." Jeff was squeezing my hand so tightly that my finger hurt from pressing on my engagement ring.

"Well, I would like to be invited as a guest. That's my only condition. Is that acceptable?"

We all laughed, and Jeff and I answered yes at the same time. "Not only are you invited to our ceremony, but there is a big party taking place at Vinnie D's. You are most welcome to attend that also," I said.

"Thank you. But under the circumstances, I should get my rest. Jeff and I will be meeting at seven tomorrow morning to get this job done so that you two may get on with your lives."

So Jeff and I were married that night in his hospital room. Martine and Rosalie stood by our side as we said our vows. The priest asked for a special blessing on our marriage. I spent my wedding night on a pull-out sofa in the room, next to Jeff's bed.

The next morning at six thirty, I kissed my beloved and said, "See you later, darling," as they wheeled him off to the operating room. I was still in my wedding gown. Rosalie took me to my apartment to change and we both prayed all the way. We were back in an hour in casual clothes. Jeff was still in surgery. It was hours before they were finished.

Dr. Sinke came out at three thirty and gave us a big smile. Everything had gone well and with no complications, Jeff could be released in a few days. I was so relieved I could hardly speak. I managed a, "Thank you, Doctor." I hugged Rosalie and burst into tears. All I could say was, "Thank you, God. Thank you, God," over and over.

Dr. Sinke said, "Molly, I suggest you go home and sleep and come back in the morning. Jeff may be awake by then. He will be closely monitored all night by his nurse. You may call here anytime during the night to inquire about him."

"Thank you, but I'd really like to stay here. I need to be as close to Jeff as I can. Please, Doctor."

"Suit yourself, but I don't have a good bed for you tonight, Molly. You'd be better off at home."

"Molly, please listen to the doctor. You really need your rest. Jeff doesn't know you're here anyway. He is still under heavy sedation," Rosalie pleaded.

Dr. Alan had come into the room and was coaxing along with Rosalie. So, reluctantly, I agreed to go.

I slept like a log that night. The doctor had given me a Valium,and at Rosalie's insistence, I took it. I awoke at six the next day, feeling like a new person. I woke Rosalie up and we called the hospital. The nurse said that Jeff was resting peacefully and I should take my time getting there. I felt great. I said, "Rosy Face, Jeff is doing fine and I'm starving. Let's wake the others and go get breakfast."

Kathy, Ron, Martine, John, Ritchie, Neil and Cecilia had all gone to the party at Vinney's the night before. They were still asleep. and so we woke them up and went to a little café around the corner for breakfast. I filled them in on Jeff's condition as we sipped our coffee. They were a little disappointed that they couldn't attend the wedding, but under the circumstances, they understood. We all ate a hearty breakfast. Everyone was calling me Mrs. Wilde, and I was so happy. Finally, Neil asked Rosalie if she was ready to give us the next good news. We were all ears.

"My dear friends," Rosalie said, "Neil and I would like you all to mark your calendars for March 14, 1997, for a double celebration. On that day, I will turn fifty-six. On that same day — I hope you're all ready for this — Neil and I are getting married."

All of us stood up and started clapping. We hugged and kissed Neil and Rosalie. We were all so ecstatic. We finished our coffee and headed for the hospital to give the good news to Jeff. When we walked in his room, he was sitting up in bed holding a pillow that was shaped like a heart. He looked a little pale, but still as handsome as ever. He smiled a big smile and we all took turns kissing him. Neil was the last to give a hug. He whispered in Jeff's ear and the two of them laughed.

"Did you tell him? Why are you laughing? Tell us what you said," Rosalie was saying.

"I just want to know what's new," Jeff said.

"Yeah. I have a confession," Neil said. "I told him yesterday when I leaned over him as he lay on the floor of the church."

"That's right," Jeff said. "His exact words to me were, 'Don't you die on me, you son of a bitch; you have to come to my wedding next March."

The nurse came in the room and told us that only two people could be in the room at the same time. Rosalie said, "Let's all leave and let these newlyweds have some privacy. And Jeff, don't forget to ask the doc the sixty-four-dollar question. See you two later."

"What question?" I asked.

"The one about the sex."

"Oh, that question."

"I already asked. Tell Rosy I'm way ahead of her."

"And the answer?"

"Oh, the doc said it depends on how quickly I recover."

"The only thing that matters is that you are okay. The rest is not that important."

"Oh, but it is. I'm figuring on about a week at the most. I love you, Molly."

"And I love you, my darling. You have no idea how much. I'm going to take such good care of you."

"Sweetheart, we are going to take care of each other. Always and forever."

FIRST ANNIVERSARY

When Jeff and I celebrated our first anniversary, we did it with all of our good friends on a cruise to Barbados. What a wonderful time we had. We had a lot to celebrate.

Rosalie and Neil had been married four months then and were deliriously happy. They were married in Holy Angels Church in Craddock with three hundred guests present. She was radiant in a beautiful ivory lace gown. Like me, she went traditional. We all enjoyed a reception at their home. Since her dad had passed away, her son gave her away. Her daughter was matron of honor. It was a happy day for all of us. I remember looking back once in the church and seeing her former husband, Jack, standing in the back and looking on. I was sure in my own mind that he wished he had treated her better. She was thin and more beautiful than ever.

Ritchie, John and Martine were doing well. Ritchie was still in the special boarding school where I had first met him. Believe it or not, Cecilia was dating a nice man that she had met in a support group for gays. Life could not have been better.

Jeff and I are living in my beach house in Cape May. We see a lot of Kathy and Ron, and look forward to their beach wedding in august. We take frequent trips to the big city to shop and see old friends. We've also picked up a few new friends; Dr. Alan Walker is one. We get together with him and his wife whenever we go to the city.

"Jeff, darling, are you truly happy here at the beach? It's quite a ways south of the Big Apple."

"I am very happy here, Molly dear. I don't mind if it's far from New York. All that matters is that you are here with me. And what about you? Do you mind that it's so far north of Channing Street?"

"Not at all."

North of Channing Street

A Short Novel
by
Gloria Spivey Flecker

ABOUT THE AUTHOR

Gloria Spivey was born in Tarboro, North Carolina on January 15, 1940. She attended grade school in Tarboro and Winton, North Carolina until the summer of 1949, when she moved with her family to Portsmouth, Virginia. She attended Craddock High School until she married and moved to New Jersey in 1956.

Gloria went to college in Atlantic County, New Jersey and Red Rocks, Colorado. She married Ben Ricciardi and raised three sons and three daughters. She lived most of her life in New Jersey, where she was employed as a Human Services Specialist in Atlantic County for 23 years. She retired in 2002 and moved to Myrtle Beach, South Carolina, where she met and married Thomas Flecker. She and Tom now share a home in Murrells Inlet, South Carolina.

Gloria has been a member of the South Carolina Writers Workshop since October, 2005.

941833

Made in the USA